CYCLIST CLUB

Part 2 of the Rodriguez Series

GEORGE MARZOCCHI

"Cyclist Club"

Copyright © 2020 by George Marzocchi

All rights reserved.

Published by Red Penguin Books

Bellerose Village, New York

ISBN

Print 978-1-952859-45-8 / 978-1-952859-75-5

Digital 978-1-952859-46-5

No part of this book may be reproduced in any form or by any electronic or mechanical means, including information storage and retrieval systems, without written permission from the author, except for the use of brief quotations in a book review.

This second book in the Rodriguez series is dedicated to my wife Terry who has been by my side through this entire journey and continues to encourage and inspire me.

A very special thanks to our sons Damien and Julian.

A big thank you to Stephanie Larkin at Red Penguin Books.

CONTENTS

Prologue	1
1. The King is Dead	3
2. Road Rage, Perhaps	9
3. Meet The Cyclist Club Members	15
4. Santiago Blinks	23
5. The Team	29
6. Mrs. Mayhew	35
7. The Two Men	41
8. Sauce to Die For	49
9. Man of Steel	53
10. Body Bag	59
11. The Ideal Inmate	65
12. Red Widow	75
13. The Cyclist Club Meets	79
14. I Don't Drink that Sh...	87
15. And the Winner is...	89
16. A Body Bag for Body Bag	95
17. Zachariah's "Athletes"	99
18. My Father the Saint	105
19. Deaf Mary	109
20. Darren Mitchell	113
21. Spider	117
22. The Last Call	123
23. Jennifer	127
24. The New Member	133
25. Bullets Fly	139
26. Techie ala Vegan	147
27. A Choice of Weapons	153
28. The Well Is Dry	157
29. David's Lesson	171
30. Say Nothing	175
31. Moscow Mule	179
32. I Scream Social	183

33. Breakfast of Champions	189
34. Hatchet Man	193
35. Club Fed	197
36. Empty Threats	201
37. Heavy Lifting	209
38. Altered States	219
39. It's Just Business	229
40. Go With Jah	233
41. A Killer is Born	239
42. Bedroom Roulette	243
43. Evil Cloaked in Laughter	245
44. Friend or Foe?	251
45. Tattoo of Death	255
46. Two Cossacks	257
47. Stalking Rodriguez	269
48. Red or White	273
49. Who's Bogie?	279
50. Tupaya Suka	283
51. The Lighthouse Inn	291
52. Aunt Shauna Says Hello	295
53. The Invitation	303
54. The Deal	307
55. Change of Plans	317
56. #82	321
57. The Stakeout	327
58. BookMark	331
59. Dressed for the Kill	337
60. Revealed	347
Epilogue	353
About the Author	355
Also by George Marzocchi	357

PROLOGUE

My name is Elizabeth McMahon. I'm a sergeant with the Las Vegas branch of the Drug Enforcement Agency. From the day Agent Rodriguez was transferred to my command, he's been a thorn in my side; but when he was transferred to Oceanview, Long Island, I knew that I would miss him. He was one of the best officers in my command. Unorthodox in his approach and like a dog on a bone when it came to cases. He's taken down drug cartels south of the border, hopped-up meth distributors in Arizona, and organized crime bosses in Brooklyn. But nothing would prepare Rodriguez for what was about to occur in Oceanview. It's as if the devil himself escaped from hell, but this devil is not called Satan or Lucifer. This devil in human form is named Zachariah. A sadistic aberration fueled by a combination of evil and mind-altering drugs. In his wake, he leaves victims killed for "sport."

Rodriguez must face this aberration head-on as the clock ticks away. Someone's life hangs in the balance, an innocent who is caught up in this evil. Someone precious to him. Rodriguez has little time to put the pieces together to find Zachariah and end it. The deadline approaches and the night draws near. The night is Friday the 13th when the Cyclist Club meets. It's the night to send Zachariah back to hell.

CHAPTER 1

THE KING IS DEAD

Jorge Delacruz sat on the terrace of his hacienda on the outskirts of Medellin, Colombia. The death of his nephew and the imprisonment of his niece had changed him. The leader of the most powerful drug cartel in South America, went from being a charismatic, level-headed businessman who ran his empire like a corporation to a paranoid and unreasonable man, quick to anger and violence. Most of his cartel associates had abandoned him to join other gangs and some he killed thinking they were stealing his merchandise or betraying him. The rain forest just outside his hacienda was a burial ground for people who ran afoul of Jorge Delacruz. He stared at the jungle as if expecting the spirits of the people he killed and buried there to rise and seek revenge. The only people who remained loyal to him and were still at the hacienda were his manservant, his staff, and his bodyguard, Carlos.

The silence was broken by his manservant yelling his name. "Mr. Delacruz, Mr. Delacruz, come quickly. There's a big fire across the river." Carlos and his manservant were already at the rear of the hacienda when Delacruz arrived. Black smoke and flames were visible through the jungle growth.

"Go and get the binoculars, the powerful ones we use for hunting," Delacruz instructed his manservant. After doing so, he handed them to Delacruz. "Are my eyes deceiving me or is that El Moreno's Palacio on fire?" He let out a loud laugh and handed the binoculars to Carlos. "Here, look, isn't that the cabron's hacienda? Die you putto, die!"

His manservant asked, "Padrone, may I see?" He looked through the binoculars as the faint sound of sirens pierced the jungle. "It seems the fire brigade has arrived. I see lots of flashing lights."

Delacruz replied, "They won't save it. It will crumble to the ground along with his merchandise. The flames are too high. I hope he burns along with it."

His manservant, still looking at the fire through the binoculars, saw two cars approaching. "Padrone, two cars are approaching from the south at high speed."

Delacruz grabbed the binoculars and observed two black SUVs coming towards his hacienda. He turned to Carlos and said, "Bring the weapons and hurry. Let's greet them properly." He turned to his manservant, "Go home to your family. This is not your war."

"No, padrone, give me a weapon. I'll stand with you."

Delacruz replied, "If we all die here, who will take care of your family?"

His manservant replied, "I'll make sure we don't die here."

"Carlos, give him the pump shotgun. There's no need to aim; just fire in their direction. Good luck, amigos." The cars were only about fifty feet away. The men aimed as they came to a screeching halt. The lead car driver's side window quickly rolled down, and a white handkerchief was waved frantically in the air. "It seems they want to talk, not fight."

A voice from the car called out, "Jorge, it's me, Miguel. I brought you some men."

Delacruz turned to Carlos. "What do you think, do we let them come in?" Without waiting for an answer, he yells, "Miguel, show yourself. Let me see it's you."

Miguel stepped out of the car with his hands up. "See, it's me. I have men who want to join us."

"Get back in the car and drive forward slowly," weapons still trained on them with caution. "Okay, all of you come out of the cars and let me see you."

The men exited the cars with their hands in plain sight. Miguel replied, "See, Jorge, I've come with men who are willing to fight and restore power to your family."

Delacruz walked up and down, inspecting the seven men standing before him. "What did you bring me? Farmers and peasants?" He turned to one of the men, "You, have you ever killed a man?"

The man looked down at the ground. "No, Mr. Delacruz, just goats and chickens."

Delacruz looked at Miguel and shouted, "Well, if I'm hungry I know who to call. After you kill them, do you know how to cook them?" Carlos let out a laugh as Delacruz continued to look at the men. He noticed three standing together dressed in suits, the telltale sign of a weapon in a shoulder holster apparent to him. He approached them. "What about you? You have the look of killers, but are you?"

One of the men replied, "We used to work for El Moreno, but he is no longer with us."

"Really? And where is he?"

"Right now he's floating down the Medellin River. He should be in Medellin in about half an hour," one of the men answered. They all laughed.

"You three are the only men that worked for El Moreno?" inquired Delacruz.

"No. There were more; but they, too, are no longer with us."

"What happened to them?"

One of the men answered, "I killed them."

"You killed them? How many and why?"

"There were six. They refused to join us, said they wanted to go home to their families, the putos. So, I forced them into a room, locked the door, and burned them alive." There was a long silence as the men glanced at each other.

Finally, Delacruz spoke. "You burned six men alive because they wanted to go home to their families? Delacruz grabbed the shotgun from his manservant and aimed it at the men. "If any of you move, I'll kill all of you. Carlos, take their weapons and search them."

The men looked at Miguel nervously as Carlos removed guns and knives from the men and placed them on the table by the pool. "So, did you bring me any money? I heard that there were many millions of dollars in that hacienda hidden away. Perhaps you brought me jewelry or artwork. What did you bring me?" The men were silent. "Nothing. You stupid fucks killed six men, burned down a hacienda worth millions, and you have nothing to give me. Do you smell that? That's the smell of millions of dollars going up in smoke. I need men, or I would send you all to hell. So, you want to join me? Let's see if you're worthy of my time. Now, let's sit down. We have a lot to discuss. When I'm satisfied that you mean me no harm, I'll return your weapons." The men sat around the table and Delacruz continued. "I had a nephew. His name was Diego. He was my dead brother's son. I raised him from the age of ten and taught him everything I know. In the beginning, I taught him how to kill; and he was good at it. He killed when he had to, but he would never lock unarmed men in a room and burn them alive for the sin of wanting to go to their families. Unlike you," pointing to the man, "he wasn't a coward. Later, he studied finance and became my financial counselor. He was one of the smartest men I knew, and my money was always safe and never traceable." Delacruz turned to the man. "You, what do you bring to the table?"

The man nervously replied, "I was El Moreno's bodyguard and his closest confidant. I did everything for him."

"Are you the one that killed him or was it you three together?"

"Jorge, what does it matter? We're here now," asked Miguel.

"It matters, Miguel, because perhaps one day they'll do it to me. So, answer me. Who killed El Moreno?"

The man answered, " I did it alone."

Delacruz sat quietly as the manservant brought trays of food, snifters of brandy, and bottles of wine to the table. Delacruz whispered something to his manservant; and he hurried off, returning a short time later with a newspaper clipping in his hand. Delacruz asked the killer his name.

The man answered, "Santiago Molina."

Delacruz handed him the clipping. "I have a job for you, Santiago Molina. Look at that page. Do you see the cop there, Rodriguez? I want you to kill him. Show me you can kill someone armed and capable of killing you. Believe me, do not underestimate this man." Molina looked at Miguel and back at Delacruz, not sure what to say.

Delacruz continued, "Well, do you think you can do it? He's a policeman in the United States, surrounded by other policemen. He was there when my nephew was murdered; and one at a time, they will pay."

Molina wasn't expecting to be tested so early on, and he was not sure what to say. Delacruz spoke again, "Okay, okay, I see that you have no words so I will speak. If you do this for me, I'll pay you half a million American dollars upon proof of his death."

"What kind of proof do you want?"

"I want to know that he is dead. How you do it is up to you. Bring me his fucking head. I don't care—just prove to me that he's dead. I'll want your answer after lunch." The men smoked cigars as the table was cleared. Delacruz waited for the staff to leave then asked Molina for his decision. Molina, still nervous, looked to Miguel for a lifeline.

Miguel said, "Jorge I'll go with him, you know, to cover his back."

"Cover his back!" Delacruz let out a laugh. "This man just single-handedly killed El Moreno and burned six men to death. No, Miguel. Let me tell you what's going to happen. I'm going to give Mr. Molina here money for plane tickets and expenses. He's going to New York, Long Island to be exact, to find this Rodriguez and kill him." Delacruz turned to Molina and warned, "If you fail, don't come back to Medellin because I'll kill you myself. If you succeed, bring me the proof and I'll give you the money. If Rodriguez kills you, I don't care. I'll send another one of you three. I'll send all of Medellin if I must until this man is dead."

CHAPTER 2

ROAD RAGE, PERHAPS

Sergeant Rodriguez was having dinner with the mayor of Oceanview and the police commissioner when his phone rang, his Caller ID alerting him that Detective Marco Spinelli was calling. He excused himself and went outside to take the call. "Hello, Detective, what's up?"

"Hi, Sergeant. We've got a gunshot victim in his car on Ocean Drive, right off exit 20. Looks like road rage. Can you drive out? We can use your help."

"Sure, I'm not that far away. I'll be there soon." Rodriguez arrived at the scene a short time later and was briefed by Detective Spinelli who advised him that Trooper Jankowski found the car with the victim inside.

"Trooper Jankowski, I'm Sergeant Rodriguez. Tell me what you found."

"Well, Sergeant, I was on routine patrol when I saw this car half in the ditch and the body inside."

"Did you notice any damage to the car?"

"I didn't see any, Sergeant."

"What about tire marks? Did you notice any?"

The trooper responded, "No tire marks or skid marks. Looks like he never hit the brakes."

Rodriguez examined the body with Detective Spinelli, "Looks like two or three headshots, Sergeant."

"The driver's side window is shattered and so is the back window. The entrance wounds are on the left side of the head."

"It looks like the fatal shots were fired from the driver's side." Rodriguez searched the road for shell casings and other clues.

"Marco, stay with the body and get forensics over here. Trooper Jankowski, walk with me down the road. I'm thinking if the car ran off the road up there, he was probably shot somewhere back here and was able to drive just a little further before he died. So, how long have you been with Suffolk PD?"

"About two years, Sergeant."

"Is this your first dead body."

"Yes, Sergeant. I've seen a few car accidents but not like this."

"Yeah, you never forget your first one, Jankowski." Rodriguez shined the flashlight from side to side as they continued down the road. They located shell casings, five of them. "Here you go. We've got three casings here and two more there." Traffic began to build behind the police car parked sideways across the road, its lights flashing. The men stopped and turned back as a motorist yelled, "When are you guys going to open the road?"

Rodriguez yelled back, "You'll be the first to know." The two men walked slowly, the flashlight illuminating the road. Suddenly,

Rodriguez stopped and pointed the flashlight at something laying on the side of the road. "What is that?"

Jankowski responded, "Looks like an old shoe. Maybe somebody threw it out of a car window." Rodriguez drew closer and replied, "That's not a regular shoe. That's a cyclist's shoe. See those clips on the bottom? They attach directly to the pedals of the bike so your foot can't slide off. These belonged to a serious bike rider."

"Sergeant, there's blood on that shoe and the road."

"I know. I saw it, too. Go get the forensic guys. I'm going to look around." Rodriguez began a slow descent down the embankment when his foot hit an object. He aimed his flashlight down at the obstruction, illuminating the mangled body of a man. Not far was a bicycle, the frame twisted and bent. He moved the flashlight over the body and noticed the victim suffered a nearly severed arm and twisted limbs. He also observed that the victim's right foot was missing.

Just then, Trooper Jankowski began his descent to join Rodriguez. Seeing him coming, Rodriguez yelled up, "Don't come down here, Jankowski. Send down the forensics team." Once the forensics team arrived, Rodriguez climbed his way up the embankment. "It's messy. Now we got two bodies. This guy is banged up. Don't go near that shoe; his foot is still in it." Jankowski is staring straight ahead. "Hey, Jankowski, are you okay?"

"Yeah, I think so." As they started to walk back, Rodriguez asked Jankowski what he thought had happened. "I think it was road rage."

Rodriguez challenged him, "Maybe, but how do you explain the shattered back window?"

Jankowski responded, "As the car drove away, the shooter fired, hitting the window."

Rodriguez countered, "The cyclist was in front of the car when he was hit and thrown down the embankment. Someone else fired at the back of the car thinking the driver was getting away."

"There was someone else involved who left the scene," Jankowski offered.

Rodriguez continued, "Think about it for a minute. We found the casings behind us, the biker's body down the embankment, and then the car." The driver was shot back there, and the biker was hit around this area."

"Look at the road. There's the blood, and the severed right foot is there. The car continued a while and stopped just before the embankment."

"Maybe it was another biker or another vehicle, but there was somebody else here who took off."

"So, Jankowski, what's your first name?" asked Rodriguez.

"It's William, but my friends call me Will. And you?"

"Rodriguez, but my friends call me Rodriguez." He stopped walking and looked back towards the biker's body. "A helmet—I didn't see a helmet."

"Not every bike rider wears a helmet" Will replied.

"You're right, but the serious riders always wear one because they know better. I'm going back to see if I can find one."

"I'm coming with you." The men reached the embankment and Rodriguez asked, " you sure you wanna come down?" "Trooper Jankowski answered, "yeah i'm ok." and they worked their way down to the biker's body. Rodriguez shined his flashlight at the biker's head and noticed marks on the biker's face.

"See those marks? I'll bet whoever else was here ripped his helmet off and took it. But why?"

Will replied, "Maybe it came off when he was hit by the car."

"No, I think his helmet stayed on. There's no visible head trauma. You know what I think, Will? He had a go-pro on his helmet. A go-pro and the whole thing was recorded. Let's go back and let the forensic guys do their thing."

As they were leaving, Detectives James McGraw and Andrew Davis arrived at the scene. Detective Davis was with Homicide and McGraw was an ex-homicide detective who was now an investigator with Internal Affairs. The men kept their distance; and McGraw shouted, "Hey, Rodriguez, why don't you let Homicide take over?"

"You need to wake up McGraw; they already took the body away."

"Fuck you, Rodriguez."

The next morning Rodriguez was in his office being besieged by the press looking for information about the previous night's events. Detective Spinelli came into his office and whispered, "The mayor is on line two. Good luck, Sarge."

Rodriguez took a deep breath and picked up the phone. "Hello, Mr. Mayor. How are you?"

"I'm fine, Sergeant. Did you get any sleep?"

"I got some. How can I help you, sir?

The mayor responded, "About last night, I want you to take this investigation over and pick a team to help you."

Rodriguez replied, "What about Homicide? Isn't this their domain? Why me?"

"Yeah, it's Homicide's job; but I think you're playing chess and they're playing checkers, so I need you on this. The press is all over it; and I've got to tell them something, so pick a team and let me know who it is."

"Fine, I'll do it, but whoever I pick is non-negotiable."

"Okay, Rodriguez. Think about it and get back to me tomorrow."

"I don't need to think about it until tomorrow. My team is Detective Spinelli with Homicide and Trooper William Jankowski. He's with Suffolk PD."

"I know Detective Spinelli, but what about this trooper? How much experience does he have with investigations?" inquired the mayor.

"Zero, but I can work with him and bring him up to speed. If he doesn't work out, I'll pick someone else."

"Are you sure you want to work with someone green on this one?"

"Yeah, I'm sure. I think he's going to be okay."

"Okay, Sergeant. I'll contact his commander. Just email me his name."

CHAPTER 3

MEET THE CYCLIST CLUB MEMBERS

Justine Godfrey grew up as the heiress to a family that made billions of dollars in the oil business. She always looked the part with her hair pulled back, dripping in jewelry, and speaking like a socialite from the '50s. Forty-five years old and single, she claimed that most men were annoying and adolescent in their actions. Most men found her snobbish and condescending. Two years ago, her parents died in a fire in their summer mansion in Greenwich, Connecticut, under suspicious circumstances. Being the sole beneficiary and the fact that she was able to escape the fire lent an air of mystery to the entire incident. Speculation wasn't proof, however; and authorities went through the evidence and eventually ruled the fire an accident. Ms. Godfrey, inheriting her family's entire fortune, wasted no time in restoring the mansion to its original glory. You can have all the money in the world and still be bored, but Justine Godfrey had a remedy for that. Ms. Godfrey was a human trafficker. Her network of contacts in the trade extended from Eastern Europe to Asia. Her associates, members of organized crime across many countries, were hardcore killers and gangsters but played by her rules. With her money, she could reach across oceans to find people to do her bidding. She was looking forward to Friday when the private club where she was a member notified her that they were meeting.

Edward Viscount (aka Eddie the Vis), as he was known, was an arrogant, self-centered, and immoral fading rock star. His career had lately taken a downturn due to drug and alcohol abuse and the fact that nobody could work with him. Today he was in Los Angeles, waking up in the Beverly Hills Hotel, having performed at a less than brilliant concert the night before. It was noon and the hot sun pouring into his room spotlighted the cocaine and bottles of Jack Daniels strewn about the room. Did I forget to mention the dead prostitute in his bed? Lying in bed and staring at her body, Eddie thought that maybe she was still sleeping. He reached over to feel for a pulse; but as soon as his hand touched her cold wrist, he screamed and jumped out of bed. He took a few hits of cocaine and reached for his cell phone. He called Jack, no last name. Jack maintained a low profile and stayed in the shadows. His job was to clean up celebrity messes, and this was quite a mess. Jack agreed to take the assignment for a rather large fee, of course. He made arrangements with Eddie the Vis to let him and his associate into the room and to then disappear for a few hours. Eddie did as he was told. A few hours later he received a text telling him that his room was ready. Eddie returned to a pristine room, no cocaine, no Jack Daniels bottles, and best of all, no dead prostitute. His cell phone chimed a reminder: "Cyclist Club Meeting Friday."

Ali Bakar sunned himself on the French Riviera, his tanned body paunchy and flabby, but that never stopped him from wearing a Speedo. Wearing a fake beard and a toupee of a mousey reddish-brown color, Ali's chosen career path was trafficking in weapons of all types. It didn't matter to Ali in whose hands they ended up so long as he got paid. He was lying on a chaise de plage (beach chair to most of us) looking up and down the beach for his contact. He summoned the waiter to bring him another drink. The waiter returned with the drink and an envelope and motioned to a man sitting at the hotel bar. The man raised his drink as if making a toast and Ali Bakar returned the gesture. He opened the envelope. The note read: "room thirty-four at five o'clock." Ali arrived at the room on time and was greeted by the contact who handed him a list of weapons, advising that Ali would receive the weapons when he paid the money. Ali never intended to pay the man. Putting a knife to the man's throat, he demanded to know where the weapons were or he would kill him. The men struggled. Ali stabbed the man repeatedly, killing him. Now, Ali didn't have the weapons and he had murdered a man for no reason. He stuffed the body between the mattress and the box spring, cleaned up the room, and cautiously made his way out the door, taking the stairs up to his room. He removed his disguise and went to the front desk to check out. The man behind the counter asked if everything was to his satisfaction as he was checking out early. Ali responded that he must leave. He had an important meeting this Friday in New York.

It was a hot night in Las Vegas and the roulette table was just as hot. Ray Salerno, a degenerate gambler and alcoholic, made money by arranging high-stakes poker games for organized crime families in Vegas; however, Ray never learned from his mistakes. He continued to gamble, and he continued to lose. He had hit the Mega Millions lottery for twenty-five million dollars but had squandered most of it due to his gambling and decadent lifestyle. His addiction to prostitutes and cocaine had made him behave recklessly, and he'd been borrowing money from a Vegas loan shark called "Freddie the Hammer." Freddie earned this nickname by, you guessed it, using a hammer to encourage people to pay their debts. Fingers, toes, it didn't matter—whichever was closest. Right now, a couple of Freddie's goons were looking for Ray because he owed Freddie $15,000; and the grace period had run out. The roulette wheel spun; and with each spin, Ray's pile of chips got smaller. The spin of the wheel mesmerized Ray until a little voice in his head told him to look up. That little voice had never failed him, and he spied two of Freddie's goons coming across the casino floor. One of them was carrying a paper bag with, you guessed it, a hammer inside. Ray ran for the nearest exit and noticed a conveniently-placed fire extinguisher hanging on the wall. He grabbed it and told himself to go for the eyes. The men turned the corner and walked into a wall of fire extinguisher foam. They rubbed their eyes, coughed, and gagged as Ray kept spraying. The bag with the hammer dropped to the floor and Ray, not missing an opportunity, began bashing the men with the hammer. Ray had morphed into Freddie—fingers, toes, whichever was closest, it didn't matter. The men rolled on the floor begging for him to stop, but Ray was already on his way to the bus station. It was sunrise in Vegas as Ray settled back in his seat. A young kid sitting across with his mother asked him where he was going. Ray answered that he was headed to New York City. He had to be there by Friday to meet some friends.

The closing bell on Wall Street signaled another upmarket. Carlyle Bolton III was a happy man. He managed his family's finances, and they were doing quite well. Carlyle learned everything he knew from his father, Carlyle II. The Bolton family made their money by investing in both small and large businesses and, when they became profitable, taking a percentage of assets. This business model wasn't lucrative enough for Carlyle, so he invested in these companies, took all the assets, fired the workers, and left a blank space where a thriving business once was. Carlyle sat in the back of a limousine as it wound its way up Park Avenue having a heated discussion on his cell phone. He was becoming agitated and his voice rose with anger. He shouted into the phone, "You told me this week! What the fuck happened?" There was a pause then he screamed again, "How tough can it be? It's just kids. If you scare them, they'll do whatever the fuck you want!" The driver began to take notice of the conversation and was looking in the rearview mirror. Carlyle screamed again, "I know it's against the law; but for me, it's like a drug!" There was another pause then Carlyle screamed, "Get them from Russia or China. I don't give a fuck! I know they're cracking down on that kiddie shit, but so what. I'm tired of looking at the same old shit." There was a pause and he remarked, "I can't on Friday. My private club is meeting." There was another pause then he responded, "If I tell you then it's not private anymore, is it asshole?" The driver had heard enough. He slammed on the brakes and pulled over. He went to the back and pulled open the passenger door. "Get out of my limousine. Now," he ordered in his African accent. The driver was about six foot four and looked like he worked out a lot, a whole lot. "I will not ask again." Carlyle said to the driver, "You can't kick me out, I'll get a cop." The driver reached in, yanked Carlyle's phone out of his hand, and said: "I think the officer might be interested in the last person you were speaking to." Carlyle replied, "I'll get a lawyer and sue your company and you." "No, you won't because I know where you live; and if you tell my company, I will tell the police. Now get out." Carlyle reached for his briefcase and his coat and muttered under his breath, "Goddam monkey." He got out of the limousine and as he walked away, the driver kicked him in the ass. Carlyle turned and exclaimed, "What the fuck are you doing? You assaulted me!" The driver smiled and replied, "That was for calling me a monkey. Goodbye."

Thomas Deville, President and CEO of Deville Marketing, ran a multi-level marketing business. The authorities called it mail fraud and a pyramid scheme. Nonetheless, Thomas made millions from this illegal endeavor. Some wondered how he had the time to verbally and physically assault his wife and children, maintain a millionaire lifestyle and run a "business." Tonight, Thomas was particularly pissed off because he suspected one of his partners was talking to the authorities. After a night of drinking and hanging out with some friends and a variety of prostitutes, he figured it was time to go home and show his family who was boss. He arrived home and began to yell, scream, and berate everyone, including the dog. Mrs. Deville decided she'd had enough; and as he raised his hand to slap her face, she grabbed a very expensive Asian vase and brought it down on Mr. Deville's head. Later, when Thomas woke up, and not having learned anything, he went into a profanity-laced tirade, shouting his wife's name. He searched the house; but there was no one there, not even the dog. Closets were empty. One car was gone, the most expensive one by the way; and all the jewelry, including his, was gone. He began to dial the police and realized that he couldn't. You know—investigations and all that. So poor Thomas Deville consoled himself with the fact that on Friday night his private club was meeting, one of his favorite things to do. He went to the liquor cabinet, poured himself a drink, and continued drinking until he passed out on the living room floor.

Jane Michaels was a State Senator who had taken the phrase "crooked politician" to a whole new level. Her appetite for lobbyist cash was insatiable. Today she was awaiting the arrival of an envelope full of cash from a Chinese solar energy company looking to squeeze out its American competition. What she didn't know was that the person delivering the money was not who he claimed to be. Senator Michaels gave her staff the rest of the day off so they would be alone. He arrived on time and the Senator showed him into her office. They exchanged pleasantries, how's the weather, how was the flight, do you have the money, blah, blah, blah. The man reached for the envelope in the side pocket of his jacket revealing a small microphone which didn't go unnoticed by the good Senator. She remarked, "Not here. These offices are bugged." Of course, they weren't, because if they were, half of Washington would be in prison. The man played along so as not to tip off Senator Michaels. She continued, "I know a quiet little place that's not too far. We can have a drink and you can give it to me there." The two had a grand old time talking, laughing, and flirting. Senator Michaels bought all the rounds, gin and tonic with a lot of gin for him, and club soda for her. Round four and the heavy guns came out, the old mickey fin for the gentleman. If Senator Michaels was anything, she was not unattractive, with a mane of blonde hair and blue eyes. She had a Midwest look reminiscent of an aging beauty queen. The flirting was over, and the scene shifted to the no-tell motel across the street where she had enough time to walk with the gentleman before the mickey took effect. It seemed that the combination of gin and fin was too much for the poor man's heart, and he expired on the stained bedspread. The wire, the money, and her disguise all left the room with her. The man, unfortunately, could not because he was dead. She returned to her office and removed the blonde wig and the blue contacts; and instantly, she looked like Sophia Loren instead of a Barbie doll. She grabbed her luggage and, in a flash, was on the 4:20 Amtrak Acela to New York for the Friday meeting.

CHAPTER 4

SANTIAGO BLINKS

Santiago Molina was at the Medellin airport. He was not going to New York to assassinate Sergeant Rodriguez. He owed it to Miguel to tell him he was running, but he wouldn't tell him where. Miguel answered the call, "Santiago, where are you?"

"I'm at the airport. I'm not going to New York, Miguel."

"What are you saying? Are you trying to get us both killed? If Jorge finds out, we're both dead. Do you understand me?"

"I'm sorry, Miguel. I lied about the whole thing. Yes, I set the fire; but I didn't kill El Moreno. I just wanted Delacruz to think I had balls, so I made up the story."

"So what happened that morning? And don't you fucking lie to me."

"I'll tell you. The night before the fire, El Moreno was on his yacht. He was partying with several women. He was drinking and using lots of cocaine. When he gets messed up, he's unpredictable; and he started fucking with me, calling me maricon and pendejo in front of the women. I could've killed him right there, but I left. When I returned early the next morning, the hacienda was quiet, and El Moreno was not in his bedroom. I went to his boat and found him dead, maybe too much cocaine. I don't know. I found his servants, "the farmers" as Delacruz called them; and they helped me set the fires. I could hear the screams of the men trapped inside. When the fire began to rage and the screams stopped, I went to the boat and threw the body overboard. Two other men showed up; and together, we vowed to never tell anyone the truth. You see, we all hated that piece of shit. That's when I called you and you took us to Delacruz. Without you there, he wouldn't have trusted us."

"Why didn't you tell the truth? Now you fucked us both. If he finds out, he'll kill me for bringing you to him. But you'll be safe somewhere, not giving a shit about what you caused."

"I'm sorry, Miguel. I'm just a fucking coward. Please forgive me. I must go. I can't tell you where I'm going. My flight is boarding. Adios."

Miguel screamed into the phone, "Santiago, Santiago, I'm a dead man, you fucking pendeho." He made a call to the two men who were with Santiago. "It's Miguel. Meet me at my hacienda. I want both of you there in two hours. I don't care what you're doing, get there. I can't tell you now, I'll tell you when we meet." The men were punctual, arriving at Miguel's hacienda at the appointed time. One of the men asked what they were doing there. Miguel hesitated then replied, "We're going to kill Delacruz and everybody in his Palacio. Santiago is not going to New York. He's running to who the fuck knows where. When Delacruz finds out, he'll send men to kill us all." The men looked at each other, not believing what they were hearing. One of them spoke: "What happens if we fail?"

Miguel poured everyone straight rum and he downed his drink in one gulp. "If we fail, we're all dead men, all of us." Miguel unlocked a cabinet above the bar and said to the men, "Take as many weapons as you like, something you can conceal, and let's go." They stopped their cars on the road to the hacienda and continued on foot. When they got to the front gate, they found it unlocked. Miguel ordered Ernesto, one of the men, to circle to the back and warn him if he saw anyone. The hacienda appeared to be deserted; and Ernesto, with gun drawn, slowly made his way through the rooms. For a man his size, Carlos was amazingly fast; and as Ernesto turned a corner, Carlos was waiting for him. He came from behind, put him in a chokehold, and broke his neck. Ernesto slid to the floor as Delacruz watched. Delacruz, holding the pump shotgun, signaled Carlos to check the other side of the house. Miguel was hiding in the bushes near the pool on one side facing the main living room. From that vantage point, he could see inside the gold-painted room. He moved slowly to get a better view and saw Carlos approaching his position. Carlos, however, didn't notice Miguel. Carlos was about thirty feet away and Miguel rose and fired, hitting Carlos in the chest. This didn't seem to have any effect, and Carlos fired back but missed. Again, Miguel fired, and again Carlos was struck in the chest; but he continued to advance. The third man ran towards the gunfire and was cut down by Delacruz who was hiding nearby. Carlos was beginning to stagger, but Miguel decided to change his position, knowing that Delacruz was close by. Miguel recognized the sound of the shotgun, understanding how lethal it was. Carlos was still on his feet and shooting wildly. Miguel fired one more shot on the run, and this one finished Carlos. His large body fell into one of the many pools on the property, the crystal-clear water turning red with blood. Delacruz shouted at Miguel, "You betrayed me, you piece of shit. I knew Santiago wasn't going to go through with it. I had him followed, and he bought a ticket to Costa Rica. He made a phone call from the airport. He called you, didn't he, you fucking putto. I had a feeling you were coming for me. So, what do I do with you, maricon? You've been with me for a long time. You're like family to me. So tell me, Miguel, what should I do?"

Miguel responded, "It doesn't matter anymore, Jorge. Perhaps we'll kill each other right here, right now, and be done with it."

"No, Miguel. I'm not dying today, but you are." Delacruz's manservant heard the gunshots as he hid in one of the upstairs bedrooms. He crept slowly to the side of the house and took Ernesto's weapon. Making his way to the front of the hacienda, he saw Miguel on the steps in front of him. Miguel had his back turned, but he heard the footsteps behind him. He turned quickly; but the manservant was quicker, firing twice, and hitting Miguel. The manservant yelled to Delacruz, "Padrone, I killed him. I'm here in the front."

Delacruz came running, shotgun at the ready. When he saw Miguel on the steps, he lowered his weapon. "Nice work, I'll see that you're handsomely rewarded."

The manservant raised his weapon and pointed it at Delacruz, saying, "Call me padrone, Jorge. Call me padrone."

Delacruz replied, "You're pointing that gun at me. Are you loco, muchacho? Put the gun down."

"No, I want you to call me padrone, then I'll put it down."

"You want me to call you padrone? Fuck you. You work for me. Put the gun down."

"No. How does it feel to be afraid, Jorge?"

"Afraid? Me, afraid of a servant, a peon like you? Go to hell." Delacruz attempted to raise the shotgun and fire, but the manservant drew first blood. Delacruz tried to raise his weapon again, but again he was hit. He fell to his knees. The shotgun had become too heavy for him to lift. The manservant walked over to him, knelt, and said, "So how does it feel to know that your servant got the better of you? I know where you hide the money, I know about the fake walls in the bedrooms. I know all the combinations to the safes; and after all these years of selling poison and watching you kill anyone who stood in your way, I'm taking it all. So, call me padrone and I'll see that you die quickly. If not, I'll kill you a little at a time, one knee then one elbow then the other knee and I'll leave you here to die." Say it, you devil." The manservant, however, forgot to do one thing after he shot Miguel. He forgot to make sure he was dead. Miguel staggered towards the manservant, gun in hand, pointing it at his head. Delacruz smiled when he saw Miguel getting closer to him. The manservant heard Miguel, but it was too late. He died instantly from a gunshot wound to the head. Miguel, who was dying, dropped down next to Delacruz. "Next time you need a manservant, Jorge, try a different agency." The two men laughed together.

"Don't make me laugh, Miguel. It hurts."

"See, Jorge, I told you both of us were dying here today. Did I not?"

"You're a son of a bitch, Miguel." Delacruz paused, "You know what I regret?"

"No, what, Jorge?"

"I regret not seeing my niece for the last time. Perhaps I can watch over her from above."

Miguel replied sarcastically, "Above?" and let out a laugh. "How many men have we sent to their graves without allowing them last words to their families? No, my friend, I'm afraid we're not going there."

The sun was setting, and a warm fragrant breeze wafted through the hacienda. Delacruz whispered, "Do you smell that, Miguel? Those are orchids, a beautiful fragrance. Perhaps they'll put some on my grave."

Miguel looked over at Delacruz and realized he was dead. He sadly replied, "Goodbye, my friend" as he, too, quietly passed away.

CHAPTER 5

THE TEAM

Sergeant Rodriguez was in his office going over reports when Trooper William Jankowski knocked on his office door. " Come in, it's open."

Jankowski entered and extended his hand to Rodriguez. "I'm reporting for duty, Sergeant."

Rodriguez stood, shook his hand, and replied, "'Good morning' is sufficient, Will. Have a seat." When Spinelli gets here, we'll go over what we know so far. So, tell me, what made you decide to become a trooper?"

"My father was NYPD, and my older brother is a cop in Atlanta. It's something I always wanted to do. It just felt natural. Can I ask you a question, Sergeant? Why did you pick me for this investigation?"

"The mayor called me and asked me to run this investigation and told me to pick my team. So, I chose Spinelli from Homicide; and since you were first on the scene, I thought you'd be the logical pick."

"But, Sergeant, I don't know how to investigate a homicide."

"Don't worry, we'll walk you through it. It's not going to be easy, Jankowski. Long hours, lots of reports, questioning suspects and witnesses. Have you ever been to the morgue?"

"No, Sergeant. Never."

"Well, it's part of the job, crime scene photos, autopsy photos. It's all part of the deal. I'll try to spare you as much as I can until you get used to it. The beginning is a little rough. So, are you in?"

"Yeah, count me in."

There was a knock on the door and Detective Spinelli walked into the office. "Come in, Marco. This is Trooper William Jankowski, the other member of the team do you remember he was the first on the scene." The men shook hands as Rodriguez put two folders on the desk. "We got an ID on the victim in the car. It's Howard Mayhew. Does the name ring a bell?"

Spinelli picked up the folder and thumbed through it. "He was supposed to be the next Bernie Madoff," and he hands the folder to Rodriguez.

Rodriguez continued looking through the folder, handing some pages to Trooper Jankowski. "That's the preliminary Medical Examiner's report. Read it, Will. What does it say?"

Will read the report to himself, then replied, "He was shot three times in the head with a .22 caliber handgun. It appears he died instantly."

Rodriguez continued, "There were five casings at the scene. The shooter was on the driver's side, and the window was up. The bullets shattered the window but didn't go through to the other side."

Will asked, "Why a .22 caliber handgun?

"Because it's fairly quiet and causes the most damage in a headshot."

"So, you think it was a hit, Sergeant?"

"Given the weapon and the character of the victim, I would say that's a good guess. The only question is the dead biker. Let's wait for the final report from the ME. We need to interview the widow. Maybe she can give us some answers. She said she's okay and is ready to talk to us. We'll head out there tomorrow. The house is in Sagaponack, one of the most expensive zip codes in the country. Shit, Mr. Mayhew was doing quite well with stealing people's money." Sergeant Rodriguez continued, "Spinelli, what do we know about the cyclist? Did we identify him?"

"I'm afraid not, Sarge. He had nothing on him; but the bike is a Pinarello Dogma F-10, about $8,000 new."

Rodriguez turned to Will. "Shit, serious money for a bike. Did the forensics team find a helmet?"

"No helmet," Spinelli responded, "not even pieces of one."

"Did the guy have any tats or piercings, something we can use for an ID?"

"Yeah, Sarge, he had three. The first is a skull and crossbones on his back by his left shoulder; the second is a half-sleeve on one arm that looks like a snake with a crucifix in its mouth, the snake bears a strange resemblance to, you guessed it, the devil. The third one—the numbers 666 vertically up the back of his left calf."

Rodriguez turned to Will. "What do you think, a cult, devil worship, or just some asshole who's trying to look tough?"

"Here, take a look, Sarge." Spinelli handed the photos of the tattoos to Rodriguez. He inspected the photos and handed them to Will.

Will examined the photos and noticed something written on the crucifix. "Sergeant, there's some writing on the cross. Do you have a magnifying glass?"

"Sure, top drawer."

Will peered closely at the tattoo and remarked, "Whoever did this tattoo is an artist. It's one of the best inks I've seen."

"Oh, yeah, how do you know?"

"I used to date a girl who was a tattoo artist, and I have a few myself. She was good, but this artist knows his shit."

Spinelli asked, "Can you make out what it says?"

Will, still looking at the tattoo, replied, "Yeah, it says, 'Jolly Roger.'"

"Well, that would explain the skull and crossbones tattoo on his back," observed Rodriguez. "What about his clothes? Any labels that can tell us where they were bought?"

Spinelli responded, "Nope, all ripped out. Nothing, not a clue; but the stuff is expensive biking gear worth about a grand."

"All that money spent and no helmet. I don't believe this guy was riding without a helmet," replied Rodgriguez. "I'm going to go out there before it gets dark and look around. I want you to come along, Will. Marco, why don't you canvas some of the tattoo parlors around town and show them those pictures. Let's meet back at the precinct in a few hours."

The ride to the crime scene was about twenty minutes from the precinct. They arrived to find a black car and two squad cars with lights flashing parked on the side of the road. Detectives McGraw and Davis were sitting inside the black car. The trooper that was assigned to guard the crime scene approached Rodriguez. "Sorry, Sergeant, I tried to stop them; but I was overruled."

"By whom?"

"The two guys in the black car. This guy McGraw did all the talking."

Rodriguez walked over and motioned for the men to roll down the window. "Good evening, gentlemen. What are you doing here? Please try not to mess up my crime scene, okay?" Rodriguez walked over to the embankment and observed two uniform officers appearing to look for something. He yelled, "I want you to get up here. Now."

Detectives McGraw and Davis exited their car and walked over to Rodriguez. "What's the problem, Sergeant? They're looking for clues."

"No, they're not. They're walking around aimlessly, stomping on the crime scene; and you're letting them."

McGraw replied, "Why are you here? This is a homicide investigation; and last time I checked, you're not a homicide detective."

"And the last time I checked, McGraw, you only investigate cops who are doing their job. If you have a problem with that, call the mayor. It wasn't my idea. The mayor wants me to take over the case."

"Why the fuck would the mayor give you a homicide case?"

"Like I said, not my idea. I want to do a proper search of the area."

"What are we looking for, Sergeant?" asked Davis.

"We're looking for a helmet. I think the guy had a go-pro, and I think somebody took it so we wouldn't know what happened. I want to conduct a complete search."

The uniformed troopers climbed the embankment to the road, and one of them asked, "Who are you guys?"

Rodriguez answered, "I'm Sergeant Rodriguez, and this is Trooper William Jankowski."

One of the troopers questioned, "So, who's in charge? We thought these guys were."

"Let's just say we're working together on this. Now let's do a search." Rodriguez turned to Davis. "What do you think, Davis, a grid?"

"Sure, Sergeant, a grid about twenty yards out." The men searched the area with no luck on finding the helmet or any additional clues.

Rodriguez and Jankowski arrived back at the precinct and found Spinelli waiting in the office. "So, did you find anything?"

"No, we did a grid of the area but got nothing. How'd you make out with the tattoos? Any information?"

"Not much. Some of the local artists say it's too high-end for them, but they were done by the same guy. They seem to think it's not a local artist, maybe someone on the west coast. Nobody recognized them, but they all agreed they were the best work they'd ever seen."

"Oh, yeah? What made them say that?"

Jankowski replied, "Anybody who knows the business can tell by technique, colors, and signature."

"Signature," asked Spinelli. "Yeah, a lot of artists sign their work; but they're discreet about it. They'll hide it somewhere in the tat."

"I think one of us needs to take a trip to the Medical Examiner's office and get a look at those tats up close. Alright, let's get out of here. In the morning Marco and I will talk to Mrs. Mayhew to see what we can find out. She knows we're coming around eleven. Will can hit some bike shops to see if anybody sells that brand.

CHAPTER 6

MRS. MAYHEW

It was a beautiful morning in May, the beginning of summer; and people were moving into their summer residences on the Island. Traffic was beginning to pile up; and the men were stuck in it, already late for their appointment with Mrs. Mayhew. Rodriguez was growing impatient. "I'm going to hit it and get out of this traffic." With lights and siren, the men bypassed the traffic and quickly approached the mansion on Rivercrest Road in Sagaponack.

They were greeted at the front gate by two security guards. One of the men approached them with a clipboard. "Good morning, gentlemen. Are you on the list?" Rodriguez showed his badge and replied," I'm Sergeant Rodriguez and this is Detective Spinelli. We have an eleven 'o'clock appointment." The security guard scanned his clipboard. "Rodriguez and Spinelli. Yeah, you're on the list; but you're late."

Spinelli leaned over and demanded, "Open the fucking gate." The security guard let out a sigh and signaled for the gate to be opened.

Rodriguez turned to Spinelli, "Decaf, Spinelli, decaf." The road to the mansion was long, bordered on both sides by beautifully-landscaped gardens and cedar trees. The road opened up to a circular drive, around which several exotic cars were parked. The men were greeted at the door by a butler who escorted them to a larger room. Mrs. Mayhew was seated and waiting for them, "You're late, Sergeant."

"Our apologies, but traffic was rough."

"I have guests coming at noon, a luncheon for my philanthropic group."

Rodriguez questioned, "You're having a luncheon?"

"Are you surprised, detective? Did you expect to find me dressed in black and sobbing like a schoolgirl who's lost her puppy? The truth is my husband was a conniving, cheating, horrible man. I was his trophy wife, but he lost interest as I got older."

Rodriguez asked, "When did you see him last?"

"Let me see...a few days before he died. You see, sometimes he would disappear for days on end."

"Do you know where he went?"

"Who knows, probably with one of his many mistresses or his shady circle of friends. My husband considered himself a financial genius; but in reality, he was a grifter and a con man, bilking rich widows out of their savings with some investment scheme or another. He made millions, but it's all gone now."

Spinelli looked around and remarked, "It seemed to work out pretty well."

Mrs. Mayhew let out a laugh and replied, "Are you referring to this house? My money bought this house and everything in it. The cars, the houses in Paris and Palm Springs, no doubt you noticed that red

Ferrari as you drove up. Well, I bought that for him on his sixtieth birthday."

"Mrs. Mayhew, if things were so bad between the two of you, why didn't you divorce him?"

"My husband had a prenuptial drawn up when I was young and naïve. You see, he knew about my family fortune; and no matter what happened, he would get half of my estate. Four hundred million dollars. So, we decided to live separate lives. He can bang all the whores he wants; and I have some young male friends who visit from time to time, you know, to help me relax. I believe the souffle is out of the oven, doesn't that smell divine? Have either of you ever had a cheese souffle?"

Rodriguez answered, "I did when I was in Paris."

"You were in Paris, Sergeant? Isn't it wonderful? You must come by and tell me about it some time."

Rodriguez glanced at Detective Spinelli and then changed the subject. "Mrs. Mayhew, do you know anybody who would want to kill your husband?"

"Sergeant, the question should be, 'Do I know anybody who didn't want to kill my husband?'"

"Can you give me some names?"

"I don't remember their names, but these three men would come around from time to time, sometimes once a month, sometimes every six weeks. They were very rude and spoke badly to my husband. When I asked him about it, he became cross and asked me to mind my own business. Sometimes he would hand them an envelope."

"Was it money, Mrs. Mayhew?"

"Probably; but as I said, he wouldn't tell me."

"Did these men ever introduce themselves to you?"

"Yes. In the beginning, they did; but I'm not sure I remember."

"When was the last time they were here?"

"It was a few weeks ago."

"When we came in, our names were at the front gate. Can you call down there and see if they're on the list?" requested Spinelli.

"Yes, that's a wonderful idea. I'll have my butler do it." A few minutes later the butler handed Mrs. Mayhew a list with three names which she then passed to Spinelli. "Gentlemen, if you don't mind, my guests will be here soon; and I'd prefer it if they didn't find two policemen in my salon."

Rodriguez handed Mrs. Mayhew his card. "Here's my card. If you think of anything else, give me a call. My cell phone number is on the back."

As they walked back to their car, Spinelli exclaimed, "That was fucking weird."

"Yeah, not exactly what I was expecting. Let's see how Will made out with tracking the bike down." Will was waiting for them at the precinct. Rodriguez asked, "So, how'd it go, Will?"

"Not good, Sergeant. None of the shops I stopped at stock this bike."

Rodriguez asked, "Can it be ordered?"

"I asked and nobody's ordered this bike in any of the stores I stopped at, Sergeant."

"That sucks. Spinelli, let me see that list of names she gave you."

"Here you go, Sergeant."

Rodriguez read the names aloud, "Josh Solomon, David Everett, and Zachariah."

"Zachariah, what's his last name," asked Will.

"No last name, just Zachariah."

The sun was setting, and Mrs. Mayhew's guests had left. The butler approached Mrs. Mayhew, "The guard just informed me that there are three men at the gate who want to extend their condolences."

"Three men—don't allow them in. Tell them to come back tomorrow."

The butler spoke into the intercom, "It's late; perhaps they can come back tomorrow."

At that moment there was a knock on the door. Mrs. Mayhew exclaimed, "Call the police."

The butler picked up the phone as the men strode in. One of the men demanded, "Put the phone down."

The butler inquired how they got past the men at the gate. "Don't worry; we didn't hurt them. We told them we were friends of your husband."

The butler looked at Mrs. Mayhew and she replied, "My husband is dead. What do you want?"

"We don't want anything; we came by to pay our respects. How did the luncheon go, Mrs. Mayhew?"

"How do you know about my luncheon?" she nervously asked.

One of the men questioned, "The two men that were here today—who were they, Mrs. Mayhew?"

"That's none of your concern; now please leave."

"We must assume they were policemen investigating your husband's death. What did you tell them?"

"I wasn't involved in my husband's personal life. We've been estranged under the same roof."

"Did you tell them our names?"

"No, I didn't tell them anything. Now it's late and I want to retire, so get out."

"Be careful who you speak to, Mrs. Mayhew; and be careful what you say. Do you understand? We'll see ourselves out. Good night."

CHAPTER 7

THE TWO MEN

It was 11:00 p.m. and Sergeant Rodriguez, unable to sleep, was watching *Key Largo*, Humphrey Bogart being one of his favorite actors. His Maine Coon cat, Bogie, was asleep by his side. "What's up, Bogie? Are you bored?" His phone rang, and he wondered who would be calling him at this hour. He picked up to find Mrs. Mayhew's voice on the other end of the line.

"Sorry for the late hour, Sergeant."

"Mrs. Mayhew, are you alright?"

"No, Sergeant. I'm frightened, and I can't sleep. Those men came back this evening."

"What did they want?"

"They said they didn't want anything, but they were threatening in their tone."

"They threatened you? What did they say; be specific."

"They said I should be careful who I speak to and be careful what I say."

"Anything else?"

"Yes, they wanted to know if I told you their names."

"I hope you told them no, Mrs. Mayhew."

"Yes, that's what I told them; but I'm scared for my safety. Can you send someone around to watch the house?"

"I'll get somebody out there in the morning. For now, I'll have a car circle the area. Now try to get some rest. I'll phone you in the morning, Mrs. Mayhew. Good night."

He began to dial the precinct but hung up and called Will instead. "Sorry, Will, I hope I didn't wake you."

"No, my girlfriend and I are watching *Key Largo* and having popcorn. Is everything okay?"

"You're watching *Key Largo*? So was I."

Will covered the phone and whispered to his girlfriend, "It's my boss, Sergeant Rodriguez. Something must be up. What's up, Sergeant?"

"I'm not sure. I just got a call from Mrs. Mayhew. She told me those men came back earlier tonight and made some veiled threats. I'm going out there to look around and I want you to come with me. I'll pick you up on the way."

Will covered the phone again and said to his girlfriend, "He wants me on a stakeout with him. That's fucking cool, right?"

"Will, I can hear everything you're saying. It's not a stakeout. We're going out there to check with the security guards at the gate and advise them to keep their eyes open, that's it. I'll pick you up."

When they arrived at the house, they noticed that the front gates were open; and the security guards were nowhere in sight. The men ran to the front gate and found the guards on the ground, unconscious.

Rodriguez drew his gun. "Will, call for assistance and cover the entrance. I'm going up to the house." He made his way up the driveway to the house—the front door was wide open. Cautiously, he entered and encountered the butler, dead on the floor with his throat cut. He then heard the sounds of a scuffle coming from the second floor and ran up the stairs to find Mrs. Mayhew. She was on her bed struggling with a man who was attempting to smother her with a pillow. Rodriguez jumped on top of the man and they fell to the floor, knocking over the nightstand. They rolled around on the floor and Rodriguez, the stronger of the two, got the upper hand, punching him in the face. Rodriguez was able to pin the man against the wall, but he was elbowed in the ribs, and the intruder was able to break away. The fight continued with the assailant throwing punches. Rodriguez was able to block them as he fought back, pummeling him with rights and lefts. The assailant recovered and grabbed Rodriguez around the neck. Facing each other, Rodriguez broke the man's hold and head-butted him in the face, stunning him. Realizing he was outmatched, the intruder pulled a gun, jumped across the bed, and ran to the head of the stairs. He turned and fired a shot at Rodriguez who returned fire, hitting the man twice. He tumbled down the steps and lay dead at the base of the stairs.

Mrs. Mayhew was coughing and gasping for air. Rodriguez ran over to her. "Just breathe, Mrs. Mayhew, breathe." Rodriguez searched the room and found no one else there. He instructed her to stay in her room. Will heard the shots and ran up the drive, seeing headlights coming right at him. The driver's side window was down, and the driver fired two shots at Will who dove to the ground. The car was traveling at a high rate of speed and narrowly missed him. He got to his feet and fired at the back of the car. Three bullets tore through the back window, hitting the driver. The car continued another fifty feet and crashed into one of the trees on the property. Mrs. Mayhew remained in her room as more police officers arrived on the scene. Rodriguez checked the man at the bottom of the stairs and discovered him dead.

Will stood in front of the house, a blank expression on his face. Rodriguez asked, "Are you alright, Jankowski?"

"I think I just killed somebody," he replied solemnly.

Rodriguez approached the car cautiously, gun in hand, and discovered the driver dead. He searched for identification and found the man's license. His name was Josh Solomon. In the distance was the sound of police officers and emergency medical service personnel.

Rodriguez returned to Will and confirmed, "You're right, Will. He's dead." Will was very quiet and Rodriguez continued, "It was you or him. He was trying to run you over. They were going to kill Mrs. Mayhew, and they killed the butler. You did what you had to do. Just so you know, it doesn't get easier. I'll get one of the uniforms to take you back."

"No, I'm going to stay with you and wrap this up."

"Are you sure? This is going to take all night. The guy in the car is Josh Solomon, one of the three guys on the list."

A uniformed police officer approached and informed Rodriguez, "We got an ID on the guy on the stairs. His name is David Everett."

Rodriguez turned to Will, "That's two out of three." They returned to the house to check on Mrs. Mayhew as she was tended to by medical personnel. At the entranceway, the butler's body was covered with a white sheet.

"How are you feeling, Mrs. Mayhew?" asked Rodriguez. "May we ask you a few more questions?"

She responded, "If not for you two, I would be dead now."

Rodriguez asked the medical personnel if they could give them a minute. "Mrs. Mayhew, the two men are on the list you gave us. Their names are Josh Solomon and David Everett. Did you see the third man? Are these the three men that threatened you?"

"Yes, they were here earlier; but the threats came from Zachariah."

"What does Zachariah look like, Mrs. Mayhew?"

"Well, Sergeant, he's very tall and muscular like an athlete."

"I'm six foot three. Is he about my height?"

"Yes, Sergeant, and he's bald with a sardonic smile."

"Sardonic smile? What do you mean?"

"When he smiled, he looked evil and menacing with crooked teeth; but other than that, he was well-groomed. I remember he wore a little too much cologne."

"Mrs. Mayhew, is there any place you can stay for the next several days? I'm afraid there's going to be an investigation team camped out here."

"Yes, Sergeant, I can stay with my son. He's not far from here."

"Would you like us to call him for you?"

"No, I'd rather not alarm him. I'll call him."

"Will, do you have any questions for Mrs. Mayhew?" Will was quiet and then asked, "When Zachariah spoke, did he have an accent?"

"Yes, I believe he did, maybe Eastern European or Russian."

Rodriguez continued, "You said he was athletic. Was he built like a football player, you know, wide with a big chest and arms or more like a runner or a swimmer, wiry with longer muscles, you know, lean?"

"He was built like you, Sergeant. I guess you would say like a football player. His thighs were very large; they seemed strange."

"What do you mean by strange?"

"Well, his legs seemed to be out of proportion to his body. They looked bigger and stronger."

"Mrs. Mayhew, call your son. We're going to go now. You're surrounded by police so you're safe. I'd like you to come to the precinct when you're better and have a facial composite done of Zachariah."

"You mean by a sketch artist?"

"No, Mrs. Mayhew, those days are over. It's all on the computer now. I'll be in touch."

The sun was rising and pouring into the car as Rodriguez drove Will home. Rodriguez remarked, "Shit, I find that if I'm out all night and I don't get to bed before the sun comes up, I might as well stay up. What about you?"

Will was staring straight ahead and replied, "Something she said about his legs being bigger and stronger."

Rodriguez agreed, "Yeah, like a cyclist. You handled yourself well tonight. Now let me tell you what's going to happen. Internal Affairs is going to investigate the shooting to make sure deadly force was justified. They're going to ask you questions. Just tell the truth exactly as you lived it. They're going to check our stories to see if they jibe. Some of the guys at the precinct may call you a hero and some may give you the cold shoulder. Screw 'em, hold your head up and keep moving. Get some rest. I'll see you at the precinct around noon. I'll fill in Spinelli."

Rodriguez called Captain Ebersole with the Brooklyn organized crime unit. Ebersole answered, "Well, top of the morning, Sergeant. Do you know what time it is?

"Yep, it's 6:00 a.m. and I need your help."

Ebersole asked, "How's McMahon? Have you spoken to her?"

"No, not recently. She's due for a call."

"Give her my regards when you do. So what's up, Sergeant?"

"Well, it's about Maxie. I need you to pull some strings with the warden."

Rodriguez arrived at the precinct after getting a few hours' sleep. Will and Spinelli were waiting for him. "Good morning, gentlemen. Let's go into my office." The men entered and closed the door. "Will, in a few days Internal Affairs is probably going to contact you. Let me know. I'll speak to them."

Spinelli chimed in, "Tell them to fuck off."

"Now, now, Marco, let's not be rude. I'll deal with them. Will, I was going to ask you to take a trip to the Medical Examiner's office with me today; but I'll let Marco do the honors. We need to find the guy who tattooed the cyclist. Get some better closeups of the tats and show them to Will when you get back. I'm expecting a call, I may be out the rest of the day."

Marco mockingly replied, "You got a girlfriend stashed away, Sergeant?"

"Yeah, it's your sister. Will, while I'm gone, run a check on those two guys from last night and find out all you can." Just then his phone rang. It was Captain Ebersole, "Hi, Captain, how'd you make out?" There was a long pause, then Rodriguez replied, "Officer Ramos on the third floor, thanks, Captain." There was another pause then he responded, "Me? I'm working on some weird shit case. I'll fill you in later. Thanks, Captain. I appreciate it."

CHAPTER 8

SAUCE TO DIE FOR

Rodriguez arrived at the Suffolk Prison on the end of Long Island carrying two plastic bags and was ushered to the third floor where he met Officer Ramos. Pleasantries were exchanged and Officer Ramos informed Rodriguez, "I need to be in there with you."

Rodriguez replied," I get it."

"I also need to look inside those bags."

Formalities out of the way, Rodriguez entered the room to find Maxie waiting for him. Upon seeing him, Maxie flashed a big smile. "Well, well, look who's here after all these weeks. Did you miss me, Sergeant?"

"Nah, who the fuck would miss you, but I did bring you something you might enjoy." Rodriguez opened the bags and said, "I have Linguine with Bolognese sauce, broccoli rabe, and a bottle of Pepsi."

"How the hell did you swing all this?"

"I pulled some strings, let's leave it at that."

While the men ate, Maxie said, "It ain't Rao's, but it's good. Too bad I don't drink soda."

Rodriguez got closer and said, "Try it, you'll like it."

Maxie took a sip from the Pepsi bottle. It was Chianti. "Shit, the only thing missing is the blow job."

Both men laughed and Rodriguez asked, "Did you ever hear of a guy named Howard Mayhew?"

"Hear of him? I used to drink with him back in the day. I heard somebody put two in his head."

"Three, yeah, a few days ago."

"You see, Sergeant, when I was moving money around for DiNapoli, I used to go down to the exchange from time to time. I got to know some of the big players, and they talked about this guy like he was the next Madoff. They thought I was an investor, and they told me to avoid this guy like the clap. I met him and drank with him a few times. He tried to scam me into investing with him, but I knew better. If I gave this guy Richie's money, he would have killed us both."

Rodriguez asked, "So how is DiNapoli? Any word?"

Maxie laughed and replied, "Nice try, Rodriguez. You know this food is pretty damn good. Where'd you get it?"

"I got it at a place called Vesuvio."

"Never heard of it. Where is it?"

"It's in Woodside."

"Ain't that neighborhood all spics now?"

Rodriguez looked at Maxie and responded, "Maxie, you do realize I'm Hispanic, right?"

"Yeah, I know. With a name like yours, you ain't German. Listen, if it makes you feel better you can call me a wop, actually I'm half a wop."

"You're hot shit. If it's okay, I'll just call you Maxie. I have to go."

Maxie replied, "Thanks for the food, Sergeant; and come again. You know where to find me. Bring more pasta. That sauce was to die for."

"Sure, Maxie, sure."

CHAPTER 9

MAN OF STEEL

Zachariah prepared to go to the gym. He cracked half a dozen eggs into a blender and poured in protein powder and juice. He downed it, reached into his bag, took out two syringes, and injected himself in each thigh. He let out a primal scream, grabbed his gym bag, and was out the door. On the south shore of Long Island was an exclusive gym named Heavy Lifting. This was the type of gym where serious bodybuilders worked out. It was not open to the public; enrollment was by referral only. It was not your typical gym. Today was an unusually busy day. Zachariah claimed a stationary bike in the corner and began his workout. All eyes were focused on him. A tall powerfully-built man with strong legs and bulging thighs, he rode the bike for over an hour, peddling non-stop with the setting on the highest resistance possible. He was shirtless, violating the gym rules; but he didn't seem to care. His back was completely covered in tattoos. Across his shoulders were the words "MAN OF STEEL." An employee approached him reluctantly. "Excuse me, sir, but you need to put a shirt on. It's management policy."

Zachariah continued to peddle, staring straight ahead. Finally, he said to the employee, "Are you management?"

The employee responded, "No, I'm not."

The answer came immediately. "Then get the fuck away from me. You're interrupting my workout." The MAN OF STEEL finished his workout to applause and departed the gym. He was driving to his home when his phone rang. "Yeah?"

The voice on the other end said, "Finish it tonight. It has to be tonight. She can identify you."

"Okay, McGraw. I'll send one of my guys."

"I don't give a shit who you send. I just want to see it on the morning news. Get it done." The voice on the other end disconnected. Zachariah was angry, and he slammed his phone against the dashboard. He continued to drive along the ocean to a house on Shore Crest Drive. In front of the house, a young Asian girl was waiting for him. "You must be Kim." He noticed that she had an expensive red bike. They went upstairs, and he threw his gym bag on the floor. He asked, "Are you ready?" She nodded, and they entered a room at the end of the hall. "Do you know what you want?"

She responded, "I was thinking of a black and white dragon on my shoulder with his claws digging into my skin leaving bright red blood tracks. It would be cool if it was breathing fire."

"Nice, which shoulder?"

"I think the left one. Can you put the claws on my shoulder like the dragon is climbing?"

"Yes, I can do that. It's going to take many sessions."

"Okay, let's get started."

After a while, Zachariah asked," I couldn't help but notice that bike. Is that a Santa Cruz Hightower?"

"Wow, how did you know that?"

"Let's just say that I've been known to ride once in a while. That's an expensive bike. What do you do for money?"

"I saved every dime I made, and I was able to afford a used one."

"It's a nice bike. I ride a Pinarello Bolide TT. Ever hear of it?"

"Hell, yeah. I heard of it; but there's no way I can afford one, even used."

Zachariah asked, "When we're done, would you like to go riding with me on the boardwalk? I know a great juice bar where we can stop for smoothies."

"Maybe next time, I'm meeting some friends for drinks."

Zachariah was annoyed and applied more pressure than was needed. He said, "I'm not hurting you, am I? Damn, this is going to be a great tattoo."

Kim replied, "Yeah, it hurts more than I thought it would. Does it always hurt this much?"

"No, I'll put less pressure. Too bad you can't go for a ride with me. You know, Kim, alcohol is bad for you when you're in training."

Kim laughed, "I'm not in training. I just love to ride."

"We're almost done for today. You'll have to come back. It's a lot of work."

Rodriguez arrived home and Bogie greeted him. After a while, Spinelli called. "So how did you make out?"

"I've got shots of the tats; and if you look closely, it looks like the letters 'MOS' are on top of the cross."

Rodriguez questioned, "MOS?"

"Yeah, that's all I was able to find."

"Okay, Marco, thanks. I'll see you tomorrow." Rodriguez fed Bogie and worked out in his home gym. In the middle of his workout, Jankowski called. "Hey, Will, what did you find out?"

"Sarge, these guys are bad news. Solomon had a warrant from Georgia for murder. The other guy, Everett, he's got warrants for rape, attempted murder, and extortion from Florida."

Rodriguez replied, "I'm not surprised. These guys have a track record. Do you still feel bad about killing that piece of shit? If you want to talk about it, I'm here. See you tomorrow." He hung up and continued his workout.

The next morning Rodriguez was in his office looking at the photos of the tattoos. Will arrived and greeted Rodriguez. "Good morning, Sergeant."

"Good morning, Will. Take a look at these and tell me what you think. Marco said the letters 'MOS' are on the cross."

Will picked up a magnifying glass to get a closer look. "Yep, it's there. I see it."

"So, what do you think, Will? Is it somebody's initials, a gang tag, can you figure it out?"

Marco came into the office and greeted everyone. "Good morning, gentlemen."

Rodriguez said," I got a call earlier today that Mrs. Mayhew is back in her home, I'm going to call her to see if she wants to come in and do a computer ID. We've got two uniforms watching the house, front and back. Let's see if she'll come tomorrow morning. Marco, any word when we can look at autopsy results?

"Waiting for the toxicology report to come back."

"I want to take a field trip to the auto impound lot to look at Mayhew's car. I got a hunch. Marco, hold the fort and see if you can get Mrs. Mayhew to come in tomorrow morning. Tell her I'll send a trooper to pick her up. Come on, Will. Let's go check out the car. Be back in a few hours."

Rodriguez and Will arrived at the pound and were escorted to the car. Both men started examining the vehicle, Rodriguez is studying the front of the car. "Will, what do you think that cyclist weighed, hundred eighty, hundred ninety pounds?"

"Yeah, I would say."

"Did you ever see a person who's been hit by a car?"

"Sure, Sergeant, it's part of the job."

"Look at the front of this car. Where's the damage?"

"Shit, Sergeant, there is none."

"I wouldn't say none. All the damage is below the headlights, and they're not cracked or busted. I'm not sure what that means, Will. What do you think?"

"Maybe the cyclist wasn't on his bike."

"That's good, Will. I would say he wasn't even on his feet. One thing's been bugging me since that night. Let's assume that Mayhew was doing fifty-five miles an hour, but he was probably going faster. This guy likes speed. He was driving this Maserati and he had a

Ferrari in his driveway. An open road and that kind of horsepower, I would guess Mayhew was flying. I would do the same thing. There's no way a cyclist could keep up, so how do you slow him down?"

Will thought about it and replied, "You create an accident, an injured cyclist in the road."

"Bingo. Did you ever hear of cadaveric spasm?"

"Sure, we studied it at the academy. It's not common, but it happens."

"When he was shot, the spasm forced his foot down on the gas and the cyclist on the ground didn't move fast enough. Mayhew was set up. It wasn't road rage. The cyclist was the bait. When Mayhew slowed down to check on him, the shooter made his move. Mayhew didn't have a chance to get out of his car. We got a shooter out there. Come on, let's get back."

Rodriguez and Will returned to the precinct and found Marco waiting for them. Rodriguez asked, "Did you talk to Mrs. Mayhew?"

"Yeah, she'll be here tomorrow at eleven. I'm sending a uniform to pick her up. How'd you guys make out with the car?"

Will explained, "There's no way it was road rage. It looks like he was set up."

"Let's get a computer composite of the cyclist and see if anybody knows him. I'll ask the Medical Examiner to send some pictures over. Let's get some shots of the tattoo also except for the 'MOS.' We'll keep that under wraps. The District Attorney's office can give them to the press."

CHAPTER 10

BODY BAG

It was a little after midnight in Sagaponack and the Mayhew residence was under lockdown. Two troopers were guarding the mansion, one at the front gate and one at the back entrance. A lone cyclist rode past the trooper's car and, without warning, lost control of his bike, falling to the ground. The trooper approached the cyclist. "Are you okay?"

"Shit, I think I hurt my knee. Can I lean on your car for a minute?"

"Sure, lean on me. Do you need an ambulance?"

When the trooper turned his back, the cyclist struck. He stabbed the trooper in the back and covered his mouth to keep him from warning the other officer. He placed him in the driver's seat of the patrol car so that it appeared he was on duty behind the wheel. The cyclist made his way silently to the back of the house and observed the other trooper walking the grounds. He put a gun to the trooper's head and walked him to the service entrance. He demanded, "Open the door or I'll put a bullet in your head." The trooper hesitated and the cyclist struck him with the gun. "Punch in the fucking code, and don't tell me you don't know it." The trooper, fearing for his life, entered the code. The cyclist then pistol-whipped the trooper causing him to lose consciousness. He crept up the stairs to the bedroom and found Mrs. Mayhew asleep. Using a pillow to muffle the sound, he shot her twice. He heard sirens approaching and sprinted down the back stairs to see the trooper dazed but on his feet. He shot him, as well, and ran across the property, disappearing behind the dunes near the ocean. In his escape, he left the bike behind. Rodriguez received a call from one of the troopers on the scene. "You need to get out here, Sergeant."

"I'm on my way."

When Rodriguez arrived, he was briefed by the trooper. "One trooper is dead, one's in serious condition at Hampton Hospital. The bullet hit him just below his vest. Mrs. Mayhew is dead. She was shot. The shooter left his bike behind."

Rodriguez asked, "Who called the police?"

"Nobody, the house has a silent alarm. The trooper said after he was shot, the assailant took off across the property and over those dunes. Troopers are searching back there now."

Rodriguez examined the bike left at the scene. He called the trooper over and asked, "You know anything about bikes?"

"Not really, but I know that this bike is worth about $5,000."

Rodriguez replied, "$5,000? How do you know?"

"I've seen them in some bike shops in Manhattan."

Detective Spinelli arrived on the scene and was briefed by Rodriguez. As the men walked to the rear of the house, Rodriguez filled him in. "The trooper was hit just below his vest, but the medics said the bullet missed vital organs. He saw the suspect run behind those dunes. Come on, let's go upstairs to the bedroom.

They climbed the stairs and attempted to go into the master bedroom. A voice down the hall yelled, "Sergeant Rodriguez, it's this one."

"Spinelli, she slept in a different room last night. Why?" The men looked around the room for evidence as the forensic team dusted for prints and photographed the scene. A member of the forensic team noted, "The shooter was in and out. We didn't find anything, no prints, some dirt on the rug, but no shoe prints.

"There are indentations in the rug, a continuous pattern from the stairs to this room."

"Yeah, those were left by cleats from the bike shoes."

"We're not going to find anything here. I got to think a few things through." Rodriguez asked the forensics team leader, "Can you get a report to me tomorrow?"

"Sure, Sergeant."

"Thanks. Come on Marco, let's go."

The next morning the men were in the office discussing the latest developments in the case. Rodriguez began, "We got one trooper deceased and one in the hospital in critical condition." Marco asked how the shooter got close enough to the trooper to stab him in the back.

"I think they staged an injury just like they did with Mr. Mayhew. The trooper went to help him; and when the opportunity presented itself, he made his move. The question now is Mrs. Mayhew. She didn't sleep in her bedroom last night."

Will responded, "Maybe she felt safer in one of the back bedrooms away from the front of the house."

"Perhaps, Will, but I think that Mrs. Mayhew would have avoided sleeping in the guest room. The shooter thought the trooper was entering the access code, but he wasn't. The alarm company said that the system received an emergency code. Instead of disarming the system, the trooper entered a special sequence of numbers linked to 911. The door was unlocked in case the trooper had to get inside quickly. The shooter didn't know that. He figured he had time to kill Mrs. Mayhew and then get out before the police arrived. When the 911 code went out, it was all hands on deck; every trooper in the immediate vicinity responded. The sirens messed up his plans; he had to kill her and get back outside before the police got to the house. He had no time to go out the front and run down that long driveway where his bike was. There was no way he was going to leave his bike behind, but he had no choice. He barely got out before the police arrived."

Will asked, "Did they get any prints off the first bike?"

Spinelli answered, "No, it was clean. They've got tons of DNA; but without prints, there's not much you can do with it. Let's see if they get anything from the second bike."

Rodriguez continued, "So, let's see what we have so far. We've got a very expensive bike present at each crime scene. Will, how many bedrooms were there upstairs?"

Will referred to his notes and replied, "Five bedrooms and two baths. Mrs. Mayhew was not in the master bedroom. She was at the other end of the house. The alarm company said they got the signal at 1:19 a.m., and the first officers to respond arrived at 1:23 a.m. That means the shooter only had four minutes to get upstairs, find the room she was in, and kill her. He then had to reverse the process and shoot the officer before running across the property and to the ocean."

"Okay, so the shooter's in good shape. Getting up and down the stairs quickly was no problem for him. How did he know which room she was in? If he had to search for her, he would've never made it out before the first unit got there."

Spinelli quipped, "Maybe he got lucky."

Rodriguez responded, "Yeah, maybe. When the trooper is better, we'll talk to him."

CHAPTER 11

THE IDEAL INMATE

Mercedes Delacruz was incarcerated at the Women's Detention Center at the Suffolk State Prison awaiting trial. Because of the Delacruz family's enormous wealth and because she was determined to be a flight risk, bail was denied. The authorities had not been able to locate the family's assets. Her brother Diego, who was killed during a drug raid, was the family's financial manager; and the Delacruz's fortune was well hidden. Mercedes had been a chameleon all her life, presenting different faces depending on the situation. In prison, she portrayed herself as the demure inmate reading books and working in the prison library. She used her looks to seduce a young, naïve guard named Eric Pullman who granted her access to a computer from time to time. By doing so, she was able to transfer funds from her offshore accounts to a U.S. bank. This helped her buy favors and quietly maintain a prison gang who would do her bidding while incarcerated. From the perspective of the guards, she was the ideal inmate, not getting into trouble and keeping to herself.

The thing about prison is that some days it's impossible to keep to yourself and avoid confrontation. Today was one of those days. Mercedes was on the lunch line when a few inmates who were part of a prison gang decided it was time to test her. The ringleader approached, "Hey, Jennifer Lopez, I want your roll." Mercedes ignored her and waited for the rest of her food. The inmate spoke again, "I'm talking to you, bitch."

Mercedes turned and remarked, "My name is not Jennifer Lopez or bitch. It's Mercedes Delacruz. My father was Arturo Delacruz and my uncle is Jorge Delacruz. They showed me how to kill with whatever I have in my hand. If I hit you in the windpipe with this tray, you'll be on the floor gasping for air. And if that doesn't teach you a fucking lesson, one day while you're in the shower soaping up that fat stinky ass, one of those hardcore bitches over there, on my command, will take a shiv and stick it up your ass. So, if you want my roll, ask me nicely or back the fuck off."

The inmate looked over at Delacruz's prison gang and said, "I got it, keep your fucking roll."

Mercedes was in the prison library when Eric Pullman the young guard entered. He walked over to her table and began to play a game with her. "What are you doing, inmate?"

"I'm reading and minding my own business."

The guard replied, "The maintenance closet needs to be straightened out. I suggest you get on it."

"Yes, officer; but I don't know where it is."

"Come on, I'll show you." They walked to a section of the library that had no cameras. The guard unlocked a door and they entered the room. Inside were cleaning materials, brooms, mops, and vacuum cleaners.

Mercedes asked, "So what do you want me to straighten out?" The guard didn't answer but instead began to open his zipper. She pulled down her prison scrubs and leaned on the sink. The guard ran his hand up and down her thighs and penetrated her. Mercedes asked breathlessly, "What about the cameras?"

"There are no cameras in this part of the library. Nobody knows we're in here." This seemed to embolden them both and he thrust even harder, covering her mouth with his hand. Mercedes pushed him deeper, and she reached her peak as he finished and collapsed on her. They rested on each other for a while, and she then asked, "May I have a computer tomorrow?"

"Sure, whatever you want."

Mercedes thanked him and smiled a wicked smile.

Rodriguez was sitting in his office. There was a knock on the door. "Come in, it's open." In walked Detectives Davis and McGraw. "Gentlemen, what brings you out here?"

"Good morning, Sergeant. We just thought that you might like some help with the case."

"Really? That's nice of you, but I think we have it under control. It's a young case and evidence is starting to come together."

Davis replied, "Tell us what you know so far, maybe we can help."

"Well, we're still trying to ID the first biker, and we don't know who killed Mrs. Mayhew." Just then his phone rang and he answered, "This is Sergeant Rodriguez."

"Hello, Sergeant, remember me?"

"McMahon, how the hell are you?" He turned to the detectives and explained, "It's my old boss from Vegas DEA. We worked on the Delacruz case together. Would you excuse us? We can finish this some other time." The men looked at each other and begrudgingly started to leave. They slowly walked to the door and Detective McGraw turned back and glared at Rodriguez menacingly.

"So, McMahon, how are you doing? This isn't a Vegas number."

"No, I'm in L.A. I got transferred a few months ago. They made me the Group Supervisor of the Western District. They promoted me after the Delacruz case. Speaking of Delacruz, I've got some interesting news. It seems there was some internal battle going on within the cartel. The bottom line: Delacruz, Miguel, his bodyguard Carlos, and some guy we think was his servant are all dead. In total, they found six bodies on the property. They all died from gunshot wounds."

"Shit, what happened, McMahon?"

"Our team in Medellin heard of defections within his ranks and that he was basically on his own. We felt it was the perfect time to storm his hacienda. When they got there, they were dead. His closest competition, 'El Moreno' from across the river, was dead also. They found his body floating down the Medellin River. His hacienda was burned almost to the ground with six charred bodies inside."

"Damn, sounds like a war."

"Not exactly, it seems Delacruz and his men killed each other. According to the ballistic report, the bullets were from guns found on the property. We flew the bodies to Florida and put them on ice."

"So, what are you saying, nobody knows Delacruz is dead?"

"Exactly, we're trying to prevent a war for his territory. Delacruz had a well-oiled organization that can run for another few months without him. In the meantime, we're going after his competition, trying to neutralize them."

"Does his niece know?"

"No, but we can't keep it from her for long, you know lawsuits and all that shit. Despite everything, she has a right to know. What's going on with you, Rodriguez?"

"Well, I'm working on some clusterfuck of a case. I've got homicides, police shootings, a dead witness, and that's all one case."

"Are you working homicide now? How did you get mixed up in that?"

"The mayor of Oceanview called me personally after one of our citizens was found shot to death in his car. It's not a case of road rage, that would be too easy."

Detective Spinelli entered the office, noticed that Rodriguez was on the phone, and said, "I'll come back." Rodriguez motioned for him to sit down.

"McMahon I've got some business I've got to take care of. We'll talk again soon."

"Sure, Sergeant. Go ahead and do what you have to do."

Rodriguez replied, "Let me know before you guys tell the world that Delacruz is dead."

"Sure, you'll be the first to know."

"Thanks."

Mercedes Delacruz was working in the prison library stocking the shelves with books returned by inmates. The young guard, Eric, entered and placed a computer on a table in an obscure part of the library. He motioned to her and warned, "You got an hour. Don't move it from here. There are no cameras in this corner. I'll be back in an hour. You owe me."

Mercedes answered, "Don't I always take care of you?" As the guard left, she whispered under her breath, "Fucking gringo asshole." She got busy using different passwords and a network of hidden websites to transfer money from international banks to banks in the United States. A total of $50,000 was transferred to five different banks, and any records of these transactions were erased. An hour later Eric returned, "Time's up. I got to get this back to the supply room."

"You can take it."

"So, what did you look at today?"

"Not much, just some stuff in my country."

Eric said, "From the Dominican Republic?"

"Dominican Republic? Do you think I'm Dominican? At least learn a little about me if you're going to fuck me. Take me back." Mercedes returned to the common room of the prison, looking for someone. She spotted her sitting with her prison gang. Mercedes walked over and stood in front of her. "I got a proposition for you." The gang leader looked up, not speaking. Mercedes continued, "If you're interested in hearing it, tell them to take a walk. If not, I'll go somewhere else." The gang leader motioned for her people to leave. Her name is Shauna Wilson, in here they call her Aunt Shauna, she's Jamaican from Negril and had been running marijuana and heroin into southern Long Island until the Colombians moved in and put her out of business. "May I sit down?"

Aunt Shauna nodded, "Go ahead, you got five minutes."

Mercedes began, "I hear you're in here for murder. You and your drug dealer friend killed a couple of rivals, is that right?"

"Yeah, so?"

Mercedes continued, "I knew most of the dealers on the Island. Where did you work out of?"

"Back in the day, we had most of the south shore in our pocket. We had cops on our payroll, a DA, and then the Colombians moved in people like you and put us out of business. They had the best shit money could buy, and you made it cheap and that shut us down. A few of the cops are still out there strutting their shit as if nothing happened. Evidence and witnesses disappeared, and we got stuck holding the bag. So tell me why I should even talk to a bitch like you? You think I forgot that spics like you put us out of business?"

There was silence and then Mercedes asked, "I want somebody killed on the outside. I need two people to do the job, and I'll pay them ten grand each."

The gang leader sat up in her seat. "Is this a setup? You don't look like the type. Around here they think you're a goody-two-shoes."

"I don't give a fuck what they say. Don't be fooled by what you think you see. Let me tell you about the mark. He's the reason I'm in here, and he's fucking smart. He knows the streets; and to make it more interesting, he's a cop."

"Why do you need two people?"

"As I said, this guy's smart. He can smell trouble a mile away. I'm thinking two might not be enough. So, if you're not interested, I'll shop elsewhere." Mercedes began to get up.

"Wait, wait, maybe I got somebody. But if you want me to kill a cop, the price goes up to fifteen."

Mercedes sat back down and replied, "Okay, fifteen each. You find the men and let me know, but don't take too long."

"I need at least a week to reach out to these guys, and there's no guarantee they'll take the job. I know an ex-cop, crooked as a fuck. His name's Darren Mitchell. He can probably set it up, but it's going to take time. He's got a network in Suffolk County. Maybe he can get some dealers that work for him to do it. You got to throw something in the pot for him. You okay with that?"

"Yeah, five grand for him to reach out, but don't take too long."

———

Spinelli dialed Rodriguez. "Hi, Sergeant. We got an ID on the dead biker."

"That's great, Marco. What did you find out?"

"His name is Yuri Ivanov. He did time in Dannemora Prison for attempted murder. He did six years of a ten-year sentence, got out less than a year ago. He's got no known address or family in the states."

"What were the circumstances of his arrest?"

"Which arrest, Sergeant? He's had a few, mostly assaults."

"Tell me about the attempted murder charge. What happened?"

"Sounds like they had a beef with a group of guys in a bar, and old Yuri nearly beat one guy to death."

"Who's they? You said they."

"It was him and a guy named David Everett, yeah, that David Everett. One of the visitors at Mrs. Mayhew's place."

Rodriguez asked, "What about the tattoo? Any information on that?"

"No, seems like a custom job, maybe a small boutique parlor, word of mouth, that sort of thing."

"Okay, thanks, Marco. See you in the morning."

Zachariah was ensconced in a palatial mansion in Southampton, Long Island. He was there to oversee the arrangements for the meeting of The Cyclist Club on Friday night. He was in the kitchen reviewing the menu with the chef and his staff. "The guests will begin arriving before eight. As they enter, I want the champagne to flow." The valets will hand them their opera masks as they arrive. They know that they are to put them on or they won't be let in. Once inside, we'll let them mingle and enjoy your wonderful hors d'oeuvres, chef. Then we'll have a short screening, followed by an intermission. That's when you'll serve dinner. There will be no speaking to the guests. After dinner, we'll return to the theater for another short screening and then brandy and cigars in the sitting room. We are not to be disturbed while in the screening room for any reason. Do we all understand? I want our guests to be waited on from hand to foot. They are accustomed to their privacy, so after we adjourn to the sitting room, you may all go home except for the valets and my security. Now I must leave. I expect you all here tomorrow at 4:00 p.m. to set up. Good night."

CHAPTER 12
RED WIDOW

The call came into Suffolk County police about a homicide on the corner of Gold Street and Fourth Avenue, a rather upscale area of Oceanview. The victim suffered severe head trauma and was pronounced dead at the scene. Rodriguez arrived and questioned the officers on the scene, "Did anybody see what happened?"

"Yes, Sergeant, this young lady here saw a bike rider leaving the scene. She was walking home from work."

"Hi, I'm Sergeant Rodriguez. What is your name?"

"Deborah Paterson."

"Can you tell me what you saw? Take your time."

"Well, I was walking home from my job at the clinic; and when I turned the corner, a guy on a bike almost hit me. He was pedaling away from the scene very fast."

"Did you get a look at this guy on the bike?"

"No, I didn't see his face. He startled me, but I did notice that he was an excellent rider."

"What about his body style, Ms. Paterson? Was he big, muscular? Could you tell?"

"He was thin, but his legs looked strong. He looked like he had a lot invested in the bike and his clothes; he looked professional."

"Professional, did you see what color his clothes were?"

"Well, when he turned the corner, his clothes looked like they were black."

"What about his bike?"

"I couldn't be sure about the clothes because it was dark, but I saw the bike. It was black and yellow."

"I know you didn't see his face, but is there anything you could tell me about him?"

"He was thin like he rode a lot and kept in shape. He was wearing a helmet, so it was tough to see his face. I noticed he had this thing on top of his helmet."

"Thing, what kind of thing?"

"I don't know, maybe a camera."

"Probably a go pro. You're right; it's a camera. Just one more question then I'll have one of my men drive you home, okay?"

"Okay, Sergeant."

"Did you see a weapon, a bat, or a pipe anything like that?"

"I'm not sure...wait, yes. Something was sticking out of his backpack. It looked like a bat or a pipe, but it was short."

"You keep saying 'he,' Ms. Paterson. Are you sure it was a man?"

"No, I'm not."

"Okay, Ms. Paterson, thank you. Give me your contact information and then I'll have someone take you home."

It was 3:00 a.m. when Rodriguez arrived home. Bogie greeted him at the door as he walked in. He opened a can of cat food for Bogie's dinner, got in bed, and tried to sleep, only to be disturbed by the ringing of his phone. "What the fuck? It's 3:00 a.m."

He picked it up and the voice on the other end said, "Good evening, Sergeant. I believe you're looking for me. My name is Zachariah. Yes, I'm the third man. Too bad about Mrs. Mayhew. How did you like my latest entry?"

"Entry, what are you talking about?"

"You know, the mayhem on Gold Street. She was a rookie, you know. Not bad wouldn't you say?"

"Yeah, just as I thought. It was a woman."

"Yes, and she performed quite well. She's the newest addition to my bevy of competitors."

Rodriguez responded, "I don't know what your game is, but I'm gonna figure it out, and then I'm coming for you. There's only one way this is going to end and that's with you dead or in prison."

Zachariah replied, "Perhaps you should be the one to keep looking behind you."

"Any time."

"Such bravado, I love it. Perhaps I'll feature you in my next short film. Goodbye for now."

The next morning Rodriguez walked into his office to find his team waiting for him. "Sorry I'm late, I had a busy night."

"Yeah, Sergeant, we know. Somebody got killed over on Gold Street."

"I got the call around midnight. I also got a call from Zachariah, the third man at the Mayhew house. He practically admitted he had something to do with that killing."

"Did he do it?"

"No, but it sounded like he orchestrated the whole thing. The killer's a woman; that's what he said."

"How did he get your cell number?"

"I don't know, but I have the feeling I'll hear from him again. Probably using one of those throwaway cell phones. He mentioned something about a short film."

Will asked, "A short film, what does that mean?"

"Not sure yet, but I have a hunch."

CHAPTER 13

THE CYCLIST CLUB MEETS

It was a warm and clear early summer night in Oceanview and the members of the Cyclist Club were arriving at the mansion. For the past year, the event had always been black-tie for the men and evening gowns for the women. Tonight was no exception, and the members were greeted with opera masks and champagne. They were searched and then proceeded to the main ballroom. They mingled in the great room, making small talk and avoiding eye contact. One of the rules of membership was not to introduce yourself or talk about your past. Anonymity was key at the Cyclist Club. A voice boomed into the room, "Good evening, ladies and gentlemen. Welcome back to the Cyclist Club. We have a special night planned, after all, it's our first anniversary and eight meetings to the day that the Cyclist Club premiered. Everyone in this room has contributed to the success of our club, and we are grateful. You should all be very proud of what we've accomplished. Our chef has a wonderful menu planned and has offerings to suit any palate. Now let us proceed into the theater so that we can begin with our night's entries."

Once the group was seated in the theater the doors slammed shut startling some of the members, the lights went down and a man walked out onto the stage in front of them. He was dressed entirely in black, and like the members, he was wearing a mask. A spotlight was focused on him. "Tonight, in honor of our anniversary, I thought we would do something different. I think we should introduce ourselves, remove our masks, and tell everyone about our past and how we got to this point. We've been together now for a year to the day without knowing who we are, so it's time. Who wants to begin?" There was silence as the members exchanged uneasy glances. "Come now, surely somebody wants to say something. Ms. Godfrey, how about you? No? Mr. Salerno or Mr. Bolton? I see we're all shy, so I suggest we watch tonight's first of four entries."

The members fidgeted in their seats, not knowing what to expect. "Our first entry comes from China. One of our cyclists had been there on vacation; and he decided to have a little fun. We know him as the 'Death Ninja.' So, without further ado, our first short film."

A screen descended slowly from the ceiling.

On the screen, we see a street in Beijing from the cyclist's perspective. It's dark and the street is shimmering as if it had just rained. As the cyclist is traveling through the street, looking from side to side for a victim. Up ahead, an elderly man is crossing the street as other bikes and a few cars go by. The man turns down a dark street followed by the cyclist. The cyclist is getting closer to the man and he reaches for his weapon, a set of nunchucks, a lethal fighting weapon. The cyclist is spinning them in his right hand; he's close enough to strike. The first blow strikes the man in the back of the head. The second blow shatters his glasses and he begins to scream. "Death Ninja" jumps off his bike, wraps the nunchuck chain around the man's neck, and drags him into an alleyway. The members of the club gasp in unison as "Death Ninja's" helmet records the man's last breath. After a few minutes, it's over. "Death Ninja" scans the scene one more time, focusing on the dead man's face, and then rides off into the night.

The spotlight returned once again as the man walked back onto the stage. "So, what did you think of 'Death Ninja'? Save your applause, the winner tonight will get $50,000 instead of the usual $25,000 in honor of our first anniversary. You'll all have a chance to vote. And now we have a special treat, a newcomer to our club who is entering for the first time. She calls herself 'Red Widow.' This one was filmed less than twenty-four hours ago." The man signaled and the spotlight dimmed out.

It's Gold Street in Oceanview, Long Island, an upscale shopping street with designer boutiques lining both sides of the street. From the cyclist's perspective, a man is walking a few blocks in front of her. She pedals hard to build up momentum. As she approaches the man, she removes a sawed-off wooden baseball bat from her backpack. The cyclist startles the man, who turns as the bat hits him on the side of the face. The audience gasps. He's stunned and begins to run, but the cyclist catches up and hits him again, causing him to stumble. The cyclist dismounts and beats the man again and again as he tries to fend off the blows. Finally, he succumbs to his injuries. 'Red Widow' continues to pummel the man. She returns the bloody bat to her backpack and rides away from the scene, almost hitting a pedestrian.

The man returned to the spotlight. "Wasn't that great, ladies and gentlemen, one of my newer athletes and her first competition. I suspect we'll see a lot more of her, 'Red Widow.' And now one more before dinner and arguably one of our better offerings tonight. Enjoy people."

It's sunset on Ocean Drive, a cyclist lies on the road feigning injury. The perspective is from the other side of the two-lane highway. A car approaches at a high rate of speed but slows down and stops when he sees the cyclist lying in the road. Before the driver has a chance to get out to check the cyclist for injuries, we see a gun from the shooter's perspective. The man in the car raises his hands as if to defend himself. Three shots ring out, three of the bullets hitting the man in the head. It happens so fast that the cyclist in the road doesn't have time to get on his feet as the car inexplicably speeds forward.

The shooter fires twice again, thinking the driver is still alive. The cyclist is hit by the car and is thrown down the embankment along with his bike. The next clip is from the dead biker's helmet as the car hits him. We see the sky and the ground going by as he tumbles down the embankment. The shooter runs down the embankment and takes the cyclist's helmet. The shooter films the scene including a severed foot in a shoe and the mutilated body of the biker.

The lights went up and the man returned to the stage. "Before we go into dinner, I have a question? Did anybody recognize the man in the last entry? He was a member of the club, though none of you knew it." Nobody responded, but murmuring sounded from the audience. "Nobody cares to venture a guess? Come on, it was all over the news."

Finally, Carlyle Bolton spoke up, "Wasn't that Harry, Harry Mayhew?"

"Very good, Mr. Bolton."

Bolton replied, "But that would mean that the Cyclist Club killed him."

"No, Mr. Bolton, not the Cyclist Club, me. You see, he was broke. As we all know, one of the bylaws of the club is that every time we meet, your dues must be paid. Not only did Mr. Mayhew not pay his dues, but he was attempting to blackmail us; and by us, I mean everyone in this room. You see, we are the Cyclist Club. We should have a moment of silence for 'Jolly Roger,' the cyclist killed that night. So now that we've gotten the first entries out of the way, I think it's time we revealed ourselves. So, who would like to begin and tell us about themselves, start the ball rolling so to speak?" There was silence as the member's eyes darted back and forth. "Everyone please remove your masks. It's time. There'll be consequences if you don't." They whispered among themselves, but no one removed their mask.

"If nobody wants to speak up, I'll be the one to break the ice. I think I'll start with you, Mr. Salerno. Remove your mask and let us see you. Members, I would like you to meet Ray Salerno, a degenerate gambler who squandered millions in lottery winnings. He spent the last twelve years of his life organizing high stakes poker games for the Las Vegas mob. As we speak, a loan shark named Freddie the Hammer is looking for Ray. It seems Ray owes him a lot of money, and Ray disabled two of Freddie's goons with a hammer. By the way, one of them is in critical condition, Ray. Just imagine what Freddie would do with that hammer if he knew where to find you. I can text him if you'd like." Ray was silent and slouched down in his chair.

"Who wants to be next, perhaps you Ali Bakar, a weapons dealer and, as of late, a murderer. Oh yes, Mr. Bakar, we know about the man at the hotel. Mask off, Ali. So, how many people do you think your weapons have killed? Tens, hundreds? I would guess more. We have the identity of the man you killed and your most recent transactions. The FBI and the State Department would be very interested in these documents, don't you think? Oh, and by the way, you should be in prison just for wearing a fucking Speedo." Ali gulped a glass of champagne and wiped the sweat from his forehead.

"I think it's time for the women in the group to be front and center. Senator Michaels, how are you this evening? Show us your beautiful face, Senator, or should I say, Jezebel? Remove your mask. I suppose you're doing better than that chap you left for dead last week. Truth be told, he worked for us. You see, we were trying to get dirt on you, but you provided all we needed. Jane Michaels, the seductress Senator with her blonde wig and blue contacts. Just think what an anonymous letter to the press would do to your reelection. I hear it's tough to run a campaign from behind bars."

"Justine Godfrey, I think I'll save you for last. That brings us to Carlyle Bolton III, or should I say Dracula? Remove the mask. The vampire who sucks businesses dry and puts people out of work. That destroys lives, Mr. Bolton; but I suppose that doesn't matter to you. As if that wasn't bad enough, Mr. Bolton is a child pornography enthusiast. He has movies custom made, sort of an a la carte menu. Isn't that right, Carlyle? It costs him thousands of dollars per film; but you have money to burn, don't you? Do you remember the chauffeur that you called a monkey? Well, he has your entire conversation recorded, including the person on the other end of the line. Isn't technology grand? Imagine the publicity, what would daddy Carlyle say?"

"And now we give our attention to Eddie Viscount, nicknamed Eddie the Vis. I could never figure that nickname out. So, Eddie, I heard your guitar hand has gotten slow, your singing sounds like someone is strangling a cat, and your career is on the rocks. But you're still a hit with the ladies. Just ask the last one you slept with. Unfortunately, she won't be able to answer because she's dead. Be careful where you buy your drugs, Eddie; apparently, you got a bad batch. By the way, Jack, not Jack Daniels but Jack the guy who cleaned up your mess, has also worked with us in the past. He's good at his job, don't you think? Take the mask off, Eddie the Vis."

"Mr. Deville, how's your family? Oh, that's right, they left you. Meet Thomas Deville, a serial abuser of his wife, children, and the family pet. When he's not slapping his family around, Mr. Deville is busy running a pyramid scheme, aka mail fraud. He cheats the elderly out of their life savings, kind of like the late Mr. Mayhew. They're the same. They're thieves without guns, no conscience, no remorse, and nowhere to go but down. The sooner the better, Mr. Deville. The sooner the better. Don't be shy, remove the mask."

"And now, the 'piece de resistance,' Justine Godfrey. Mask off, please. Whatever you do, don't get between Justine and a pile of money. It's tragic how your parents died, burned in a fire, determined to be an accident. An accident? We know better, don't we,

Justine? We know it was arson, planned, and carried out with your blessing. Money was the motivator, wasn't it? Her hobby is human trafficking, isn't it, Justine? It pays well." Justine stood up and yelled, "My life is nobody's business. We should have remained anonymous. Why are you doing this?"

"Why, I thought you'd never ask. I'll tell you why. I'm trying to avoid another Harold Mayhew; the last one was messy. Do you understand, if any of you had half a fucking brain you would see that all of you have become an insurance policy? If you go to the police, I tell them all about you and The Cyclist Club. And if you think I'm going down with you, think again, because I've got the kind of connections in this town you can only dream of. Now to the dining room. Dinner is served."

A few hours later with dinner finished, they were ushered into the theater. The door shut behind them with a thud. The spotlight was again focused on the stage and the man walked into the light. "Welcome back, members. The last entry is a 'tour de force' for a cyclist who calls himself, 'Body Bag.'"

From the cyclist's perspective, we see the murder of the trooper and Mrs. Mayhew as she lies in her bed. She's startled when he enters the room; but before she could react, he shoots her. The members see him run down the stairs and shoot the trooper who was guarding the back in the chest. He runs across the property and over some dunes. They see the ocean as he runs.

The lights went up; the room was silent. The man on stage remarked, "And now it's time to vote. As usual, your vote is confidential. One vote per member, please. Before we relax with brandy and cigars, I just want to clarify that the woman in the bed was Mrs. Mayhew. She was talking to the police about her husband's death, and that was a big problem. Problem solved. Don't forget to pay your dues before you leave. I regret to inform you that starting at our next meeting, the dues have gone up from $25,000 to $30,000. You see, some greedy policemen need to be paid off. Such is the cost of doing business, I'm sure you'll find the extra money. And now, in honor of our anniversary, I've invited some friends for your carnal pleasure; and they brought gifts. We have cocaine, marijuana, and a variety of pills. Not my cup of tea, but please indulge yourselves. This mansion has ten bedrooms. Feel free to satisfy your every perversion."

CHAPTER 14

I DON'T DRINK THAT SH...

It was a beautiful day in the Hamptons and Zachariah was biking the two-and-a-half-mile boardwalk on Oceanview Beach. He rode to the end of the boardwalk and stopped at the last bench. Taking a container from his pack, he downed a greenish drink. A few minutes later a car stopped on the boardwalk and the driver walked down to the bench.

"Good morning, Detective. I bought you a kale smoothie like the one I'm enjoying." Zachariah attempted to hand Detective McGraw the drink.

McGraw replied, "I don't drink that shit."

"Too bad. It's good for you, especially after a night of debauchery. Oh, and did I forget to mention fucking. I was at my best last night. I had two at a time at one point, or was it three? I can't remember."

Detective McGraw responded, "Listen, given all the shit that's going on around here, I think you should suspend the meetings for a while."

"Suspend? Why nobody knows who we are or when we meet. Am I right, Detective?"

"Yeah, that was okay when those cases were assigned to me. I covered your ass, Zachariah; but listen to me, this case wasn't assigned to me. The mayor gave it to a guy named Rodriguez, and he's tight-lipped about what he knows."

"Oh, yes, Rodriguez, I read about him in the papers. I called him the other night and introduced myself. I felt that since I'm being hunted, it was the least I could do. I think I might reverse the scenario and perhaps I'll hunt him. What do you think?"

"You called him? Are you fucking nuts? If you fuck with this guy, you're going to bring us all down. Suspend the meetings, and I'll figure out a way to throw him off the track." McGraw watched him drink the smoothie and asked, "How can you drink that shit?"

Zachariah paused and looked at McGraw. "No, Detective, I'm not suspending the meetings. In fact, I may have another meeting sooner rather than later."

Zachariah handed Detective McGraw an envelope. He leaned into Zachariah and warned, "Take my advice and back off Rodriguez. You have no idea who you're fucking with."

Zachariah once again attempted to hand McGraw the smoothie and said, "One for the road."

McGraw responded, "I told you I don't drink that shit." Zachariah smiled and continued to drink his smoothie while looking out over the ocean."

CHAPTER 15

AND THE WINNER IS...

Zachariah dialed a number on his cell phone. The voice on the other end answered, "Hello, Zachariah."

"Good morning and congratulations, 'Body Bag.' You were the grand prize winner last night."

"So, I won 25,000 bucks, no shit."

"No shit; and as a matter of fact, being that last night was our club's first anniversary, I doubled the prize."

"I won $50,000. Fuck me! Thanks, Zachariah."

"You deserve it, a witness and a policeman all in one night. Now, how would you like to make an extra $10,000 for you and $5,000 for a friend."

"Sure, what do you want me to do?"

"There's a certain Sergeant Rodriguez who's hunting me, but I'm staying one step ahead of him. I think he needs to be discouraged a little. Perhaps you and a friend can do a ride by if you know what I mean. Don't kill him, just rough him up, a blunt object to the body, you know. He's in Oceanview, a few towns east of here. He's a Sergeant at the 101st precinct. He's tall and built like me. He has black hair and dark eyes. You'll know him when you see him. He struts around like a fucking rooster. I want you to take him down a few pegs."

"When do you want us to do it?"

Zachariah angrily replied, "Why are you asking me such a stupid question, as soon as possible. Why do you think I called you? Let me know when it's done. I'd like to call him and gloat a little."

"Yeah, sure, Zachariah."

Rodriguez left the precinct; and as he walked to his car, he observed a cyclist approaching. He continued to walk straight ahead and past his car. The cyclist passed him, and Rodriguez noticed the helmet with the camera attached. Behind him, the cyclist made contact with another rider and they peddled toward him at full speed; but Rodriguez was ready for them. The first cyclist had a pipe in his right hand. As he got close, Rodriguez anticipated the swing. He punched the cyclist in the face, knocking him off his bike. The second cyclist turned and pedaled toward Rodriguez with a metal bat in his hand. He picked up the pipe and smashed the second cyclist in the face, knocking him off his bike. The cyclist rolled on the ground screaming, "You broke my fucking nose!" as blood streamed down his face. The first cyclist picked up the bat and swung. In one motion, Rodriguez deflected the blow with the metal pipe. The cyclist charged again and swung at Rodriguez, hitting him in the chest. His bulletproof vest cushioned the blow and he rushed the cyclist, hitting him in the ribs and stunning him. The cyclist attacked again, and Rodriguez dodged the swing. He hit the cyclist in the mouth with the pipe, shattering teeth and breaking open his lip as his attacker screamed in pain. The second cyclist had enough and quickly rode off on his bike. Rodriguez drew his gun and aimed at the man; but a car came into view, allowing the cyclist to escape.. The distraction allowed the first cyclist to ride away. Rodriguez aimed but paused and holstered his weapon. Shooting someone in the back was never his style. He picked up the metal pipe and put it in his trunk.

Arriving home, he gingerly removed his bulletproof vest to discover a large welt where the bat had hit him. He felt for broken ribs, but the vest cushioned the impact. The damage appeared to be superficial. His cat Bogie looked at him, waiting for his dinner. "I'm sorry, Bogie. Here you go." He opened a can of cat food and took a shower.

The following morning Zachariah was enjoying his usual half dozen egg smoothie when his phone rang. Zachariah picked up, "So, 'Body Bag,' how did it go? I didn't see anything on the news. What happened?"

"What happened? Who the fuck is this guy? He knocked out six teeth and gave me a concussion. This guy's crazy. I'm in the fucking hospital. We didn't get near him. He's fast and he's strong. He fucked both of us up. I'm dizzy and I can't see straight. The nurse had to dial your number."

"You gave this number to a nurse? You're lucky this number is unknown or I'd break your fucking neck. Where the fuck is your friend?"

"I don't know, he took off."

"Did you tell him who I am? Tell me the truth."

"No, I didn't tell him. I wouldn't tell him. My head is pounding and I've been puking all morning. I gotta go throw up again."

"Yeah, go puke, you fucking moron." Zachariah hung up, drank his smoothie, and injected himself in the thighs again, a double dose this time. He went to the gym and was greeted at the door with a smile by the receptionist. Her greeting ignored, he went straight to the stationary bikes. Someone was using his favorite bike and he stood next to the man. "That's my bike you're on."

The man, not looking up, replied, "I'm not done."

Zachariah said," Yes, you are. Use another one."

The man quickly looked up, intimidated by Zachariah, and responded, "Sure, I can use another bike, no problem."

Zachariah replied, "Thank you, you're a gentleman."

Rodriguez arrived at the precinct carrying the pipe in a plastic bag and called Will into his office. "Will, I need you to do something for me. Take this pipe to the lab and have them check for prints and DNA. Here's the paperwork as well as my report. Give it to them when you get there. I want to see if we can match it to the bike left at the Mayhew house."

Will took the pipe and studied it. "What the fuck is all this stuff on here?"

"That stuff is dried blood."

"And what's this white thing sticking to the blood?"

"It's probably a piece of a tooth. Don't lose it."

Will looked quizzically at Rodriguez. "What the fuck happened?"

"I got a visit from a couple of Zachariah's flunkies when I left last night."

"They came to your place?"

"No, they attacked me downstairs. I expect he'll call me today to fuck with me a little more. Go ahead, Will. Get that over to the lab. I'll wait for Marco."

About half an hour later Marco walked into Rodriguez's office, "Good morning, Sergeant."

"Hey Marco, were you able to get that list done?"

"Yeah, apparently there are fifteen gyms in a two-mile radius."

Rodriguez remarked, "Fifteen, and forty percent of the country is obese, go figure. Let's start with the one furthest out and work our way back."

"What if this guy works out at home like you do, Sergeant? We're not going to find him at a gym."

"Right, but we have to try."

CHAPTER 16

A BODY BAG FOR BODY BAG

On the way back to the precinct, Rodriguez's phone rang. Rodriguez looked at Marco and nodded. He answered and put the phone on speaker. "Hello, Sergeant. I must say you did quite a number on my friends last night. I hear an echo. Are we on speaker? Is someone with you?"

Rodrigucz motioncd to Marco to be quiet. "No, I'm driving alone. Go ahead, you have the floor."

"One of my friends is in East End Hospital, you might want to visit him. It seems you gave him a concussion, and you took some of his teeth as souvenirs. I think it's quite humorous."

Rodriguez replied," I'm not playing your games, Zachariah. Sounds like a setup, so go fuck yourself. Is that all you have to say?"

"It's not a game, Sergeant. He's probably still there."

"Yeah, I'll check it out. Anything else?"

"Are you a bike rider, Sergeant? My friends tell me you're strong and quite fast on your feet. You remind me of me."

"No, I'm a runner. I always felt that bikes are for pussies like you. I'm going to catch you, Zachariah; and you're going to prison for the rest of your life. Anything else is bullshit. Bye."

"Marco, call East End Hospital. See if anybody was admitted last night or early this morning with a concussion and facial injuries."

Marco complied. "It seems a guy went to the emergency room at ten last night and said his name was Josh Solomon. He just walked out of there against the physician's advice."

Sergeant Rodriguez remarked, "Josh Solomon, the dead guy at the Mayhew house. This guy took his identity and now he's gone."

Mercedes entered the prison cafeteria looking for Aunt Shauna and noticed her sitting with her prison gang. As she approached, Aunt Shauna dismissed the people at the table. Mercedes questioned, "So, how's it going with our deal?" Aunt Shauna looked around and motioned for her to sit down. Mercedes continued, "So, it's been three days. Any news?"

"I'm working on it. Mitchell may have a couple of guys; but who is this fucking guy? Nobody wants a piece of this deal."

"So, what's up? You got somebody or not?"

"Yeah, I may have; but you got to come up with more cash."

"More, what the fuck are you talking about?"

"It's a cop, and the word on the street is this guy Rodriguez is crazy. As I said, I may have a few guys; but they want more cash. 20 each should get it done, besides why don't your uncle get somebody to do it?"

"He can't make a move. The COPES is watching him along with the gringo DEA."

"What the fuck is the COPES?"

"That's the Colombian secret police, crazy bastards. So, what do you want out of this, Auntie?"

"Me...I want you to watch my back."

"Watch your back? What about your crew?"

Aunt Shauna laughed "My crew, those bitches would stick me in a minute if I gave them the chance. I suppose that would be merciful, but the thought of dying scares the shit out of me. I'm doing life plus ten, so money don't mean shit now. Just watch my back."

Rodriguez and Marco headed to East End Hospital to interview the nurse on duty in the emergency room the night Rodriguez was attacked. They questioned Amy Vazquez about the events of the previous night and learned that the person admitted to the emergency room suffered facial injuries, lost six teeth, and experienced symptoms of a concussion. The following morning he had the nurse dial a number on his phone. During the call, the nurse said that the man was agitated and angry but didn't mention the person on the other end by name. She didn't remember the number. Shortly after the call, he signed himself out. He seemed anxious and was in a hurry to leave.

As Rodriguez and Marco were driving back to the precinct, Marco remarked, "That was a waste of time, we got nowhere."

Rodriguez agreed, "Yeah, it seems this guy Zachariah is an elusive prick. He'll fuck up eventually and we'll be there to slap him down and put him away. Let's check a few more gyms, then we'll head back. It's getting late."

When they returned to the precinct, Will was waiting for them. "Sergeant, I just got the call. We got a body by the dunes off Ocean Drive." They sped to the scene with lights and sirens blaring.

When they arrived, they were greeted by a trooper who filled them in. "Sergeant, a guy walking his dog found the body over here. It looks like the victim was beaten to death, it's pretty bad." Upon examining the body, they observed that half a cell phone was jammed into the victim's mouth.

Rodriguez reminded the trooper, "If you're handling any evidence, get some gloves from the Medical Examiner." Rodriguez donned gloves and removed the cell phone, put it in an evidence bag, and handed it to Forensics. He opened the victim's mouth and observed gaps where teeth should be. "This is one of the guys that attacked me last night."

"Shit, Sergeant, look at his face. Somebody beat him very badly."

Rodriguez examined the body. "The beating didn't kill him; his neck was broken. I did that to his face last night." Will and Marco gaped at each other. Rodriguez continued, "Let me know as soon as you find anything on that phone." He also observed a tattoo on the body. "Will, check out this tat. What do you think?"

Will remarked, "It's good, but not like MOS."

"Yeah, the colors just aren't there."

"Sergeant, look. He's got one on his back, too, right above the shoulder. It says, 'Body Bag.'"

"That's a good one. Looks like it was done by the same artist, MOS."

CHAPTER 17

ZACHARIAH'S "ATHLETES"

Zachariah returned to his house on Shore Crest Drive after a twenty-mile bike ride. He made himself a protein drink and put on "The Flight of the Valkyries" by Richard Wagner. The only light in the room was the red-orange glow of the sunset. He sat on the sofa and opened a mahogany wooden box. He removed a smaller antique glass box filled with a white powder and two gold straws. He put a small amount of the powder on the table in front of him and snorted it. He turned up the volume and continued to snort the powder. He took off his clothes and posed in front of a mirror and moved to the music as he posed. He picked up a barbell and exercised violently while letting out primal screams. He continued to look at himself in the mirror as the music played. This continued for an hour. When he was done, he put on bike shorts and walked to a bookcase. He slid it to the side, revealing a staircase to the basement. He went down the steps into a well-lit room that was warm and humid. An electric fan in one corner produced a low-pitched hum as it struggled to cool the area. There were six rooms in this part of the basement. Each room was furnished with a full-sized bed, a stationary bike, a private bathroom with a stand-up shower, and a television. Instead of doors, each room had bars like a jail cell. Four of the six rooms were occupied, kidnap victims of Zachariah. He went to the first room and commanded, "Jennifer, it's time. Get on the bike." He moved to the other rooms. "David, get on the bike. Andrew, Sara, get on your bikes."

Jennifer rebelled and cried, "I'm not doing this shit anymore. Let me out you freak!"

"Jennifer, let's not have another one of your episodes. Get on the bike. Remember, you have to exercise for two hours in the morning and one hour in the evening. Now get on the bike, Jennifer."

"No, I'm not, fuck you."

"Come on now, you're upsetting the rest of the athletes."

"We're not athletes, we're your fucking prisoners!" she screamed. "Let me out!"

Zachariah moved in closer to Jennifer and warned, "If you don't do as I say, I'm going to make an example of you. Now get on the bike."

David advised," Do it or he's going to hurt you, Jennifer." In the background "The Flight of the Valkyries" continued to play. Everybody was on their bikes and Zachariah pushed them like a coach.

For an hour he yelled and screamed at them to pedal faster and faster. "Very good, team. You performed well today." He removed four syringes from a cabinet behind him and handed one to each. "Inject yourselves, half a syringe in each thigh. Jennifer, you first, half in each. Do it." Jennifer did as she was told and the rest followed. "I have a great dinner planned for you tonight. It's skinless chicken, boiled broccoli, and a vegetable smoothie."

David said, "I'm not eating that shit."

"Well, David, then I guess you're not eating at all. You're an athlete, you need to eat like one. I'm going upstairs to prepare your dinner and you'd better eat it. After dinner, we'll go upstairs and I'll do more work on your tattoo. You're progressing beautifully and soon you'll be competing. 'Hatchet Man' has a great ring to it, don't you think."

Zachariah watched them eat their dinner. He said to David, "David, do you remember 'Red Widow?'

"Yeah, what about her?"

"Well, I have great news for all of you. She performed in one of my films recently. She had a magnificent debut. The members of the club loved it. I know that when you're ready you will also perform beautifully, all of you will. Now eat up. I have a special dessert for you, milkshakes."

Jennifer sobbed and Zachariah cajoled, "Come on, Jennifer, don't be sad. Soon you'll be a star in one of my films. Did you know I competed in the Tour De France three or four times? I don't remember exactly. For four years I was the coach of the Russian team and we were the best, but we were not allowed to win."

Andrew asked, "What do you mean?"

"Well, you see, Andrew, they accused us of using PEDs."

"PEDs? What's that?"

"Performance-enhancing drugs, Andrew. You need to know these things if you're going to be on the team. They banned us year after year. They said we tested positive, all lies. The results were rigged."

Sara asked, "Is that what we're injecting?"

"That's none of your concern, you'll keep injecting until I tell you to stop." Zachariah started to get agitated, "You must listen and do as I say if you want to be on my team. Now I'll get your milkshakes."

Sergeant Rodriguez received a call from the Suffolk County Police Lab. "Hi, Sergeant, this is Dr. Aslam. We concluded most of the toxicology tests on the dead cyclists. Both of these men had a smorgasbord of drugs in their systems. We found a PED that was banned in the United States in the '70s. There was also a trace amount of a drug they used to call 'truth serum' used by the KGB and the CIA during the Cold War. These aren't drugs that you can find in your local pharmacy. The most disturbing thing we found were traces of an experimental drug that was being tested in the '60s and '70s for mind control. This drug was being tested by both Russia and the CIA. Again, our results are not conclusive. We'll know more in a few days. We also found quantities of LSD in almost equal amounts in our testing. How can two separate individuals have almost the same amount and types of drugs in their systems?"

There was silence and then Rodriguez asked, "How does somebody get their hands on these drugs?"

"It's almost impossible, Sergeant. Perhaps the dark web; but even then, near impossible."

"Is it possible to recreate these drugs if one had the formulas, doctor?"

"Yes, but even the formulas themselves have been outlawed for years. Now, Sergeant, I have to get back to work, I'll contact you when we're done with our testing."

Rodriguez inquired, "Is there anything that would indicate that someone has these drugs in their system?"

"Yes, a few of the tell-tale signs are aggression, a tendency to be quick to anger, mood swings, and profuse sweating due to increased metabolism."

"Thank you, doctor."

CHAPTER 18

MY FATHER THE SAINT

Rodriguez returned to his apartment and was greeted at the door by Bogie who began weaving in and out of his legs. That was Bogie's signal that he was hungry. "I know you're hungry, Bogie. Here you go." While Bogie ate, Rodriguez opened a box of old photos. He looked at the pictures and thought back to his childhood growing up in the Dominican Republic. He was the oldest of two children, his younger sister, a twin, was born with a debilitating rare disease. His father, Santos Rodriguez, was a policeman in the Dominican Republic and his mother was a teacher. They called his father the "Saint." When he was sixteen, his family moved to the United States. He finished high school in Florida and was awarded a football scholarship to Florida International University. The family settled into life in Miami. His father became an agent with the Miami DEA, and his mother was hired to teach at a local high school. When he was twenty years old, his father, Santos Rodriguez, was involved in an incident that would change his life. After a ten-month investigation into shipments of pure heroin coming into Miami, the DEA got a break in the case. An informant came forward and gave authorities the location of a warehouse where the heroin and millions of dollars were stored. Rodriguez's father was one of four agents who were first on the scene. They uncovered 200 pounds of heroin worth almost 50 million dollars and 2.5 million dollars in cash.

When it came time to catalog the confiscated drugs and money into evidence, it was discovered that eight hundred thousand dollars and fifty pounds of heroin were unaccounted for. The agents were questioned continuously for days, and then one at a time. In the course of questioning, the agents lied and cast doubt on Rodriguez. This doubt led to a more in-depth investigation. By the time the investigators were finished, Rodriguez was the chief suspect in stealing the money and drugs. The other agents testified against him, and he was suspended and eventually dismissed from the DEA. It was clear that he was framed for the actions of the other agents. In all his years as a member of law enforcement, he never had a blemish on his record. All his life he wanted to be a cop, and this put a strain on his family. Eventually, he started drinking and would retreat into his own world. His family urged him to seek help; but being a proud man, he refused. Alcohol and depression began to take their toll and culminated in his suicide. The younger Rodriguez found his father's body when he came home from football practice one afternoon. That was a turning point in his life, and he left college and joined the Police Academy. His mother died of a broken heart shortly thereafter. His sister was placed in an adult care facility as her condition continued to worsen. He often thought about revenge against the men who lied and framed his father, but he was always able to push those thoughts aside and carry on. But as he looked through the newspaper clippings of the case, those thoughts began to resurface. His father and the three agents were shown at a press conference where the drugs and the money were on display. The newspaper clippings progressed through the investigation to the point where his father was dismissed from the force. The agent's names were Juan Ortiz,

Darren Mitchell, and Abraham Persaud. Sergeant Rodriguez made up his mind to find the three agents to get a confession and clear his father's name.

As he tried to get some sleep, thoughts of finding these men and getting closure kept him awake. He found some comfort when Bogie jumped up and snuggled next to him. The next morning he called McMahon, his commanding officer when he was with Las Vegas DEA, for help in finding the men. She informed him that Ortiz died in the line of duty six years earlier. Persaud retired to Florida; his last known address was in Miami. Mitchell was also retired and living in the New York area. Unfortunately, Mitchell had moved several times and there was no permanent address for him. She advised him that the agent in charge was Captain Richard Anderson.

CHAPTER 19

DEAF MARY

Mercedes received a late visit to her cell. One of the guards handed her an envelope, letting her know it was from Aunt Shauna. The guard warned her, "I ain't your errand girl, next time it's going to cost you."

Mercedes replied, "Get it from Shauna, now excuse me." The note contained a few short words, "Library tomorrow at two."

They met in the library at the appointed time. The guard told them, "You have ten minutes then I'll come to get you."

Aunt Shauna turned to Mercedes as the guard strode off. "Remember what we talked about? I may have somebody."

"You may have, may have don't mean shit. Come on, Shauna, don't waste my time. Let me know when you have somebody. Listen, I want Rodriguez dead, the sooner the better. I've got the money waiting. It's theirs." Just then, Mercedes noticed someone watching them from between some books. She said, "Who is that, Shauna? Hey, why the fuck are you watching us?"

The woman stepped out from behind the books and Aunt Shauna remarked, "Oh, that's Mary. Don't worry, she's a fucking retard. She's deaf.. She can't hear shit so she can't say shit. She works in the library. She stabbed her boyfriend to death with a pair of scissors. Claimed he was smacking her around and that's how she got deaf, so she stabbed him, a lot. Nine times, that must have been a fucking mess. Retard or not, she got fifteen years."

Aunt Shauna waved Mary away, and as she turned and walked away, Mercedes called her to get a reaction, but Mary kept walking and didn't turn around.

Aunt Shauna said, "What's up, Delacruz? Don't believe me?"

"Yeah, I believe you. Find me those guys, the money's waiting."

Mercedes had been following Mary, not trusting that she was completely deaf. Eric came to escort her to the library, and she brought up Mary's name to see if she could glean any further information. "I didn't know that Mary worked in the library."

"Yeah, she comes Mondays and Wednesdays, mostly in the afternoon. Why do you ask?"

"No reason, it amazes me how people with handicaps can work normally."

The guard laughed, "Well, don't underestimate our friend Mary, she's not as handicapped as you think."

"What are you talking about?"

"What I mean is, first of all, she stabbed her boyfriend nine times. She claimed that all the beatings made her deaf. Thanks to modern technology, she's got a hearing aid that goes inside the ear courtesy of the taxpayers."

"You're telling me she can hear."

Eric says, "Yep, better than we can."

Mercedes said, "Take me back, it's time for lunch."

"You want to go back now? I thought we were..."

"Just take me the fuck back, Eric."

Mercedes found Aunt Shauna. "We need to talk."

The other people at the table looked at Aunt Shauna and she said, "Go ahead, give us a minute." As the women started to leave, she said to Mercedes, "This better be good."

"It is. Do you know that bitch Mary, the retard? Well, she ain't so fucking retarded."

"What are you talking about?"

"She has a hearing aid that goes inside the ear."

Aunt Shauna says, "Yeah, so?"

"So, the bitch can hear; and she probably heard every fucking word we said."

"Come on, Delacruz. Don't be paranoid. She didn't hear shit."

"Find those guys, Shauna. I want it done."

CHAPTER 20

DARREN MITCHELL

Darren Mitchell, retired DEA agent, still used his badge and illegal firearm to shake down drug dealers. He confiscated the drugs and then distributed to dealers he had working for him. He knew all the places to go to extort and pick up some extra cash. He was in law enforcement for 20 years, started his career in Vice and Morals in Philadelphia. Eventually, he joined the Florida DEA; and the lure of money and drugs was too much for him. His lifestyle included strip clubs, prostitutes, and drug use. He resigned from the DEA when his spending habits began to draw attention to himself.

Today was Darren Mitchell's lucky day. It seemed that word of his escapades on eastern Long Island had made it to Zachariah's inside man at the police department, Detective McGraw. During their last meeting when McGraw picked up his envelope, he told Zachariah about Mitchell. A few days later Mitchell received a text from The Cyclist Club offering admission, a once-in-a-lifetime offer to become a member. Mitchell was intrigued and responded, "*Tell me more.*"

The text came back, "*We meet once a month or every six weeks. A gourmet dinner is served, and the champagne flows and flows. We screen short films created by The Cyclist Club team of athletes under the guidance and coaching of Zachariah. We then enjoy cordials, cigars, and more in the smoking lounge. If you are not interested in this membership offer, please destroy this invitation. There is a reason you were selected, so please do not give this invitation to anyone else. If you wish to join us, you must pay your dues of $30,000 in cash the night of the meeting. I would like to remind you that this is a private and very selective club, so confidentiality is a must and you are not to bring a guest.*"

Mitchell replied, "*Why is it $30,000, that's a lot of money.*"

The text came back, "*If you wish to join, those are the dues per meeting. If you don't have the money, destroy the invitation. Well, what's it going to be?*"

Mitchell thought for a minute and then texted, "*I have the money.*"

"*Excellent, Mr. Mitchell, so can we count you in?*"

Mitchell responded, "*Is this Zachariah?*"

The return text questioned, "*Will you be joining us, Mitchell? Yes or no?*"

He answered, "*Yes.*"

Mitchell drove to the seedy side of Oceanview bordered by abandoned railroad tracks on one side and a marsh on the other. His mission was to scare off a drug dealer who wandered into his territory by teaching him a lesson. With him was a low-life punk named Jimmy who did Mitchell's dirty work. Jimmy"s intimidation weapon of choice, besides a .38 caliber handgun, was an icepick. They drove past rusted-out cars and boarded-up homes and stopped behind an abandoned paper mill next to an overgrown marsh.. A short time later a car arrived, and two men stepped out and surveyed the scene. Jimmy said, "I got this, Mitchell." He exited the car and approached the men. Mitchell watched from the car as the men talked. The discussion continued for a while with Jimmy gesturing angrily.

Mitchell was beginning to doubt his judgment in letting Jimmy talk to them. He began to exit the car and walk over when one of the men reached behind his back. Jimmy pulled the icepick from his pocket and stabbed the man in the throat. The man fell to the ground as Mitchell ran over, screaming, "What the fuck are you doing, Jimmy?" The other man pulled a gun and shot at Mitchell but missed. Jimmy shot him at close range. The man fell, fatally wounded. Mitchell screamed, "Why did you kill 'em? What the fuck are you doing?"

"He was reaching for a gun, Mitchell." Mitchell searched the body but didn't find a weapon.

"He wasn't armed, you stupid fuck. Now we have to get rid of these bodies.

"It looked like he was reaching."

"Shut up, Jimmy." Mitchell looked around. "Let's drag them to the marsh." The bodies were left about 100 yards from the road. Mitchell ordered, "Take their wallets, and let's get out of here."

"What about their car?"

"Leave it. Some assholes will strip it in a few days."

Jimmy went through their wallets and pockets and handed Mitchell a large roll of money. "Shit, there's got to be about 10 grand here."

"What about the other guy? Check him, too." Jimmy handed more money to Mitchell. "Grab their jewelry and their watches and let's go." On the way back to Oceanview, he called a guard at the Suffolk State Prison. "I took care of our little problem."

CHAPTER 21

SPIDER

Rodriguez walked into the precinct and noticed that Detective Spinelli had already arrived. "Good morning, Marco. When Will gets here, come into my office." Rodriguez closed the door behind him and began a search for Abraham Persaud. He found three people named Abraham Persaud living in Florida City, a dangerous area outside of Miami. He compared the last known addresses given to him by McMahon and found a match. There was a knock on the door and Will and Marco came in. The men sat down, and Rodriguez said, "I'm going to be away for a few days. I need to take care of something. While I'm gone, I need you guys to keep an eye on things."

"Is it something we can help you with, Sergeant?"

"No, Will, but thanks anyway. I'll be gone for the weekend and should be back on Tuesday."

Marco asked, "What about Bogie?"

"He'll be okay. My neighbor Vivian is going to take care of him until I get back. He's in good hands. She's a real cat lover about your age and hot, she's perfect for you, Will."

"No, thanks. I have a girlfriend, Sergeant."

"Our friend Zachariah has been quiet. Hopefully, he stays that way for a while. Assholes like him surface from time to time, so just be ready. I'll let you know if he contacts me. While I'm gone, check on some more gyms in the area and go out five miles or so and check those. This guy's a gym rat. Check more bike shops, tattoo joints, you know what to do."

Rodriguez dialed a number in Miami, contacting someone he arrested early in his career for selling illegal guns. A woman answered, "Yeah, this is Spider."

"Hello, Spider. Do you know who this is?"

"Not sure, but it sounds like a cop I know from up north. Rodriguez, is that you? How have you been? "Did a woman make an honest man out of you yet? "No Spider, what about you? "Nah you know nobody's good enough for me." They both laughed and Spider says, "You know you're famous down here after that Delacruz thing."

"Am I? Is it a good famous or a not so good famous."

"Neither, it's a watch your back famous. When you shut him down, you put a lot of guys down here out of business."

"Speaking of business, Spider, are you completely out of it?"

"For you, no. After what you did for me down here with that asshole who almost killed me, I'm sure we can work something out. What do you need?"

Rodriguez warned, "Not over the phone. I'll be there on Saturday. Are you still in the same place?"

"Yeah, see you then. Call me when you're downstairs." Rodriguez drove from Miami International Airport to a seedy neighborhood in Florida City about forty miles away. He parked in front of a rundown graffiti-covered building with bars on the windows. He recognized some of the graffiti as gang tags and thought back to when he was in the gang unit early in his career.

He called Spider. "Yeah, you here?"

"I'm downstairs, right in front."

"I'm coming down to get you." Spider opened the front door. She hadn't changed in the ten years since Rodriguez saw her. She always reminded him of Halle Berry. The time she spent in prison didn't age her. She said to Rodriguez," Look at you. You've been working out, baby. Damn, you look good."

"Thanks, Spider. You haven't changed either, you're still hot."

The two of them laughed together then Spider asked, "So what can I get you, baby?"

"I need two, can't be traced, that I can hide. One there," pointing to his ankle, "and one in my jacket pocket."

"I got it; I think I got just the ones you're looking for. Come on, let's go upstairs."

Rodriguez looked around the apartment. "Did you fix this place up yourself? It's beautiful."

"Yeah, mostly; but I had help from some ex-gangbangers who are part of a neighborhood clean-up effort. Just some guys trying to get away from all this shit and make a better life."

Rodriguez asked, "Why do you stay here if it's this dangerous?"

"Well, in the first place, I was raised in this apartment so there's lots of memories: two brothers, two sisters and me. They all turned out right and moved away. We see each other around the holidays. I go there, they don't come here; and as far as the dangerous part, people in the neighborhood know me and they don't mess with me. Watch this, baby." She picked up the TV remote and aimed it at a cabinet that looked like a bar and then entered a code. Instantly, a secret door opened. Inside were ten guns all loaded and neatly cushioned in foam. "And you know there's always one at my bedside. After all, a girl has a right to protect herself. Go ahead and take a look, I'm sure there's something in there for you. Be careful, they're all loaded." While he handled the weapons she asked, "Do you want a drink?"

"Sure, you got Scotch, a little ice?"

"Coming right up. You see something you like? Check out the third gun on the right."

He replied, "Shit, it's a Walther PPK, the James Bond gun."

Spider agreed, "That's right, it's my personal favorite. If you want it, it's yours." She handed him the drink, looked him in the eye, and said, "See anything else you like?"

He replied, "Yeah, I do." Taking her drink out of her hand, he picked her up and carried her into the bedroom. The following morning, he left the apartment, Spider waved from the window and Rodriguez smiled and waved back. He was on his way to an address in Florida City, the last known address of Abraham Persaud. He arrived at an old house on a corner lot, shabby and in need of repair. He was greeted at the door by a woman in her fifties, unkempt and dressed in a stained housecoat. She had a cigarette hanging from her lips, "Yeah, can I help you?" she asked in a raspy voice. "Are you here about the mortgage"

Rodriguez replied, "No, I'm looking for Abraham Persaud. Does he live here?"

"What do you want him for?"

"I'd rather discuss it with him. Are you his wife?"

The woman let out a belly laugh culminating in a loud grating cough. "No, I'm his sister, lucky me."

Rodriguez asked, "Do you know where he is?"

"Yeah, check the bar two blocks down on the right. Are you a cop or something."

"No, he used to work with my father in the DEA. I was down here, so I figured I'd look him up."

"Yeah, well the bar is a good place to start. He practically lives in the fucking place."

He asked, "One more thing, do you know a guy named Darren Mitchell?"

She slammed the door in his face.

CHAPTER 22

THE LAST CALL

The name of the dive was The Last Call, and Rodriguez thought that it certainly was. He walked in and observed three men sitting at the bar. He took a photo of Persaud out of his pocket and noticed him at the end of the bar. The bartender asked, "You want a drink?"

Rodriguez replied, "You got any coffee?"

"No, but I can brew a pot."

Rodriguez handed him twenty dollars and said, "Brew it."

He walked to the end of the bar and sat next to Persaud. Persaud turned to him and said, "It's a big bar, why are you sitting next to me, you queer or something?"

"No, Abraham. I'm not queer. My name's Rodriguez. My father was Santos Rodriguez, but everybody called him 'Saint.' Do you remember him?"

"No, I don't know anybody by that name."

Rodriguez took out the newspaper clipping and showed him the news story with their pictures. "See there's the four of you. Did you know that Ortiz was dead? What about Mitchell? Do you know where he is?"

"Mitchell, how the fuck would I know? I gave up trying to find him a few years ago. I'm done trying to get revenge. When Mitchell became part of our team that little prick was 25 years old. He didn't know shit from a hole in the wall. Me and Ortiz taught him everything. Then how does he repay us? He skips with all the money and the drugs. So if you think you're going to shake me down, I'll save you the trouble. I ain't got a pot to piss in. Mitchell got it all. It's called the triple cross, so take a walk."

"I don't want money. I want to clear my father's name because we both know he had nothing to do with the missing money and drugs. You and your asshole partners ruined our lives. My father put a gun to his head and pulled the trigger. I found him when I came home from football practice. Imagine a twenty-year-old finding his father with his brains splattered against the wall."

"Well, aren't you the good son. Let me tell you something. It was a long time ago and nobody gives a fuck anymore."

Rodriguez moved closer and warned, "Say nobody gives a fuck again and watch what happens."

"You can't threaten me. I'll call the cops. I'm sitting here minding my own business and you threaten me. That's against the law."

Rodriguez showed his badge and said, "I know."

"Well, well, I guess it's true what they say—like father, like son. Listen, your old man wasn't exactly innocent. He knew we were on the take, stealing money, drugs, taking bribes; and he didn't say shit."

Rodriguez replied, "Yeah, and if he told someone he would have been the victim of friendly fire. I know how it works, Persaud."

The bartender brought his coffee, Rodriguez took one sip and pushed it to the side. The bartender asked, "How's the coffee?"

Rodriguez answered, "Interesting." He leaned into Persaud and continued, "Now finish up. You and I are going to the Miami DEA regional office. We're going to see Captain Anderson, and you're going to tell him how you and the others framed my father. Don't make me drag you out of here kicking and screaming."

Persaud guzzled his beer and said, "Miami's a long way off. Let me take a leak and then I'll go, but ain't nothing going to happen." Persaud walked into the bathroom and Rodriguez stared straight ahead. A few minutes later a single gunshot rang out, followed by a thud. The bartender and the other men at the bar ran to the bathroom. They managed to open the door a crack and looked inside. Blood and bits of brain matter were splattered on the wall. They tried to open the door all the way, but the body was blocking it. The bartender exclaimed, "Jesus Christ, what the fuck happened?"

Rodriguez walked out. "Keep the change." He made his way back to Florida City and stopped at Spider's building. He called her from downstairs.

She answered, "Rodriguez, are you okay? Where are you?"

"I'm fine, are you busy? Can I come up?"

"Sure, I'll let you in." When he walked into the apartment, Rodriguez handed her the guns. "I didn't need them."

She asked, "You want to tell me about it?"

"No, it's okay. Now get dressed. I'm taking us to dinner in Miami. Is Italian okay?

Spider replied, "Italian is fine as long as it's Fresco's."

"Fresco's—the lady has expensive taste."

She asked, "Rodriguez, is this a date?"

He responded, "Of course."

CHAPTER 23

JENNIFER

"The following afternoon as Rodriguez was on his way to the airport, he called Marco. "I'm heading to the airport, what's going on?"

"Not much, Sergeant. Things have been quiet, but you did get a call from Captain McMahon from L.A."

"Okay, I'll call her later when I get home. My flight gets in around seven, so I'll see you in the morning." Rodriguez arrived home and found his neighbor Vivian sitting on the couch with Bogie on her lap. "Hi, Vivian. Bogie, did you behave for your Aunt Vivian?"

"Sure, he was a good boy; but you're running low on cat food, Mr. Rodriguez."

"Thanks, Vivian. I'll pick some up."

"Mr. Rodriguez, may I ask you a question?"

"Sure, go ahead."

"You're a sergeant, right?"

"Yeah."

"Do you look for missing persons?"

"I do if it's connected to a case I'm working on. Why?"

"Well, I'm not sure. It's a girl in my class. Her name is Jennifer Morse. More than a week ago she stopped coming to class, and I'm worried about her."

"How close are you to her?"

"We're classmates. We used to always have lunch together in the cafeteria."

"Did it ever occur to you that maybe she dropped out of college or moved away? Do you know her family? They might know where she is."

"No, I never met them. From what she said, they don't get along."

"I get it. Look, all I can do is give this information to the people in Missing Persons. When was the last time you saw her?"

"It was in class a week ago Friday."

"Was she seeing anybody, boyfriend, girlfriend?"

"No, she always said she wanted to meet somebody nice."

"Did you ever meet Jennifer's friends?"

"A few of them, sometimes they would pick her up after school."

"Do you have an address?"

"She never told me where she lived exactly, but she has a two-bedroom apartment near the boardwalk on Seaside Avenue. She told me she had a roommate named Gina."

"Did she ever talk about her?"

"Yes, she told me that she went to visit her family in China; and when she came back, she was acting strange."

"Strange how?"

"She was cold and distant and was exercising a lot."

"What does Gina look like?"

"I don't know, I never met her."

"Did Jennifer have a job?"

"Yes, she worked at the hospital. She wanted to be a nurse."

"What about this girl Gina? Did she work?"

"Come to think of it, Jennifer said she didn't; but she always had the rent money."

"Do you know if she's into drugs or where she hangs out?"

"She wasn't into drugs as far as I know. She and Gina were serious bike riders."

"Serious? What do you mean by serious?"

"I guess they rode a lot together."

"Do you know where she rode her bike?"

"She said they would ride on the boardwalk mostly on the weekends."

"Did you ever see her bike?"

"Yes, it was black and yellow. It looked very expensive."

"Did you say black and yellow?"

"Yes, why? Sergeant, does it mean anything?"

"Maybe, I'm not sure."

"Do you have any pictures of her?"

"I have a picture of a group of us at a party, but that's it."

"Okay, send it to me and let me know which one she is, and I'll see what I can do."

Zachariah was watching the captives that he calls his "team" exercising on their bikes. Just like a coach, he was barking orders at them. After the session, he moved his chair closer to David's cell. He called David over. "I think in about a week you'll be ready to star in one of my films. Do you understand what that means, David?"

"I'm not sure, Zachariah."

"Well, do you remember Red Widow? She starred in one of my films and she was wonderful."

"I remember her, but I'm still not sure what you mean by 'film.'"

"Let me come right to the point. If I asked you to kill somebody for me, would you do it?"

Jennifer screamed, "Don't listen to him. He's a fucking psycho. Don't let him into your head."

"Would you kill Jennifer if I asked you to?"

"Of course, Zachariah."

"Did you hear that, Jennifer? David said he would kill you if I asked him. Do you want me to ask him, Jennifer?" Jennifer sobbed loudly and didn't respond. "That's what I thought. When you're ready, David, I'll supply you with everything you need to compete."

David asked, "Compete in what?"

"It's a contest between you and my other team members. You'll have to pick a weapon and kill someone, and you can win lots of money. You like money, don't you? All you have to do is kill for it. I'll explain further as we get closer to your debut. Now it's time for your medicine and lights out." Zachariah handed them each a syringe. "Half in each thigh, as usual. Next week I'll be upping the dosage to a full syringe in each thigh. You're ready for more medicine. Good night, no talking, and no television. You are athletes and you need to rest."

As he was leaving, David called to him, "That's a great name 'Hatchett Man.'" Zachariah paused on the stairs and smiled, revealing his crooked teeth

---

Aunt Shauna passed a note to Mercedes in the prison cafeteria. "Library tomorrow at two." Mercedes persuaded Eric to let her into the library before her scheduled time. Aunt Shauna was waiting in the shadows. Mercedes said to the guard, "May I have the computer today, Eric? Please? I'll have a surprise for you when you come back." Eric went to retrieve the computer and locked her in the room.

Aunt Shauna stepped out from the shadows. "Hey, Mercedes, my old man came to see me today; and I got some news about our deal. He's been doing business with Mitchell. It seems Mitchell knows Rodriguez; and he wants Rodriguez dead, too. He said he knows a couple of guys who will do it. They want the money upfront cause it's a cop. I'll let you know where to send the money. Here comes your boyfriend, I'm out."

At that moment Eric returned with the computer and Mary was with him. Mercedes said, "Hi, Mary. How are you today?" Mary appeared frightened, and she moved closer to Eric.

Eric said, "Mercedes, would you mind showing Mary how we catalog the books?"

"Sure, I don't mind. I'll show her. Come on, Mary. We can start back here, follow me." Eric motioned to Mary to go with her. Mary followed Mercedes, but she was afraid and kept looking back for Eric. They arrived at a secluded part of the library where there were no cameras. Mercedes grabbed Mary and pushed her up against the shelves. "I know you can hear, and I know you heard what I said to Aunt Shauna. If you repeat it, I'll kill you. Did you hear that?" Mary nodded her head in the affirmative, her eyes wide open in fear. Mercedes moved her hand between Mary's legs and taunted her, "Maybe I'll let Aunt Shauna have some of this before I do. Remember what I said, not a fucking word."

CHAPTER 24

THE NEW MEMBER

Darren Mitchell was having breakfast at his favorite restaurant, the Route 25A Diner. It was located in Ocean View at the end of Gold Street. It was a family-owned place with a '50s vibe to it. The food was delicious and served family style and was popular with the locals. It was before the summer season kicked off on Long Island so it was mostly empty. Detective McGraw walked in and sat down next to him. Mitchell said sarcastically, "Have a seat."

McGraw responded, "Nice of you to invite me."

Mitchell replied, "I got a text from that guy you gave my number to about joining some fucking club."

"Yeah, Zachariah. Are you going to join?"

"It's $30,000 every time we meet. It's a little steep, don't you think?"

McGraw replied, "From what I hear, it's worth every dime."

"So why don't you join?"

"Come on, Mitchell. Do you think I can afford 30,000 grand every few months?"

"No, I guess not." Mitchell lowered his voice and leaned closer to McGraw, "This guy Rodriguez from your precinct. Somebody wants him dead."

McGraw leaned back and looked around the room. "Who?"

"Don't worry about it. I know two guys who said they'll do it."

'Why are you telling me this, Mitchell?"

"I'll tell you why. Because with him out of the way, you'll probably get the Mayhew case."

"That's it. You're going to kill a police sergeant, so I get a case he's working on. Are you out of your fucking mind? I shouldn't be listening to this."

McGraw got up to leave and Mitchell said, "You want to hear the rest?" McGraw paused and sat back down. "About fifteen years ago I was working with the DEA in Florida. I was a rookie, young, 25-26 years old. These guys were going to show me the ropes. Santos Rodriguez was one of my partners. Yeah, the same. It was his father. We were a bunch of cowboys back then, shaking down dealers, stealing evidence, and selling the shit we used to steal. His old man wanted no part of it, and he threatened to go to Internal Affairs. We set him up and ruined his career. He lost his job, his family, and eventually, he killed himself. I thought it was over, forgotten about; and now after all these years Rodriguez is looking for me to even the score for his old man."

"How do you know that."

"I heard he was in Florida a few days ago and caught up with this guy Persaud, one of the cops who was in on the setup. He was in a bar when Rodriguez found him and ten minutes later, Persaud eats his gun in some shithole bathroom. I got a call from his sister. She told me all about it. She said he was asking about me. I ain't going out that way, McGraw. I got a good thing going here, and I'm not leaving. I figure it's just a matter of time before he finds me."

McGraw sat staring at Mitchell, "Unless you got something else to say, I'm out of here."

"Wait, there's more here's the deal. With Rodriguez gone, I don't have to keep looking over my shoulder. You and Davis get the Mayhew case, it'll make you both famous, and I'll give you $50,000. All you have to do is look the other way and slow-walk the investigation. There's no risk to you."

"So let me get this straight. You're going to have Rodriguez killed, and you're going to pay me to monkey wrench the investigation."

"Yeah, this Mayhew case is big. There could be a fat promotion in it."

McGraw paused and then replied,"50,000 bucks. How do I know you have it?"

"I got at least fifty times that stashed away. So, what's it going to be?"

McGraw thought about it for a while. He stood to leave and responded, "You got a deal, but I want the 50 grand up front. And don't think about fucking with me or I'll deliver you to Rodriguez myself. Enjoy your breakfast. Let me know when you set it up."

Aunt Shauna was in the recreation room watching Jerry Springer with some of her gang. Mercedes walked in and sat next to her. "How the fuck can you watch this shit?"

Aunt Shauna looked at her, "Is that what you came to tell me? It's alright anyway. It's good you're here. I got some news on Rodriguez. He's going to be dead soon. I found the shooters." Aunt Shauna handed Mercedes a piece of paper, "Transfer the money to those three accounts. When it's there, I'll give the go-ahead. The sooner the money's there, the sooner he dies."

Mercedes took the paper. "Give me a few days."

Aunt Shauna moved closer to Mercedes, "Don't forget our arrangement, Delacruz. You and your Latina bitches watch my back. You see these hoes sitting here with me? I don't trust any of them. See you." She went back to watching TV.

It was a beautiful day on Long Island as summer approaches. Zachariah was sitting on his terrace overlooking the ocean. As usual, he was drinking a vegetable and protein concoction. In the background, "The Isle of the Dead" by Rachmaninov was playing. From his vantage point, he noticed Kim, one of his clients, arriving on her bike for another tattoo session. He shouted, "Hi, Kim. Come on up. I'll let you in." Zachariah welcomed her, "Come in. You must be thirsty after the bike ride. Would you like a protein drink? I can make you one like mine."

"Sure, what's in it? It looks refreshing."

"It's a personal favorite of mine, some protein powder, kale, apples, and other vegetables. I used to drink it all the time when I was training for the Tour de France." They sat looking out over the ocean making small talk and drinking the smoothies. "So, let's have a look at that dragon on your shoulder." Kim took her shirt off and Zachariah admired his work. "Wonderful, it's coming along nicely. It's going to be a masterpiece. Let's go into the parlor and do some more work today." Zachariah got his instruments ready.

"So, I see you rode your bike again today. It's perfect weather for it."

"I don't ride that far, just a few miles."

"Well, a few miles is quite a distance."

"I live in Seacrest, but not the nice part."

"Is that where you're from? Are your parents there?"

"No, my parents are in Japan. I'm here studying."

"Okay, Kim. Are you ready to get started? I promise I won't hurt you too much. Today we're going to work on the body of the dragon. I would imagine the rent in Seacrest is high. Do you have roommates?"

"No, I live alone. My parents send me money from time to time."

"I see," Zachariah reached for a syringe as he spoke. "Yes, this is healing nicely, and the definition in the face is superb." Zachariah injected her with the drug.

It worked fast and Kim began to feel the effects quickly. She asked," What did you inject me with?"

"Just something to help you relax, not to worry."

"Why is the room spinning? What did you give me?" Kim's voice began to trail off as she lost consciousness.

Zachariah slid the bookcase to the side and went down the stairs. "Hello athletes, we have company, another competitor has joined us. She will replace David as he moves into the first round of competition. I'm very proud of you, David. You've qualified to move on. I'm proud of you all." He returned upstairs, brought Kim down, and put her into one of the other rooms. "Everybody, meet Kim. She'll be coming to in a little while. Please make her feel comfortable. Jennifer, please no negativity, okay? She will begin her training tomorrow. For now, let her rest. Now, I'll be out for a while. She'll need some new clothes and training gear. I'll be back soon. David, while I'm gone make sure Jennifer stays positive for our new athlete."

"Sure, Zachariah."

McGraw was in the precinct when Darren Mitchell called him. "Let's meet at the diner. I've got something for you. Tonight at 8:00." Mitchell entered the diner with a briefcase and sat at McGraw's table. He leaned in and whispered to McGraw. "It's set up for Friday night when he leaves the precinct."

"How will they know it's Rodriguez?"

Mitchell replied, "Delacruz gave my contact a detailed description."

"Delacruz, the drug dealer? Is he the one behind the hit?"

"No, the niece Mercedes; and what difference does it make? You're getting paid, so who gives a fuck. Remember our deal, you look the other way and drag your feet on any investigation."

"So, who are these guys Mitchell?"

"If you're worried about getting it done, don't worry, McGraw. These are hardcore motherfuckers. Trust me, Rodriguez is a dead man. By the way, you need to do one more thing for that money. I want you to be there when it goes down. You don't have to show yourself, just make sure it's done the right way. Make sure he's dead. You want something to eat?"

"No, it's okay. I kind of lost my appetite."

"Take the briefcase on the way out. It's all there in cash. Now, where's this fucking waitress?"

CHAPTER 25

BULLETS FLY

It was a balmy night on Long Island; summer was in the air. Rodriguez left the precinct and was driving the six miles to Oceanview. He was meeting the police commissioner for dinner. He turned onto Ocean Drive; and after a few miles, he noticed a car behind him. At this time of the year, Ocean Drive was not a well-traveled road. He suspected that he was being followed. His suspicions were confirmed when he sped up and the car kept pace. He sped up again and made a sharp left turn, but the car stayed with him. He saw the car picking up speed and was attempting to come alongside. He weaved toward the car and it backed off. The car was on his right again, and it was getting closer. He accelerated, attempting to keep a safe distance. Then a shot rang out and the back window shattered. Rodriguez made another turn and the car stayed close. He continued at a high rate of speed hoping to lose the pursuit vehicle. He turned back onto Ocean Drive, but the car was still behind him and gaining. Another shot rang out. Rodriguez realized that he was getting close to town and he couldn't keep up this speed. The cars were now driving on

Ocean Drive, reaching speeds of 100 miles an hour. Despite the speed, shots were still being fired at him. They dodged other cars that were on the road with many near misses. The chase car was beginning to gain on Rodriguez and soon they were side by side. Again, he weaved to the right cutting the car off and swiping the front of the car. The lights of the town were becoming more visible and he saw an opportunity to end the chase. Rodriguez made a sharp left-hand turn, climbed one of the dunes, and went airborne, almost flipping over. His car slammed back onto the road, narrowly missing a telephone pole. The gunmen were not so lucky. As their car climbed the dune, it slammed head first into the pole, flipping over twice, coming to rest on its roof. This area was desolate: the beach was on the right and the nature preserve was on the left. Four large homes were nestled at the end of the road. Rodriguez sat staring out the windshield, his pulse racing, realizing how close he had come to dying. He pulled his gun and slowly exited the car. Broken glass littered the ground and sparkled in the car's headlights. The smell of gasoline permeated the air and a fog began to settle. The driver had exited the wrecked car and was seriously injured. He limped towards Ocean Drive, gun in hand, attempting to flee. Rodriguez continued watching as the gunman picked up the pace. He was unable to run, having suffered a leg injury. Rodriguez, with his gun drawn, followed him. He shouted for him to stop, but the gunman ignored the command. Rodriguez commanded again, "Stop or I'll shoot, last warning." The man turned and raised his gun. Rodriguez fired two shots, and the gunman fell dead. Rodriguez turned his attention to the passenger who was crawling on the ground seriously wounded. Rodriguez stood above the gunman. "Who sent you to kill me?"

The gunman replied, "Fuck you."

"I'll get you an ambulance. Just tell me who wants me dead. Who sent you?"

"I ain't telling you shit."

"Give me a name or I'll leave you here."

"Fuck you, cop."

Rodriguez got in his face and responded, "I want answers, or I'll leave you here. No ambulance."

The assailant caught his breath, defeated, then replied, "Mitchell, it was Mitchell."

Rodriguez asked," Darren Mitchell?"

"Yeah, but some bitch in prison paid for it."

"Who?"

"Delacruz. The guy you killed told me it was Delacruz. She paid for it. Get me an ambulance, I'm hurting, man."

Rodriguez replied, "How much to kill me? How much."

"Twenty thousand each. Get me an ambulance."

"Where's Mitchell?

"I don't know who Mitchell is. I told you the guy you shot set this up with some bitch in prison."

Rodriguez asked, "You don't know Mitchell? You don't know where he lives?"

"I swear I don't know him."

"If you don't know where Mitchell is, you're no fucking use to me." Rodriguez looked around then fired a shot at the gunman, killing him. He went to the overturned car, found a gun, and dropped it near the body. In the distance, the sounds of sirens were getting closer.

Detective Spinelli was one of the first to arrive on the scene. He exited his car and hurried over to Rodriguez. "Are you alright, Sarge? What the fuck happened?"

"I'm okay. Two guys tried to kill me, how did you get here so fast?"

Detectives McGraw and Davis arrived shortly thereafter and approached Rodriguez. McGraw was the first to speak, "What happened here, Rodriguez?"

"You don't waste any time do you, McGraw? Who called you?"

"We got an anonymous call of shots fired."

"Are you psychic, McGraw? How did you know a cop was involved?"

"The person said she saw lights like the kind on a police car."

"If she did, they weren't mine. Excuse me, McGraw. I'm a little busy right now."

"I could question you officially in the office."

"Go ahead, set it up."

"You don't want to go through that do you, Rodriguez? The PBA gets involved, the press, and not to mention the commissioner."

"Do what you got to do, McGraw. All I know is you got here pretty fast. I wonder why?"

"You got something you want to say to me, Rodriguez? Go ahead."

"Yeah, somebody just tried to kill me and I'm a little busy now. So get the fuck out of my way and stay out of my investigation."

Rodriguez finished up at the scene and Marco drove him home. The car Rodriguez had been driving was impounded for evidence. There was an eerie silence in the car. Marco was the first to speak, "Did you know those guys?"

Rodriguez looked at Marco. "No. They didn't say anything. They just started shooting. They were trying to kill me, don't know why or who, that's it. Make a left at the next corner. I'm down on the right. Thanks for the lift. I'll see you tomorrow. Good night, Marco." Rodriguez fed Bogie and then collapsed on his bed. Bogie snuggled next to him a few minutes later and they both fell asleep.

The morning sunlight pouring through the window woke him. He had overslept and called Marco to let him know he would be late. As he was getting ready for work, his phone rang. It was McMahon. "Good morning, Rodriguez. I saw the news this morning, are you alright?"

"Yeah, I'm fine. What did the news say?"

"Something about road rage and that it was being investigated internally."

"Road rage, that's pretty funny."

"So, tell me, Sergeant, what's the real story?"

"These two guys were trying to kill me; I was defending myself."

"Do you know who they were?"

"I can't talk about it right now."

"Okay, Sergeant, but this isn't the only reason I called. We're going to release the news about Delacruz's death next week. There's a press conference scheduled for Wednesday. Things have cooled down thanks to the COPES. The Colombians in a joint effort with our agents rounded up many of his dealers and some guys at the top, of course, not without some gunplay."

Rodriguez replied, "What I'm about to tell you can't go any further than this call. The men that tried to kill me were hired by Mercedes Delacruz."

"From prison? How the fuck…who told you?"

"One of the guys who tried to kill me told me before he died." There was silence on the phone. "I can't tell you any more. I've got to go. I'm already late for work."

McMahon asked, "Did you tell the authorities about Delacruz?"

"No, I'm going to handle it in my own way. Please keep this conversation between us."

"Take care, we'll talk soon."

———

Rodriguez arranged a visit with Maxie the next afternoon. When Maxie saw Rodriguez, his eyes lit up. "Sergeant, I thought you forgot about me."

"No, not me. How are you doing, Maxie?"

"This joint is starting to take its toll on me. It don't matter, I ain't going to rat Richie out."

"Maxie, I need you to do me a favor."

"Favors are expensive here, Sergeant. Know what I mean?"

"Yeah. I get it, Maxie. Hear me out. This is right up your alley. I need to freeze all of Delacruz's assets, the big man as well as his niece."

Maxie sat back in his chair and stared at Rodriguez. He began to laugh and shook his head from side to side. "That's hot shit, Sergeant. How am I supposed to do that?"

"Do you remember when I first came to see you? You said you knew who the mastermind was behind the Delacruz and DiNapoli deal. You knew who set the whole thing up. You told me you figured it out by following the money. You also told me that you were skimming off the top and you knew the account numbers. Can you freeze the accounts using those numbers?"

Maxie looked at Rodriguez in silence. After a while, he responded, "If I do this, what do I get in return, Sergeant? A bowl of pasta, wine? You got to do better than that, a lot better."

Rodriguez sat back in the chair and sighed, "So what do you want, Maxie?"

"Listen, Sergeant, even if I wanted to freeze the accounts, I can't do it from here."

"I get it, Maxie. So what am I supposed to do, I want those accounts frozen."

Maxie thought for a minute. "Maybe I can help you. I know a guy who can do it on the outside, almost as good as me. He's a strange dude, but he knows his shit."

"What about the account numbers?"

"That's the easy part, Sergeant. They're up here," pointing to his head. "I got a photographic memory when it comes to numbers. Ask Officer Ramos for a pen and paper." Officer Ramos overheard the request, and he handed them to Rodriguez. Maxie wrote for about five minutes, folded the paper, and handed it to Rodriguez. "I wrote the address on the outside of the paper. When you get to his apartment, slide this under the door. He'll know what to do. Don't waste your time trying to read it. It's in code. This guy is a shut-in. His whole life is computers. When you meet him, speak softly or he'll go into his shell. I know it sounds weird, but that's how he is. He's 55 years old, doesn't own a TV, hates music, and he never got laid. He lived with his mother until she died and left him the house. He even gets his food delivered, fucking weird."

"What do you want in return, Maxie?"

"I'm going to leave that to you, Sergeant. I think you'll do the right thing."

"You got it, Maxie. Thanks."

CHAPTER 26

TECHIE ALA VEGAN

Rodriguez arrived at an address in Woodside, Queens. It was a private house on a corner lot in need of repair. Rodriguez rang the bell and then heard footsteps approaching the door. "Who is it?"

"Maxie sent me. I'm slipping a paper under the door. It will explain why I'm here." Rodriguez looked around and slipped the paper under the door. After a while, he heard the click of three locks and the door opened a crack. A voice asked," How do you know Maxie?" Rodriguez responded, "I'm the one that put him in prison."

The door opened a little further. "Come in." The man at the door was short and stocky. He was balding and pale and looked as if he hadn't seen the sun in months. He was wearing thick glasses due to all those hours in front of the computer. "My name is John. My mother died and left me this house. You didn't lie to me about locking up Maxie. That's why I let you in." The house looked like it hadn't been cleaned in years, and it smelled of old cat litter and cabbage. The walls were covered in velvet wallpaper with a loud, brash pattern. The house was uncomfortably hot.

Rodriguez looked around and said, "Nice, but it needs some work."

"You don't have to be polite. My mother had about twelve cats in this fucking place. It's old and disgusting. I'm going to sell it soon and go off the radar. Do you believe some schmuck is willing to pay almost a million bucks for this house?"

Rodriguez asked what happened to the cats. "The neighbors adopted most of them, and I kept two of my favorites. I miss them. They died last year a few months apart. Maxie said your name is Rodriguez. Is that your first name?"

"Rodriguez is fine."

"Just Rodriguez, strange. Let's go into the living room."

They went into a room filled with electronic equipment, computers, laptops, and monitors. Rodriguez looked around and said, "Amazing."

"Yeah, it's a lot, isn't it? I guess you might say I'm addicted. So, according to Maxie's note, you want to freeze these accounts."

"Can you do it, John?"

"Are you questioning my ability, Rodriguez?"

"No, I'm not. I apologize."

"The only question is are you in a hurry? I can do this, but it's going to take some time. Are you hungry, Sergeant?"

"Yeah, I'm starved."

"Why don't you go out and get us some lunch while I work on this. I'm 100% vegan, so shop accordingly."

Rodriguez went outside and called Detective Spinelli, "Hey, Marco, how's it going?"

"Hey, Sarge. Are you okay?"

"Yeah, I'm good, taking care of some personal business. What's going on there?"

"Nothing, it's so quiet it's scary. Detective McGraw was here, and he was asking me questions about the Mayhew case."

"Really? What did you tell him?"

"I told him he's got to talk to you."

Rodriguez replied, "He seems very interested in this case. You did the right thing. I'll deal with him. I get the feeling Internal Affairs will be interviewing me soon about the other night. I'm going to be out for the rest of the day. Call me if anything comes up."

Rodriguez returned to the house with lunch and John greeted him at the door. "How's it going, John?"

"Slow, I was able to break the firewall of four out of the ten accounts. I think those are frozen. There's one more thing I need to do to make sure. Come on, let's eat. So, what did you get me, Rodriguez?"

"I got you a Greek salad."

"Does it have cheese?"

"Yeah, why? Don't you like feta cheese?"

"Rodriguez, do you know what vegan means?"

"Yeah, you don't eat meat."

"I guess you don't know any vegans, do you? We don't eat meat, dairy, eggs, fish, and on and on. What did you get for yourself?"

"I got myself a falafel on salad with no cheese."

Rodriguez was about to take a bite when John said, "Stop. I'll trade you my salad for the falafel since you almost screwed up lunch."

"But I had an urge for a falafel."

"Sorry, Rodriguez; but if I eat anything that came into contact with this cheese, I'll go into shock and won't be able to finish." Rodriguez immediately handed John his falafel. "I knew you'd see it my way," John said with a smile.

The men eat in silence. The only sound was the click, click, click, of the keyboard. After a while, John said, "Six firewalls down." He asked, "Who do these accounts belong to?"

"I'd rather not say."

"The reason I'm asking is that in 24 hours, the person or persons who own these accounts will be notified that their firewall was breached. Until then, nobody can touch the money. They will be asked to send the bank a secret code, kind of a password; and that will restore the account to active status. The point is that if the message makes it to the account holder, this is all a waste of time. Is there a chance of that?"

"No, John. One of the account holders is dead and the other is in prison and will be there for a while."

"Shit, Rodriguez, do you know anybody who's not in prison?" The men laughed and John said, "Another one down, two left."

"Where did you learn how to do this?"

"CIA, I was there for twenty years. After retirement, I taught coding and programming and that's where I met Maxie. He's the smartest guy I know when it comes to this, next to me, of course. There goes number ten."

"How do you know they're frozen?"

"Trust me, Rodriguez, they're frozen. Now can I ask you a question?"

"Why are you freezing them?"

"I can't tell you that."

"Okay, Rodriguez. I get it." John turned the keyboard to Rodriguez and said, "Put the account numbers in and watch what happens." As they were each entered, a red line appeared next to the number. John explained, "The red line means they're frozen. Unless they answer the message, they'll stay frozen."

Rodriguez extended his hand and said, "Thanks, John."

"Sorry, but I don't shake hands. I'm a bit of a germaphobe. Next time you see Maxie, tell him how I helped you out."

"I'll do better than that, John."

Rodriguez was driving back to Oceanview when Dr. Aslam called. "Good afternoon, Sergeant. I have more information on the toxicology test on the two cyclists. The results are alarming, Sergeant. First, as I originally thought, there were traces of a mind-altering drug in both cyclists; the clinical name is in the report. Even though the amounts found were low, the effects of this drug can be catastrophic on the human mind. It was used experimentally by the KGB and the CIA during the cold war. Testing was done on subjects that were held in confinement for some time and given regular doses. When combined with the Stockholm Syndrome, the captive can be manipulated to do anything the captor wants them to do. The result is that the person will eventually go insane, suffering massive amounts of brain damage; and death will come painfully. Picture the worst headache you've ever had times ten, Sergeant"

"How long before that happens?"

"If these drugs are used consistently, perhaps nine months to a year."

There was silence on the phone and then Rodriguez asked, "You said that the captive can be manipulated, would that include murder, Dr. Aslam?"

"Yes, it's possible. I'll have my courier bring a copy of the report to the precinct."

"Thank you, Doctor."

CHAPTER 27

A CHOICE OF WEAPONS

Zachariah was watching his cyclists train. The basement was hot and humid, and his patience was wearing thin. He barked at Kim, "Pedal faster, Kim. You're not keeping up. I insist that my athletes give it all they've got so come on, pedal!"

Kim shouted, "Let me out, I don't want to do this!"

Zachariah turned to Andrew and said, "Andrew, please convince Kim to train with us. Make her aware of the consequences if she doesn't."

"Do as he says, Kim. He's serious."

"Exactly, Andrew. I'm serious about my athletes. I want you all to succeed and be competitors. So come on, Kim pedal. I want to see a positive attitude. That's better."

Kim pedaled faster and faster and began to scream, "Let me out!" again and again. Zachariah covered his ears, and he yelled for Kim to shut up. He shouted it over and over. Kim continued to pedal, as did the other captives. Kim was screaming at Zachariah to let her out. Zachariah lost his patience. He grabbed a syringe filled with a clear fluid, opened the gate, and rushed in. Kim jumped off the bike in fear and cowered in the corner as he injected her with the syringe. He caught her as she collapsed and placed her on the bed. He angrily warned the others, "Next time I'll hold all of you responsible. When she wakes up, tell her that." Zachariah yelled, "Inject yourselves! Now!"

Andrew asked, "What about dinner?"

Zachariah responded angrily, "There is no dinner," as he stormed up the stairs. The next morning Kim and the others were awakened by someone or something coming down the stairs. There was a frightening thump, thump, thump, and Zachariah entered the room dragging a large suitcase. He placed it down in front of David's gated door. David took two steps back in his cell, not knowing what to expect. Zachariah turned the suitcase toward David and said, "Open it."

David was apprehensive and asked, "What's inside?"

Zachariah appeared anxious and responded, "Oh, come on, David, open the damn thing." David reached through the dark gray bars and slowly clicked open one latch then moved slightly back as if expecting something to jump out. He reached through and opened the other latch. Zachariah let out a sigh. "Open it, David, all the way." David flipped open the top and avoided looking into the suitcase. Zachariah shouted, "Look inside, David. Don't be a coward. Look now." David slowly peeked inside and saw a tangle of metal pipes, baseball bats, and knives, some rusty and bloodstained. All can be, and some have been, used as lethal weapons. There was one weapon that stood out—a hatchet. Zachariah said, "It's time to choose your weapon." David went directly for the hatchet, picked it up, and retreated to the back of his room. He swung the hatchet from side to side, testing it for speed and balance. Zachariah said, "Good choice, Hatchet Man." He unlocked the door. "Come out and come close, David. I want you to strike me with the hatchet as hard as you can." The other captives yelled for David to do it. Zachariah repeated, "Come on as hard as you can, David. Do it." David just stood there with the hatchet in his hand, staring at Zachariah. "You can't do it, can you, David?"

"No, I can't hurt my trainer and my coach."

"David, if I asked you to kill Kim with the hatchet would you do it? You will kill if I command, wouldn't you?"

"Yeah, I would do it."

Zachariah smiles and says, " you truly are Hatchet Man."

Zachariah took the hatchet from David and ordered him to return to his room. "In a few days, you'll participate in your first competition using the hatchet as your weapon of choice. Now everybody on your bikes. Kim, I'm expecting a lot from you because I want you to succeed, so let's go. Have a good workout then I'll bring your breakfast."

CHAPTER 28

THE WELL IS DRY

Rodriguez drove to the Women's Detention Center in Riverhead. Captain Ebersole arranged a visit with Mercedes Delacruz. Rodriguez arrived at the prison and was met by a guard. As they walked, some of the inmates shouted at him. Some were calling him pussy magnet and big dick, among other things. Rodriguez found it amusing. The guard escorted him to a room alongside the library. A few minutes later Mercedes was led into the room by Eric, her prison lover. When she saw Rodriguez, the surprised look on her face said it all. "What the fuck are you doing here?"

Eric warned her, "Remember what we talked about, inmate."

"'Inmate?' Fuck you, Eric. You didn't call me inmate the last time you were fucking me." He looked at Rodriguez who stared straight ahead. Eric, more commanding this time, responded, "Sit down, Delacruz."

She sat across from him and said, "So, what do you want?"

Rodriguez leaned in and said, "You didn't expect to see me, did you? You wasted your money on those two assholes you hired to kill me. They're both dead, but one of them told me about Mitchell."

"I don't know anybody named Mitchell." She stood up and shouted, "Take me back to my cell."

Rodriguez replied, "Sit down, we're not done." Mercedes looked at Eric and he confirmed, "You got an hour, so I suggest you have a seat."

She sat back down, leaned into Rodriguez, and said, "That's right, I paid for those guys to kill you."

Rodriguez responded, "You want to kill me for doing my job. What did you expect me to do, look the other way while you and your family move cocaine into Long Island? It's my job. That's what I do."

Mercedes replied, "When you killed my brother Diego, was that your job, too?"

"It wasn't me who pulled the trigger. I was busy staying alive at the time. I want you to know that."

Mercedes leaned in again, "And I want you to know to keep looking behind you all the time. I'll keep sending them until one kills you. That's what I want you to know."

Rodriguez sat back in the chair for a moment and then he leaned forward angrily, "You keep sending them, and I'll keep killing them. Now, I want you to know something. Your uncle is dead and so are Miguel and Carlos. All of your accounts and your uncle's accounts are frozen."

Mercedes replied, "There's no fucking way my uncle is dead. You're lying."

"No, I'm not. According to the ballistics report, they killed each other; and all the money, every cent, is beyond your reach."

"You can't do that. The money is protected by firewalls. It can't be touched without the account numbers. You're out of your mind, Rodriguez. It can't be."

"Tomorrow there's going to be a press conference, and they're going to announce it. You made a big mistake sending someone to kill me. All you did was piss me off. Never scratch dried shit, Mercedes. Let's see how much juice you got in this fucking place now. I'm going to find Mitchell, and I'm going to kill him. He owes me from way back; so if you happen to be in contact, tell him I'm coming for him."

Mercedes responded," I told you, I don't know Mitchell."

"I'm out, inmate." Rodriguez got up to leave.

Mercedes shouted, "Get back here! You can't do this. I'm fucked in here. Do you understand? You motherfucker, get back here! I won't survive in this fucking place without that money."

Rodriguez was at the door and he looked pointedly at Eric. "Be careful with this one, Eric. She's a black widow. Now let me out."

Rodriguez was on his way back from the prison when Zachariah called him, "Mr. Policeman, so nice to speak to you again."

"Call me Sergeant. I worked hard for the stripes. What do you want?"

"I'll be unleashing my newest competitor soon. Are you ready?"

"Is that why you called me? I'm disappointed. I thought you called to give yourself up."

Zachariah laughed, "A sense of humor, I like that. Be alert, Sergeant. My newest competitor will debut soon." Zachariah hung up. During the call, David sat with Zachariah who explained, "You see, David, a lot of the competition is psychological."

David asked, "Who was that?"

"That was Sergeant Rodriguez. He's the policeman that's been pursuing me to no avail, of course."

David asked, "Do you want me to teach him a lesson, Zachariah?"

Zachariah laughed, "No, David, you're not ready for this one. Sergeant Rodriguez is in a class all his own. When the time comes, I will deal with him personally. Do you realize what's expected of you, David?"

"Sure I do. I have to kill somebody."

"Yes, you do; but I'll coach you. I have some training films to show you that will explain it all. If you beat the other competitors, you can win big money. Come here, let me show you something." Zachariah showed him Kim's bike. "Do you like this bike? I gave yours to Red Widow. This one is superior to yours. Do you like it?"

"Damn, a Santa Cruz Hightower! Yeah, I like it."

"Great because it's yours. Tomorrow we'll go shopping for riding clothes, only the best for my athletes. Now let's go downstairs and take your medicine—full syringes, one in each thigh. In the morning we will increase your workouts, and we'll look at the training films. In a few weeks, you should be ready for your first competition."

Zachariah addressed the captives, "Congratulate David. Soon he is going to compete in the first round. Let's all wish him luck. Just think, you'll all be competing soon. Kim, I think I'll introduce you to Red Widow. When she first began training with me, she was resistant just like you; but over time she developed into a fine athlete. I believe you can do the same." Zachariah watched as they injected themselves then turned off the lights. He wished them goodnight and went upstairs.

Mercedes found Aunt Shauna in the recreation room and approached her. "We need to talk." Aunt Shauna nodded to her gang and they left the table. Before Mercedes could speak, Aunt Shauna said, "I heard."

"Heard what, that Rodriguez is still alive because you sent two fucking amateurs to do the job? He came to see me just to tell me he killed them both."

'What else did he tell you?"

"What are you talking about?"

"I'm talking about your uncle. He's dead, it just came over the TV. Did he happen to mention that?" Mercedes' expression changed. "Yeah, that's what I thought. He told you, didn't he? Go mourn for your uncle. We'll pick this up some other time."

"I want that moncy back. you didn't keep your side of the bargain. Didn't I tell you he was fucking nuts? I warned you. You sent two assholes to do the work and now you owe me."

Aunt Shauna listened for a while and then replied, "The money's gone, your uncle is dead, and you come out with this bullshit about money. Get the fuck out of here."

Mercedes stared at Aunt Shauna, "This isn't over. I want that money back."

Zachariah was sitting on the last bench on the boardwalk when Detective McGraw walked up and sat down next to him. "Good morning, Detective. I saw the news yesterday. That incident with Rodriguez and the two dead men from a few nights ago, was that you? It seems this Rodriguez has nine lives. What do you think?"

"I don't know what you're talking about, Zachariah."

"Well, according to the reports, two men tried to kill the policeman."

"I know about it. I'm a cop, remember?"

"The reports indicate that these were two very bad men, but the sergeant managed to kill them. I'm both sad and disappointed."

"Why did you ask to meet? You want a shoulder to cry on or something?"

"No, I'm concerned that Rodriguez might be the downfall of The Cyclist Club and just when we're recruiting new members and training more athletes. My new competitor will be in the first round soon. I'm optimistic he'll be great."

"So, what do you want from me?"

"Well, McGraw, since he can't be killed, I was thinking maybe you should destroy his reputation so he's taken off the case."

"No way, he'll see that coming a mile away."

"Are you going to lie to me and tell me you didn't know anything about it? Do you enjoy the envelopes stuffed with cash I give you after the meetings? I believe you do. You seem to shove them into your pocket fast enough." McGraw remained silent. "That's what I thought. So figure something out to get him off the case. You're with Internal Affairs. Perhaps an investigation into the shooting of a few nights ago might find a procedural misstep. If not, create one." Zachariah turned and looked at McGraw menacingly. "Goodbye, Detective." He turned back and stared at the ocean. "I would offer you a smoothie for the road, but you told me you don't drink that shit."

Rodriguez arrived at the precinct and Detective Spinelli informed him that Detective McGraw wanted him to call. Rodriguez removed his jacket, sat behind his desk, and dialed the phone. Detective McGraw picked up, "Good morning, Sergeant, nice of you to call."

"What can I do for you, McGraw?"

"I went to see the Medical Examiner as part of my Internal Affairs investigation yesterday, and he told me that one of the gunmen that tried to kill you was shot at close range."

"Really? Did he also tell you about the gun?"

"Yeah, he said there was a gun found near the body; but his injuries were very severe and he was near death."

Rodriguez responded, "So?"

"So, I think that at that moment he was more concerned about staying alive than killing you."

"Yeah, maybe; but you weren't there, so you don't know shit. Now, I need to get to work so if you'll excuse me."

"That's not good enough, Sergeant. I'm going to initiate a formal inquiry."

"Go ahead. Do what you want; but at that inquiry, you can explain how you got to the scene a few minutes after it happened. You said the person who called it in said that she saw lights like on a police car. I didn't have my lights on, so somebody's not telling the truth here. Were you following us? Go ahead, start your inquiry. I'm busy solving this case." Rodriguez hung up the phone. He called Detective Spinelli, "Marco, can you come in here? I need you to do something for me."

Three days later Sergeant Rodriguez reported to Internal Affairs and was sworn in. The presiding officer was Captain Forrester. Present were Detective McGraw and three members of the Internal Affairs investigative team. Captain Forrester was the first to speak, "Sergeant Rodriguez, please tell us what happened that night."

Rodriguez paused for a moment and then replied, "That night I left work at 6:30 p.m. and started driving on Route 25. I was meeting the Police Commissioner for dinner in Oceanview. After a while, I realized I was being followed. I tried to lose the car behind me, but I couldn't. We were hitting 90-100 miles an hour at some point. They started shooting at me, and I was in no position to return fire. On Meadowside Drive, I did an extreme left turn and went up on a dune. I went airborne and came down on four wheels. The car behind me wasn't as lucky and rolled a few times. I'm not sure how many, but the car wound up on its roof."

"Sergeant, do you remember how many shots were fired?"

"Five or six, I think. The driver was able to get out even though he had a leg injury. He turned and aimed his gun at me. I had no choice but to shoot."

McGraw said, "What about the guy on the ground? Was he shooting at you, too?"

Captain Forrester said, "McGraw, knock it off. Sergeant, what about the guy on the ground."

Rodriguez replied, "I walked over to check on his injuries and to question him. When I got there, he had a gun aimed at me, so I killed him to save my life. It was clean."

McGraw exclaimed, "Bullshit, Rodriguez. The ME said the guy was critical. The last thing on his mind was trying to kill you."

"Like I said, you weren't there, McGraw, so you don't know."

"I know that you shot somebody while he was on the ground, and you say it was a clean kill. I say bullshit."

"That's enough, McGraw. One more and I'm writing you up. How far away were you from the shooter on the ground?"

"About ten feet when I saw the gun pointing at me."

"Did he say anything to you?"

"No, not a word."

"We have IDs on the men. Let me know if they sound familiar to you. The guy on the ground was from Queens. His name was Tyrone Evans. He's got a ton of priors, everything from assault to armed robbery; and he spent most of his adult life in prison. The other guy was Anthony Rickert. Same deal with him, long rap sheet for drugs and assault. You're lucky, Rodriguez. Any idea why they would want to kill you?"

"No, I never heard of them before. Now, can I ask a question?"

"Sure, tell me. I'll ask it."

"I'd like to ask Detective McGraw how he got to the scene so fast."

Captain Forrester addressed Detective McGraw. "How about it, Detective? Do you want to tell us?"

"Yeah, it was an anonymous call and we responded."

"'We?' Was Detective Davis with you?"

"Yeah, we were on our way to get something to eat."

"You said the call was anonymous. What did the person say?"

"She said she saw the lights and assumed it was the police and called it in."

"Sergeant, did you have your emergency lights on?"

Rodriguez responded, "No, Captain, one of my investigators is outside. His name is Detective Marco Spinelli. He has information relative to the case."

"I can't do that, Sergeant, not without a subpoena."

"How about a letter from the Police Commissioner?" McGraw upon seeing the envelope shifted in his seat as Rodriguez handed Forrester the letter.

Captain Forrester read the letter and motioned to one of the investigators, "Let him in." Spinelli entered and was sworn in. "So, what can you tell us, Detective? What do you have to say?"

Spinelli hesitated and then began, "A few days ago, I went to Meadowside Drive. It's a cul de sac with four houses on it. Behind the homes is the ocean, and on the south side, there's a nature preserve. Those four houses are the only ones for at least a quarter-mile. I was able to question all of the residents of those homes. Every one of them said they didn't see lights that night. Only one resident heard the gunshots, and he's an old man. He told me he was suffering from PTSD; and when he heard the shots, he locked his doors but didn't call the police."

"Detective Spinelli, how did you get to the scene so fast?"

Spinelli hesitated and looked at Rodriguez. "I was following Sergeant Rodriguez." Rodriguez looked surprised and said, "You're following me? What the fuck, Marco? Why?"

"Language, Rodriguez, or I'll have you removed. Go ahead, Detective."

"Sergeant Rodriguez was being threatened by Zachariah, the chief suspect in the Mayhew murders, so I was following just in case Zachariah made a move. I thought I could be the Sergeant's backup."

"Has this guy Zachariah surfaced?"

Rodriguez interrupted, "No."

"You can request protection, Sergeant, if you or your family is in danger."

"That's okay but there is no family, just me. I'll take care of myself. Thanks anyway."

"Okay, Sergeant. So, Detective, you're telling us that nobody on that cul de sac saw lights that night. Is that correct?"

"Yes, that's correct."

"And you said you spoke to all the residents on that street. So, the question is who's not being upfront here? Detective McGraw, do you have anything to add? Nobody saw lights that night. It goes against what you said."

"Yeah, as I said, the call was anonymous. I think they want to stay that way."

"Perhaps, Detective, perhaps." Captain Forester eyed McGraw suspiciously. "Detective Spinelli, is there anything else you want to add?"

"No, I think that's it."

"I do have one more question for you, Detective Spinelli. How far behind the cars were you that night?"

"I was far behind. I couldn't keep up with them. They were driving too fast. I was doing 80, and they lost me."

"What kind of car do you drive?"

"I'd rather not say, Captain."

"Well, I need to put it in my report so what do you drive?"

"Okay, I drive a Saturn."

"A Saturn? Really? I thought they stopped making those."

"Yeah, everybody says that."

"Which model, Detective?"

"The wagon."

Captain Forrester tried to suppress a smile. "Okay, unless there's something else, I'm going to adjourn. When we get the final coroner's report, you'll be notified as to our decision. We may bring you back for clarification down the road. Good afternoon, gentlemen."

Rodriguez stopped Spinelli in the hallway and asked, "How long have you been following me, Marco?"

"Since the last call that you got from Zachariah."

"Where I've been is just between us, Marco. Remember that and don't ever follow me again."

"Spend that time with your family. I can take care of myself." Rodriguez walked away then turned and said, "Thanks for watching my back, but I'll take it from here. You got it?"

"Sure, Sergeant."

Darren Mitchell waited in the diner for Detective McGraw. He called a meeting after the failed attempt on Sergeant Rodriguez. Detective McGraw entered the diner and stood in front of Mitchell. "You want something to eat, McGraw? I ordered the meatloaf. Try it, it's the best around."

"Meatloaf? Are you fucking kidding me? What happened with your two hardcore motherfuckers? Rodriguez killed them both, and what the fuck was the car chase all about? All they had to do was wait for him to leave the precinct and put two in his head. No drama, no bullshit. This ain't Hollywood."

Mitchell took a drink from his bottle of beer and warned, "Keep your voice down, McGraw, and have a seat." McGraw sat and Mitchell leaned closer. "If it's that easy, why didn't you do it, McGraw?"

"Because I can't be upfront. Did you forget I'm a cop? You came to me with this shit, remember?"

"Calm down, McGraw. Have a drink. It's not the end of the world. I'll figure something out about Rodriguez. Meanwhile, enjoy the 50 grand. It's free money. You didn't do shit for it." The waitress brought the food and Mitchell observed, "Look at that meatloaf. Isn't it beautiful? This guy, Zachariah. What's his story with this Cyclist Club shit? I told him I was going to join."

McGraw responded, "He's a scary dude. He used to be a professional bike racer. His team tried to compete in the Tour de France but got bumped for drugging, you know steroids and all that shit. He was coaching the Russian team; and each time he tested, he was disqualified. He's a fucking psychopath. Human life don't mean shit to him."

"So why are you doing business with him?"

"I like money. Every time he has one of those meetings, I get paid."

Mitchell asked, "The case that Rodriguez is working on, do you think he's involved?"

"I know for a fact he is."

"You know, if you were to break the case, you could write your own ticket and box Rodriguez out at the same time. You don't have to kill him. You'll be a hero."

"I'm not going to cross Zachariah. I enjoy living and I don't give a fuck as long as the money keeps coming in."

"People are dying and you don't give a shit?"

"As long as I'm getting paid."

Mitchell paused and looked at McGraw." "It's true what they say about you."

"What's that?"

"That you're a piece of shit."

"I'm a piece of shit. You set up your partner and he kills himself and I'm a piece of shit. Fuck you, Mitchell. I hope you choke on that meatloaf." McGraw stormed out of the diner.

CHAPTER 29

DAVID'S LESSON

David watched the go-pro videos with Zachariah. "You see, David, these are the competitions that I was talking about. Does the blood and graphic violence bother you? If so, you're not ready for the competition. Do you remember Red Widow? This is one of hers. Want to guess who the bike she's riding belongs to?"

"I don't know Zachariah, who?"

"It's Jennifer's bike. It's a beauty, but not as nice as yours. I'll bet you're curious how the Cyclist Club works. Right, David?"

"Yes, I am."

"Let me tell you about it. When the time is right, I'll alert the competitors that the competition is underway. I contact them by phone and it's a call to arms. They know what's expected of them. Right now, we have 12 competitors in total. We have a sister club in Russia and the Ukraine that's controlled by my assistant coach. They ride their bikes into the streets and cause a bit of mayhem while filming it with their helmet-mounted cameras. Are you familiar with the go-pro? Each competitor must have one kill, and they have one week to do it. At the end of the week, they submit their entries, and the judges decide on the best and most exciting kill. The winner receives $25,000 and is declared the champion. We do this once a month or every six weeks. The members and I have a meeting where we serve gourmet food, champagne, fine wine, and screen the competitors' entries. At times, I'll invite some special guests to help our members relax, if you know what I mean."

"Sounds great! Can I come, Zachariah?"

"No, David, you may not. You're a competitor, not a member. Now, this is one of my all-time favorites. It's from a competitor named Body Bag. Let's watch it together. It's one of the most exciting films I've ever screened. The policemen in this film were guarding a witness who was going to testify against me. Of course, they'll never catch me. Now watch how he feigns being injured falling off his bike and, of course, the stupid policeman tries to help. Body Bag seizes the opportunity by stabbing him in the back and then puts him back into the car so that he looks like he's on the job. Body Bag was clever. I liked him. Too bad I had to kill him."

"You killed him? Why?"

"Don't look at me like that, David. He did something unforgivable. Now he forces the policeman guarding the rear of the estate to open the door and then pistol whips him. Here comes my favorite part. He's upstairs in the witness's bedroom. He shoots her twice and it's over. It's too bad about Mrs. Mayhew, but she was talking to the police about her husband's business. She was young and attractive although pretentious. I could never understand what she saw in an ugly fat old man like Mr. Mayhew. I killed him personally; but unfortunately, one of my athletes also died that night. If you listen carefully, you can hear the sirens in the background approaching the house. Too late, stupid policemen," and he let out a maniacal laugh. "See, David, as he runs away he shoots the policeman and Body Bag disappears into the night."

"Why did you kill him?"

"The short version, David, is that he failed me. I don't tolerate failure. Tomorrow I'll contact the other competitors and announce the next competition in which you'll be a part. Are you nervous about competing?"

"A little."

Zachariah slapped David in the face and said, "Don't ever tell me that you have any doubt in your ability. I trained you, and you will be a champion."

David was stunned by the slap. "Why did you do that?"

Zachariah gave David a handkerchief. "Your lip is bleeding. Clean the blood off and go back downstairs to your room. I'll bring your dinners down shortly."

CHAPTER 30

SAY NOTHING

Mercedes was in the library when Aunt Shauna entered with two of her prison gang members. Mercedes saw them coming and reached for a makeshift knife hidden between two books titled *Say Nothing* and *Inner Peace*. She tucked the weapon into her prison scrubs and moved to the part of the library where Eric told her there were no cameras. The women approached her, and Mercedes looked past them, searching for Eric. Aunt Shauna motioned for the women to stop and she walked over to Mercedes. "This ain't what you think, I just want to talk."

"Go ahead, talk."

"I know you've been talking shit about me around here. This shit's got to stop. Somebody might be listening. I get it, the guys I sent fucked up; but I can't get the money back. It's gone. They're both dead. There are no guarantees in this shit."

"So, what are you saying?"

"I'm saying there ain't no refunds in the game, so don't ask me again and back the fuck off. I can't get you your money back. You're uncle's dead, you got no more juice in this joint. We don't want a war, so stop talking shit."

Mercedes moved in close and said, "Remember when you told me you were afraid to die? Well, are you still afraid?" Mercedes pulled the knife from behind her back and stabbed Aunt Shauna repeatedly. Aunt Shauna's eyes widened in shock as she saw the blood. She attempted to lunge at Mercedes but was stabbed again. The two members of her gang were frozen in place. Aunt Shauna fell to the floor, her eyes lifeless and staring at the ceiling. Mercedes casually wiped the knife off on Aunt Shauna's scrubs and returned it to the hiding place. She warned them, "You didn't see shit. If you tell anybody, I'll do the same to you two bitches. Go out that way. There are no cameras there. Now get the fuck out of my way," and she casually walked past them. She saw Eric approaching the library door and screamed frantically, "Let me out! They're trying to kill me! Hurry up, please!"

Eric quickly opened the door and saw Aunt Shauna lying on the floor alone in the library. He asked, "What the fuck happened?"

Mercedes embraced him, "Eric, thank God you're here. There were two of them. They came in and started stabbing her. I went to see if I could help her, but then they started coming after me so I ran for the door."

"Did you see their faces?"

"No, I didn't. They had their faces covered. I think they went out the back exit."

Eric exclaimed, "Shit, I'm fucked. This was on my watch. I'm so fucked! Did they say anything, anything at all?"

"No, they just started stabbing her. They stabbed her over and over."

"I have to call this in. Do you want to go to the infirmary? Are you okay? There's blood all over you."

"I know. it must have happened when I tried to help her."

The investigation into Aunt Shauna's death lasted a few days with no conclusion and zero suspects. Mercedes was above suspicion, being a model inmate. The two witnesses to the murder wouldn't dare rat on Mercedes, and some of the guards stepped forward as character witnesses for her. Eric was disciplined and eventually assigned back to his post at the library. That area of the library still had no cameras, so nothing had changed. Status quo. The authorities did the usual lockdown and searched cells but found nothing. Aunt Shauna was written off as just another victim of prison violence. Case closed unless some new evidence was discovered.

Mercedes was emboldened and strutted into the cafeteria followed by her gang. She sat at what used to be Aunt Shauna's table. At the table were what was left of Aunt Shauna's gang. Mercedes talked to the two women who were at the murder scene. "Thanks for keeping your mouth shut about what you saw. I know you bitches wanted to do her yourselves, but none of you had the balls. Did you know she was afraid of you? She asked me to watch her back. Yeah, that's right. She thought one day one of you bitches was going to do her. So now that she's gone, I got a proposition. The four of you can stand alone and get fucked over by everybody or you can join us. Together, we can run this joint."

One of the women said, "Your uncle's dead. How the fuck are we going to run this place? Your name don't mean shit no more."

"Maybe, but if we stand together, ain't nobody in this joint is going to fuck with us." Mercedes moved in closer to the women and she demanded, "So, who's in? Let me know now." All four of Aunt Shauna's gang responded yes. "Good. Now let's break this up. The fucking guards are eyeballing us."

Mercedes reported for work at the library. Eric was on duty. "Hi, Eric. I'm ready for work. What do you need me to do today?"

"Before you get to work, tell me what the fuck happened to Shauna."

"What?"

"Shauna dying the way you told it. Is that the way it really happened?"

"You mean Aunt Shauna getting stabbed? Yeah, that's the way it went down, Eric. I was putting books on the shelf. She came in, and we started talking. Next thing I know, these two bitches came in and started stabbing her. When I went to see if I could help her, they started coming for me; and that's when I ran for the door. You saved my life, Eric. I'm grateful."

Eric replied, "You know, I was wondering why all this happened where there are no cameras; and they took off through the only exit that's not monitored."

Mercedes responded, "They probably knew where the cameras were."

"Yeah, you're probably right. Maybe I'm reading too much into it."

"So, what do you need me to do?"

"I need you to come into the maintenance closet with me."

"Really? Didn't Rodriguez tell you to be careful around me?"

"Fuck Rodriguez. I want you in there now."

CHAPTER 31

MOSCOW MULE

David and Zachariah were eating dinner together upstairs in the main house. Zachariah informed him that he was thinking of calling a meeting of the Cyclist Club within two or three weeks. "In the next few days, I need you to step up and compete. We may have some international entries this time around. I've been in contact with some of my competitors overseas. The competition will be stiff, with some experienced cyclists. I started The Cyclist Club in Russia three years ago; but the authorities started getting close, too close, so I came to the United States. I find the police here are not as, shall we say, ruthless as they are in Russia where people disappear for speaking out against the Rossiyskaya Federatsiya or, as you say, the government. I was a chemist and was recruited by the secret police. Did you ever hear of the FSB, David?"

"Yes, they're like our CIA."

Zachariah laughed, "The CIA, that's funny. Amateurs, strictly amateurs. No, they are a lot different. The FSB has no feelings, no emotion. They don't operate for the good of the masses, they operate for the profits of the oligarchs and the communist party elites. So, while I was working for the FSB, I developed a chemical cocktail that you and the others are using now. This cocktail makes you stronger and gives you unlimited endurance. Unfortunately, my athletes got caught using it at several Tour de France competitions; and my team, of which I was the captain, was disqualified four years, or was it five years, in a row. We appealed but were turned down and were told to withdraw from future competitions. I believe we were eliminated without justification. The doctor who conducted all the tests was from Soviet Georgia, and his results were biased. That's when I started the Cyclist Club. The Russian police were getting close to finding me, and I had to leave Russia. But before I left, there was something I had to do. I found out where he lived, and one night I waited as he came home from his lab, and I killed him and his wife most brutally. I left Russia immediately after."

"How did you kill them? Tell me."

"David, I think you have an appetite for murder and mayhem. You're going to be a welcome addition to the competitions. I made them suffer, David. I injected the doctor with the same cocktail that we were using, but it was ten times the amount mixed with another chemical. I watched as he convulsed and eventually drowned in his own blood. I found his wife hiding upstairs; and after I had my way with her, I killed her with the same cocktail. The next day I was on a plane on my way to the United States. You see, I had diplomatic credentials from the government that allowed me to skip the usual red tape. The only obstacle in my way now is Officer Rodriguez and perhaps a policeman named McGraw. You know, I was thinking if the time ever comes to dispose of this McGraw fellow, I'll let you do it. He's more your skill level than Rodriguez would be. How's the food, David? It's my mother's recipe. I was thinking that tomorrow we'll train outside on the boardwalk. It promises to be a nice day. The air will do us both some good."

CHAPTER 32

I SCREAM SOCIAL

The next morning at the precinct, Rodriguez called Will into his office. "Sit down, Will. There are two reasons I called you in here, the first is a question. Did you know that Marco was following me? Just yes or no will do."

"Yes, Sergeant, I did. We were taking turns."

"Thanks for being honest. I appreciate you guys, and maybe I was a little harsh on him. If the situation was reversed, I probably would have done the same thing; but as far as I'm concerned, it's over. The next thing is how's your bike-riding skills?"

"Better than most. I run mostly, but my girlfriend and I used to ride a lot. I have a Fuji Outland and all the riding gear."

"Great. Clear your calendar for today. Turn whatever you have over to Marco, and we'll take care of it. I want you to cruise the boardwalk. Do you know what you're looking for?"

"Yeah, I do, a big baldheaded ugly prick with crooked teeth."

"I wouldn't have put it that way, but bingo."

"Can I bring my girlfriend with me?"

"No, Will, it's too dangerous. If you see someone who fits the description, don't engage him. If you can follow safely, do it; but you mustn't engage. He can't know he's being followed. It's important, Will."

"Got it, Sergeant. I'll get going."

The weather was beautiful in late spring and the boardwalk was crowded. The sea air and sun brought people out of hibernation. Strollers, joggers, and cyclists were all out today. Will was leisurely pedaling up and down the boardwalk. His eyes scanned side to side searching for his target. Ice cream and snack shops were open. Souvenir shops were hawking pre-season sales. Will had been riding for a little over an hour when he spotted a pair of cyclists coming towards him. One was tall and muscular wearing a baseball cap and sunglasses. The other was smaller and younger but also muscular. Will focused on the older man's thighs. They were noticeably out of proportion to the rest of his body. It was Zachariah, there was no doubt. Will allowed them to pass and then turned around. He followed at a distance so as not to attract attention. The men ahead of him sped up and began to break away. Will had to pedal harder but managed to keep up. Zachariah and David were picking up speed and Will was having a hard time keeping them in view. He changed gears—the largest gear in the front and the smallest gear in the back. The bike was now at the peak gear ratio for the maximum speed. The only limitation was the endurance of the rider. Will was beginning to lose sight of them.

As if on cue, the two men slowed down and stopped at an ice cream shop. They parked their bikes on the side of the shop, away from the other bikes there. "David, would you like some ice cream?"

"I thought sweets were out of the question while in training."

"Yes, they are; but today is a special day. Come on, look at all these flavors." The men walked into the shop. Will parked his bike and entered behind them. Zachariah and David placed their order and sat on a bench outside the shop enjoying their ice cream. Will sat at the other end. He pulled his bike closer to him to attract the attention of the men. Zachariah was looking at the bike and he remarked, "I see you ride an Outland."

Will responded, "Yeah, I love it. It's a great bike."

"Interesting. When I started training a long time ago, that was one of my first bikes. Now I'm riding a Pinarello Bolide. See it? It's right behind you."

"Wow, it's a beauty. You said you were training. Are you guys professional riders?"

"Well, I am; and I'm coaching David here."

"Nice. Do you guys compete?"

"Not really. I'm just giving David the benefit of my knowledge."

"Do you guys ride here a lot? Maybe we can ride together one day."

"No, I don't think so. We mostly train indoors. It's better for the focus. There's too much distraction out here, you know, all these pretty girls."

"My name is William, and you?"

"Well, my friends call me Man of Steel. Time to go, David."

"But I'm not done with my ice cream."

"Yes, you're done. Dump it and let's go."

"Okay, see you guys around."

Zachariah replied, "Yes, William, see you around." The men pedaled away.

Will followed them, but they gained speed, and he lost them in the crowd. Will rode further down the boardwalk and called Rodriguez. "I met our boy today."

"What do you mean 'met?'"

"Yeah, we spoke. He was with another guy named David. We had ice cream together. It was creepy."

"Slow down, Will. Tell me what happened."

"I saw them on the boardwalk and followed them to an ice cream shop, and we had ice cream. You know the initials MOS? It stands for Man of Steel, that's what he calls himself. He didn't tell me his name, but it was him. He was wearing shades and a baseball cap. He was trying to hide his identity. He had tats covering one arm."

"So, Zachariah is Man of Steel. How old would you say he was?"

"I would say late-thirties."

"This is huge, Will. Nice job.

"Mrs. Mayhew was right. His thighs are a fucking freak show."

"Where are you now, Will?"

"I'm still on the boardwalk not far from town. I tried following them, but they sped up; and I lost them in the crowd."

"Okay, ride around for a while and don't come back here today. Make sure you're not being followed and go home. One more thing, this guy he was with, did he say anything?"

"No, he was quiet. Zachariah did most of the talking. Mrs. Mayhew was right. He sounds Russian or Eastern European, he had an accent."

"Did he call David an athlete or a competitor?"

"No, but he said he was coaching him. It seemed more like controlling him."

"Coaching him? Did he say for what?"

"He said something about giving David the benefit of his knowledge."

"The last time he called me, he said he had a new competitor. David must be his new competitor. Things are starting to make sense. Nice work. I'll see you tomorrow and be careful."

CHAPTER 33

BREAKFAST OF CHAMPIONS

Zachariah brought breakfast to his competitors. He opened David's door and they went upstairs where Zachariah had breakfast prepared for him. David was impressed by the food and he complimented Zachariah.

"So, David, what do you think of the breakfast I prepared?"

"Looks great. Can you tell me what some of these things are?"

"Sure, this is kasha. It's a porridge made from different grains. It's a typical Russian breakfast. These are butterburs, a kind of a sandwich with butter and ham. I figured you'd be more comfortable with eggs, pancakes, and sausage so I made those, too." While the men ate, Zachariah remarked, "I think you're ready to go out tonight. How do you feel about that?"

"Great, I'm ready. So this is for real, you want me to kill somebody tonight."

"Yes, David. Don't be stupid. That's what all your training was about."

"I get it, Zachariah. I'm ready."

"Wonderful. I knew you would be. I have a question for you regarding that young man we met yesterday, I believe his name was Will. I wonder if we could persuade him to join us. I like Kim, but I don't think her heart is in it. I'm willing to give her some time, but I feel it's taking too long. It doesn't seem worth it."

"Do you want me to take care of it for you?"

"You mean kill her? No, David, not yet. If she doesn't step up, I have my own plans for her. Now let's rest and then we'll train together."

Rodriguez got to the precinct early and he called Marco. "Good morning, Marco. Are you on your way in?"

"Yes, should I pick up some coffee?"

"You read my mind. Sounds great."

Marco arrived shortly thereafter and went to Rodriguez's office. "So, Marco, do you have any plans for tonight?"

"No, Sergeant, I don't. Why?"

"I've been thinking about something for a while. I think the cyclists who are involved in these murders are being controlled by Zachariah. We have Mr. Mayhew, Mrs. Mayhew, the victim in Oceanview, and last but not least, the two guys on bikes that attacked me. I want to cruise Oceanview for the next several nights."

"What are we looking for, Sergeant?"

"A cyclist on an expensive bike with a hidden weapon. Sounds crazy, doesn't it? But I have a hunch. The last time he called me, he said he had a new competitor. The new competitor is this guy named David."

"How do you know that?"

"Will spoke to them yesterday. He's sure it was Zachariah, and the guy with him was named David."

"Fuck me, Sergeant. Why didn't he put a bullet in his head?"

"Come on, Marco. You know better."

At that point, Will entered the office. "Good morning. Where's my coffee?"

"Sorry, Will. Marco said screw him, let him get his own coffee."

"He's pissed because you didn't put a bullet in Zachariah's head yesterday. Here's your coffee. Tell us about your encounter with Man of Steel yesterday."

Marco exclaimed, "Man of Steel? You're saying Zachariah is MOS?"

"Yes, he is. That's a huge piece of the puzzle." Rodriguez continued, "Zachariah is practicing mind control over his victims, calling them competitors. The Medical Examiner, Dr. Aslam, found traces of a mind-control drug used by the KGB and some hallucinogenic drugs in the dead cyclists in almost equal amounts. What are the odds? He also said that these drugs will eventually cause brain damage. We're fighting the clock on this, gentlemen. We need to find this guy David and have him tested for these drugs. Marco and I are going to drive around Oceanview tonight to see if we can spot David. Will, I'll keep you updated as we go along. Hang loose. We may need you."

CHAPTER 34

HATCHET MAN

The sun was setting on the ocean, and the reds and oranges of sunset had become a steely blue-gray. Stars were disappearing as clouds moved in from the ocean. The moon, round and bright earlier, was now cloud covered as a cool wind came off the water. The night had an ominous feel to it. Rodriguez and Marco were leaving the precinct headed for Oceanview. On the other side of town, David was suiting up for his murderous ride. Zachariah was encouraging him. "You're going to be a champion, David. I can feel it. Now, remember to catch it all on the camera that's fixed on the helmet. The Cyclist Club members want to see all the gory details." Zachariah handed David two syringes. "Now, David, one in each thigh and you'll be ready to go. I'll ride along for part of the way, and then you'll be on your own."

"Do I come back here when I'm done?"

"Yes, David. You'll be here a while longer."

The men left the house biking towards Oceanview.

Spinelli and Rodriguez were driving through town. The restaurants were beginning to shut down, and the streets were becoming empty but for a few people strolling. They drove slowly, looking up and down streets and alleyways. They encountered bike riders and couples out for an evening ride, but they were recreational riders and not what they were looking for. At a red light, a cyclist crossed in front of them going down an alleyway behind some restaurants. He was wearing professional cyclist gear, and his bike was expensive. Rodriguez said, "Let's follow that guy, I noticed a camera on his helmet." They turned down the same street and the cyclist came into view. They followed him at a distance. The cyclist looked back and realized he was being tailed. He quickly turned down a one-way street and picked up speed as he rode into a construction area and disappeared. The men drove around the construction site slowly, looking from side to side. The cyclist had either left the scene or was hiding. As they drove down a one-way street, they were shocked by what they observed. Two blocks ahead, they discovered a man with a hatchet in his hand hacking at a person lying on the ground. They turned on their emergency lights and siren and sped towards the cyclist. He jumped on his bike and darted down a one-way street in the opposite direction. Rodriguez stopped and dropped Marco off, "Check on him and call it in. I'm going after him." Rodriguez was unable to turn down the street, so he climbed onto the sidewalk and glimpsed the cyclist a few blocks ahead. He sped up and the cyclist turned into a narrow alley and waited at the end. Rodriguez entered the alleyway, but halfway through it narrowed and he could go no further. The cyclist taunted him, as Rodriguez put the car in reverse. He rolled down the window, pointed his gun, and yelled for the cyclist to give himself up. He wanted to take the cyclist alive, and he waited for his next move. "Come on, give it up."

The cyclist pedaled out of the alleyway slowly in the opposite direction and Rodriguez drove out in reverse. Marco called to inform him that the victim was deceased and that backup was on the way. Rodriguez searched the area as a chill descended on the deserted streets of Oceanview. From his right side, the cyclist darted past his car and the pursuit continued. Rodriguez was attempting to route him back towards Marco's position so that back up could assist, but the cyclist had different plans and he took Rodriguez to a more desolate section of Oceanview. Rodriguez was gaining on him and the cyclist made a sharp right turn. Rodriguez said to himself, *this fucking guy is good*. Rodriguez attempted to also make the sharp turn but climbed the sidewalk and knocked over some garbage cans. He slammed the car in reverse and backed up down a one-way street. Still driving in reverse, he spotted the cyclist and continued the chase. The car spun and was now facing forward. The cyclist was now within range of Rodriguez, but he pedaled toward a building under construction. The cyclist rode up a ramp and went airborne. He came down the other side and disappeared into the building. Rodriguez said out loud, "Damn, this guy can ride." Tires screeched as he slammed on the brakes. The chase temporarily came to a halt, but the pursuit continued as Rodriguez circled the block looking for him. The cyclist was nowhere, and Rodriguez cursed himself for losing him. He circled the block, his eyes searching the darkness for the cyclist. Rodriguez thought to himself that the cyclist was taunting him since he had many opportunities to disappear into the night. Suddenly, he appeared in front of Rodriguez and began pedaling faster toward an intersection. He approached the intersection as the light was about to change. Out of the corner of his eye, Rodriguez saw a carting truck approaching at the same time. He turned off the lights and siren and slowed down, attempting to warn the cyclist by blowing his horn, but it was too late. The cyclist and the truck met in the middle of the intersection, the impact killing the cyclist instantly. He landed fifty feet in front of the truck. Marco radioed that backup had arrived, and Rodriguez informed him the cyclist had been struck. Will arrived on the scene just before EMS personnel and police forensics. Will identified the cyclist as David, one of the men on the boardwalk. Rodriguez discovered Hatchet Man's helmet with the go-pro attached. Unfortunately, the camera was smashed beyond repair. The night air had turned cold and the sky was gray with clouds. The blue and red lights of the emergency vehicles were the only thing illuminating the scene, and they reflected off the yellow tarp covering the body. A small crowd had begun to form. In the crowd wearing a baseball cap pulled down covering most of his face was Zachariah. With his collar pulled up against the cold, he was just another spectator to the gruesome scene. He casually got on his bike and rode away.

The sun was coming up as Rodriguez and Marco left the scene. "Did Will make a positive ID?"

"Yeah, it was David. This is a big setback, Marco."

"I'll bet he's got a tattoo signed by MOS."

"The Medical Examiner will let us know. Take the day off, Marco. We can't do anything till the ME's report comes in. I'm interested in the toxicology report."

"Thanks, Sergeant. What about you?"

"I've got some business to take care of. Go ahead. Spend the day with your family. See you tomorrow."

CHAPTER 35

CLUB FED

Rodriguez called the Police Commissioner, "We had another killing last night, Commissioner; and the suspect also died."

"Yes, I heard. Last time we spoke, you felt these cyclist deaths were related to the Mayhew case. What about Zachariah? Are you any closer to finding him?"

"One of my men has a description of him. I'm going to run it past the sketch guys and then Identikit the sketch."

"How did he get that close to him?"

"On the boardwalk a few days ago. They actually spoke. There was another guy with him. His name was David. He's the deceased suspect from last night. The guy he killed was a night watchman on a construction site."

"Alright, Sergeant. Keep going with the case and keep me updated. Let's put this prick away. By the way, that other thing is a go."

"That's great. When?"

"Today. They said this afternoon around one o'clock.

"No strings attached?"

"No, Sergeant, no strings."

"Thanks, Commissioner. I appreciate what you did."

Maxie was in his cell playing chess with his cellmate, a burglar nicknamed "Tommy the Climber." He got that name because of his ability to scale the sides of buildings and break into apartments as high as the sixth floor. If he could get a hand and foothold, he was climbing. His luck took a bad turn when he attempted to break into an apartment while the tenant was still at home. Imagine his surprise when the tenant, bat in hand, pushed him away from her window causing him to fall three floors. The garbage piled neatly on the sidewalk saved his life. After recuperating from a broken arm and a few broken ribs, he became Maxie's cellmate. His climbing skills were about as good as his chess skills, as Maxie was beating him badly at the game.

Two prison guards approached his cell; one unlocked the door and handed Maxie a box. He said, "Pack up your stuff, Maxie. You're taking a ride."

"Ride where? I like it here." At that moment, Rodriguez showed up. "Pack your stuff, Maxie. You're going to South Shore Correctional."

"Rodriguez, what a nice surprise. You look like shit."

"Thanks, I didn't sleep much last night."

"Are you still working on the Mayhew case?"

"Yeah, pack your stuff. Let's get going."

"Anything I can help you with, let me know."

"Thanks, but not now. I got no time."

"South Shore—ain't that the place with the tennis courts and movies and all that shit?"

"Yeah, Maxie, for white-collar assholes like you."

"What's the catch, Rodriguez?"

"No catch, Maxie. You helped me and I'm returning the favor."

"Ebersole again."

"No, it was me. I called the Commissioner and he probably got the State Attorney General involved. I had to beg a little, but it worked. As I said, you helped me, and I did something for you. Go ahead and pack your shit. There's a car waiting. Good luck, I'll be in touch."

"How can I thank you, Rodriguez?"

"You already did by introducing me to your friend John."

"I guess he was able to help you, the fucking weirdo. Tell me he ain't weird, Sergeant."

"Yeah, he may be weird; but he knows his stuff. Take care, Maxie. I'll be by to see you."

Rodriguez was on his way back to Oceanview when he received a call. The screen displayed, 'Unknown'.

"Yeah, go ahead."

Zachariah sounded hysterical." You motherfucking policeman. Because of you, my star is dead. He was a wonderful young man, and I had a lot of faith and hope in him. He was championship material and you killed him." Zachariah sounded as if he was on the verge of tears.

Rodriguez chided him, "Are you done, asshole? A lot of people are dead because of your stupid competitions. Yeah, I know all about it. I've had a change of heart, Zachariah."

"Oh, yeah? What is that, policeman?"

"I've decided that you're not going to prison."

"What are you saying?"

"I'm saying that when I find you I'm going to put a bullet in your fucking head."

Zachariah was screaming something in Russian as Rodriguez hung up. He dialed Dr. Aslam, "Hi, Doctor. We had another dead cyclist last night."

"Yes, I know, Sergeant. I have a toxicology screen scheduled for this afternoon."

"I have a request, Doctor. Can you fast track those results for me? I'm sure that the combination of drugs will match the combinations found in the first two cases."

"Of course, Sergeant. I'll call you when they're done."

"I have one more question, Doctor. Was the greatest concentration of drugs in the thigh muscles of the other cyclists?"

"Interesting you should ask that. Yes, you're correct, Sergeant."

"I believe you'll get the same results in this case."

CHAPTER 36
EMPTY THREATS

McGraw was having lunch at the Route 25A Diner. He was reading the news account of the previous night's killing in Oceanview when he received a text from Zachariah, "Meet me at the place in one hour."

McGraw texted back, "I told you to never text me on this phone."

The response warned, "One hour. Don't make me come looking for you."

McGraw arrived at the last bench on the boardwalk to find Zachariah pacing back and forth. "So what's so important that you interrupted my lunch?" Zachariah just stared at him saying nothing and then replied, "This policeman Rodriguez must die. The sooner the better. He caused the death of my newest competitor last night."

"Yeah, I heard he got hit by a garbage truck or something."

"I had big plans for David."

"Didn't we already have this discussion? I asked you to back off with The Cyclist Club bullshit for a while. But you had to go and poke the bear, and now you pissed him off. You don't know him. He ain't letting up till one of you is dead."

Zachariah, still pacing, stopped and drew closer to McGraw, "Listen to me, it's time to earn the money I give you. I want him dead. I don't care if you have to kill him yourself. I want him dead."

"Hey, Zachariah, listen to me. I told you I ain't putting myself out there."

Zachariah was agitated and screamed, "You fucking coward! What are you afraid of? He's a man just like we are."

"No, he's not like us. He's unpredictable, a loose cannon. Remember those two men that tried to kill him?"

"You mean the ones you hired."

"No, I told you it wasn't me. He shot one guy while he was lying on the ground injured and unarmed."

"So don't you have investigators that look into that?"

"Yeah, Internal Affairs and they just closed the case, called it a clean shooting. That's what the fuck I'm talking about. He knows how to get away with this shit."

"What about your friend Mitchell? Won't he do it?"

"Mitchell? Are you kidding? He's an arrogant asshole. Rodriguez would have him for lunch. Rodriguez is already looking for him. He has a beef with him because of what Mitchell did to his old man."

"Really? What was that?"

"It's a long story; but if Rodriguez gets a hold of this guy, it isn't going to be pretty."

"Are you and Mitchell good friends?"

"As I said, he's an arrogant asshole. It wouldn't mean shit to me if he disappeared."

"So, McGraw, there's your answer. Figure out a way to get them to confront each other. It shouldn't be too hard to do. Maybe we'll get lucky and Mitchell kills Rodriguez."

McGraw laughed, "Oh, yeah, I'd love to give you odds on that one."

"Why don't you send one of your cyclist douche bags to kill him?"

Zachariah backhanded McGraw across the face, his eyes widened with anger. "Don't you ever curse my athletes again or I'll break your neck."

McGraw was stunned by the slap, "You're fucking nuts. I'm out of here. If you ever touch me again, I'll kill you." McGraw stalked away wiping the blood from his lip.

"Remember what I said, McGraw. Figure it out or the money dries up."

McGraw responded, "Don't forget who you're fucking with. I know all about you and your club."

"Empty threats, McGraw, just empty threats."

Mercedes sat in the prison cafeteria with her new prison gang. She spied Mary as she walked in and looked pointedly in her direction. Mercedes said to her crew, "You see that bitch over there? I don't trust her. She's always in my business. Me and Shauna did this deal and she heard every word. If she says something, I'll never get out of here."

One of the group asked, "What kind of shit did you and Shauna have going on?"

"Shauna hired a couple of guys to kill one of the cops who put me in here. She overheard it all in the library."

Mary was leaving the cafeteria and glanced back at Mercedes. "Why the fuck does she keep looking at me?"

One of the women at the table said, "Shauna told me she was deaf."

"Deaf my ass. She isn't deaf. She may have been at one time, but now she's got an implant in her ear. She hears better than we do."

"So what do you want us to do, Delacruz?"

"I want one of you to keep an eye on her. Tell me where she goes and who she talks to. If anybody finds out that I paid people to kill a cop on the outside, I'm going to supermax. Keep an eye on her and let me know what's up. I got to go." Mercedes made her way to the library looking for Eric and found him in the library talking to Mary. Mercedes eyed Mary suspiciously and interrupted, "Eric, can I speak to you?

"Yeah, when I'm done, inmate. This conversation is confidential."

"It's important, Eric."

"What's this Eric shit? It's CO to you, inmate. Now go stand over there till I'm done." When Eric finished his conversation with Mary, she left the library.

"Why the fuck did you call me 'inmate?'"

"Cause I told you when we're not alone I'm the CO and you're the inmate."

"I'm sorry CO, I just wanted to ask if I can have a computer tomorrow."

"I'll think about it, inmate. Now I'll take you back to your cell. It's lights out soon."

The next morning Mercedes reported for work at the library. Eric was already there and had placed a computer on the desk. "Good morning. You got one hour."

"Thanks, Eric. I'm sorry about yesterday."

Eric replied, "You got an hour, then I take it back." As usual, Eric left the room and Mercedes began typing busily. She entered the account numbers and all indicated that the accounts were locked. Mercedes was visibly upset. She tried different password combinations, but the accounts remained locked. Mercedes was frantic. She tried her uncle's passwords, but they also failed to unlock the money.

Eric returned to the library to tell Mercedes her time was up. Mercedes tried to bargain for more time but to no avail. Eric ordered, "Get to work, inmate, enough computer time."

Mercedes was already agitated, and she confronted Eric, "There you go again with that 'inmate' bullshit."

"You are an inmate, so get busy. All those books need to go back on the shelves."

Mercedes was returning the books to the shelves and preparing to deliver books that inmates had requested. From her vantage point, she noticed Eric talking with a guard. They were standing in the area of the library that had no cameras. Mercedes watched as the guard handed Eric an envelope. Eric looked around, thumbed through the contents, then stuffed the envelope into his shirt. Mercedes walked out from behind the shelves to see their reaction. The guard glared at Mercedes and quickly walked away. Eric saw Mercedes approaching, "I thought I told you to put those books back on the shelves."

"I'm done. They're all on the shelves."

Eric looked at Mercedes suspiciously, "What did you see just now?"

"Nothing."

"Bullshit, Mercedes. You saw the envelope, didn't you?"

"Why are you so antsy, Eric? What are you hiding?"

"Go distribute those books, inmate, and come back. We're not done."

Mercedes smiled, "Okay, Eric," and then pushed the cart with the books out of the library.

When she returned, Eric was waiting for her. "Put the cart back. We have to talk. Mercedes rolls the cart into the corner and walks back. "So Eric what do you want to talk about?" "You better keep your mouth shut and don't repeat a fucking word of this but some of the COs around here got side businesses going, and he's one of them. I found out about it, and he pays me to look the other way. Let's just say we worked out a deal."

"What kind of business, Eric?"

"I don't ask as long as I get paid."

"Does he have a way of bringing in shit from the outside?"

"Like I said, I don't ask."

"Eric, this is huge. Do you think it's drugs?"

"No, probably not. I think it's things like booze, smokes, a little weed maybe."

"I want in, Eric. I want to talk to this guy."

"No fucking way, inmate. It's lights out soon, let's go."

Mercedes casually replied, "Sure, Eric, take me back." And she smiled that wicked smile again.

CHAPTER 37
HEAVY LIFTING

Zachariah strode into the private gym he belonged to called Heavy Lifting. Here, he was a superstar well known for his long workouts on the bike and the weights. He noticed a young woman on a training bike logging serious miles. He climbed on the bike next to hers and began his workout. Twenty minutes later she began the cool-down phase, but he continued to pedal in high-resistance mode. She looked over at him and noticed his tattoos. her attention to them didn't go unnoticed by Zachariah. As usual, a crowd had formed to watch his workout. This attention made him pedal harder and faster. Eventually, he slowed down and threw his arms into the air as if he'd won a race. In his mind, he'd just won the Tour de France. He pedaled slowly, winding down, and looked over at the young woman. She caught his eye and said, "I've never seen anybody do that before."

"I'll take that as a compliment, thank you."

"That was pretty amazing. Do you do that all the time?"

"Yes and sometimes more, but I don't want to deprive someone of using the equipment. What's your name?"

"It's Stacy."

"Nice to meet you. I'm Zachariah. I couldn't help noticing your tattoos, Stacy. They're different. Where did you get them?"

"I got them done out here in Riverside."

"Where did you get yours, Zachariah? They're the best I've seen. Are they local?"

"No, I got them done in Russia by a friend of mine under my direction, of course."

"Are you a tattoo artist?"

"Yes, are you thinking of getting another one?"

"Actually, yes. I want to add to the ones I have. Do you have a studio?"

"No, I don't. I work out of my home. What were you thinking of getting, anything in particular? I have photos of my work that I can show you if you'd like to see them."

Stacy replied, "Why don't I give you a call and we'll see."

"I don't have a card, you see. I only work by referral."

"I see, so why don't we set something up for Thursday or Friday night. Is that okay?"

"Thursday is fine, say about eight 'o'clock. The house is on Shore Crest Drive, number 26."

"You live on Shore Crest? That's a beautiful area."

"Yes, it is. My house is on the ocean side. It's got great views."

"Great, I'll see you then."

Zachariah watched her leave and then continued his workout.

The house sat on half an acre. It was a modern two-story with a two-car garage. It was beautifully landscaped with beachgrass and cypress trees. Zachariah was not convinced that Stacy would show up, but he prepared the needles and inks for the session. It was 8:30 and he resigned himself to believing that she was not coming. He started putting away the tattoo equipment when the doorbell chimed. He answered the door to find Stacy standing there with a male friend. Zachariah was a bit annoyed upon seeing them. "I was beginning to think you weren't coming. Who is this?"

"Sorry, we're late. This time of the year it can get crazy out here."

"Yes, I suppose, and who is your escort?"

"This is my friend Robert."

"Robert, meet Zachariah."

"It's nice to meet you, but I wasn't aware you were bringing someone."

"I hope you don't mind."

"No, it's quite alright. Come in and I'll show you samples of my work." The three of them sat on the terrace. It was a balmy night and the ocean was a bit rough. In the distance, the sound of large waves crashing on the shore could be heard. "I made a pitcher of a fruit and vegetable health drink earlier. Would either of you like a glass?"

Stacy replied, "I'd love a glass."

"And you, Robert? One for you?"

"I'd prefer a beer if you have."

"Sorry, all I have is vodka."

"Great, I'll have vodka on the rocks."

"So Stacy, do you see anything you like?"

"Yeah, I like this one with the tiger jumping through the flaming hoop."

"Beautiful but complicated. We won't be able to finish it in one sitting obviously. I trust you'll be able to come back."

"Sure, you tell me when."

"Let's see how far we get tonight. Okay, let's get started. My studio is in the back. By the way, where do you want this one, Stacy?"

"I want it on my upper thigh, very upper. I hope that doesn't freak you out."

Zachariah smiled, showing his unsettling crooked teeth. "You'd be surprised what parts I've tattooed, Stacy."

Robert followed them to the back. "I'm sorry, Robert. This area is private. I'd rather you didn't come in. We won't be too long."

Zachariah handed Stacy a robe for her to change into. "So where on your thigh do you want the tattoo?"

"I want it to be seen only by someone I'm intimate with. How about here?" She indicated an area on her upper thigh just below the thong line.

"I would say that is pretty high, Stacy. Okay, let's begin. You do realize it's going to hurt in such a sensitive area."

Robert was on the terrace enjoying the view and the balmy night air and he poured himself another vodka. Zachariah was working on the tattoo, making small talk with Stacy. "So how long have you and Robert been together."

Stacy laughed, "Oh, Robert's not my boyfriend. Our relationship is platonic. We're like brother and sister. He's from Nebraska. He's here looking for work."

"And you, Stacy? Are you from Nebraska, too?"

Stacy laughed, "No, Pittsburgh."

"Is that where your family is, Pittsburgh?"

"Yes, my family is still there." Stacy winced from the needle.

"I'm sorry, did that hurt? Let me change to a fresh needle." Zachariah turned his back on Stacy and prepared a syringe of a strong sedative. "Okay, let's continue, shall we." He put his hand over her mouth and injected her with the drug. Stacy was fighting and trying to scream, but his grip was too strong. Eventually, she went limp and fell unconscious. He noticed her beautiful hair and smooth skin. He moved close to her and sniffed her hair and slid his hand up and down her thighs. A voice echoed in his head, *Don't touch her, that's dirty, don't touch her. Now you have to kill the boy, kill the boy, kill the boy.* The voices were getting louder, and Zachariah held his ears so as not to hear. The voices turned into a chant, *Kill the boy, kill the boy, kill him.* Zachariah sat with his head in his hands, the voices pounding in his head. He saw that Stacy was still unconscious and realized he couldn't let Robert know what happened to her. He prepared another injection and hid it under the sheet covering Stacy. He ran outside yelling for Robert, "Come quick, something happened to Stacy."

Robert ran into the room and Zachariah was calling Stacy's name. He instructed Robert, "See if you can revive her. I'll call 911. I was working on the tattoo and she passed out." Robert leaned over to check on Stacy and Zachariah injected him with a much stronger dose than he gave her, a lethal dose. "What the fuck was that? What did you stick me with?" Robert's legs began to buckle, and Zachariah grabbed him before he fell to the floor.

"I'm sorry, Robert. I'm so sorry. Go to sleep now. The angels are waiting for you." Zachariah was staring into space as he continued, "Sleep, sleep, go to sleep." Robert went limp and Zachariah let him slide down to the floor. The voices in his head began to taper off and eventually subsided. He lied down next to Stacy and fell asleep.

Zachariah awakened later to realize it wasn't a dream when he noticed Robert's body on the floor. Stacy was beginning to stir. He looked at his watch and was startled to see that he had been asleep for two hours. He prepared another needle and injected her again. He took the vodka and drank straight from the bottle. He then went down to the basement and quietly opened the door to one of the empty rooms. The other captives were asleep and he was careful not to wake them. He picked up Stacy, carried her downstairs into the room, and placed her on the bed. She moaned slightly as he gently put her down. He awakened Andrew and they both went upstairs. "I need you to help me, Andrew. We need to dispose of a body."

"Did you say body? What happened?"

"Don't question me, just do as I say. We can toss him off the Channel Bridge. The currents will take it out to sea. It's 1:00 a.m. It'll take us at least a half-hour to get there. Hurry, let's get him into my car." They arrived and parked on the side of the bridge with the lights off. They sat for a while in silence. "We have to be quick about it, Andrew. I'll open the back. Are you ready?" Andrew struggled with the body and Zachariah yelled, "Come on, Andrew! You're stronger than that."

"Sorry, I didn't think he'd be that heavy."

"Come on, lift or I'll throw you over with him." They got the body on the railing and Zachariah rolled it off and into the ocean. The body traveled 70 feet down into the dark water below. They looked over the edge but couldn't see a thing. The loud splash was the only confirmation they had that their mission was successful. The water under the bridge was known for its treacherous currents and it's had its share of suicides. In the distance, lights were approaching and they quickly got back into the truck. On the way back, Zachariah told Andrew about Stacy. "I'm counting on you to calm her down when she awakens. Don't tell her what happened to Robert. You must do as I say. Stay positive and tell her how good the training is. Sara can help you keep her and Jennifer positive since Sara will be in the next round of the competition. After her, it will be your turn to compete, Andrew." They arrived at the house at 3:00 a.m. and Andrew returned to his room downstairs. Everyone was still asleep, and the house was quiet. Zachariah collapsed on the couch and slept like a baby.

Rodriguez was awakened by loud purring. It was 7:00 a.m. and Bogie was hungry. "Okay, Bogie, I know you're hungry as usual." While Bogie ate, he showered and was out the door. He arrived at the precinct to find Will waiting for him. They exchanged greetings and Will remarked, "I want to hit the boardwalk today. Maybe I'll run into him again."

"I don't think that's a good idea, Will."

"Why not? I can follow him."

"Stay away from the boardwalk."

"Why, Sergeant?"

"Come into my office, Will. Here's why." They entered the office and the door closed behind them. "Cause he knows you're a cop. I got this just a few minutes ago on the way in." Rodriguez put his cell phone on the table, "Mr. Policeman, I met Will on the boardwalk; and we enjoyed an ice cream together. I like him. I feel that he would make a great addition to my team of athletes. He was there the night David was killed. Did you think you could fool me? When I finish with you, I'll make him one of my competitors. I'm sure he'll be splendid. Goodbye for now." There was a pause then Rodriguez said, "Listen, Will, I was thinking that I should transfer you back to Suffolk County PD. This guy knows who you are. It's too dangerous."

"No way. I don't want to go back. He knows who you are, too."

"Yeah, but with me it's different. I should have never pulled you into this."

"I can take care of myself. I'm staying here with you and Marco."

Rodriguez looked at Will, "Okay, Will, but I want you to stay away from the boardwalk. He knows you work for me, so he'll stay away, too. And be careful when you leave here. Make sure you're not being followed. We'll figure something out, but for now, get over to Identikit and give Officer Jacobs the description of the guy on the boardwalk. Let's see what we got. If Marco is here, please send him in."

A few minutes later Detective Spinelli arrived. "You wanted to see me, Sergeant?"

"Yeah, have a seat. So what do we know about this Zachariah? We know he's a cyclist. Will said he had a bike worth about 12 grand. He sounded like he was from Russia or Eastern Europe, and according to Will, he's about forty. Will said he had a strong accent which indicates he hasn't been in the country that long." Rodriguez paused suddenly then said, "That's it, Marco. The Tour de France. That's the biggest event for cyclists in the world."

"You think he was in it?"

"It's kind of a long shot, but it's worth a try."

"We don't even know if Zachariah is his real name."

"Start with five years ago and go back. See if you can find the names of entrants in the race from Russia. Maybe we'll find Zachariah in there somewhere."

CHAPTER 38

ALTERED STATES

Zachariah was at the Tour de France as coach of the 2012 entrants from Russia. His assistant coach was Alexi Petrenko. Together they trained a team that was considered by the experts to be the best cycling team in the world. Zachariah insisted that all the competitors on his team be Russian. He and Alexi drilled the team hard, beginning their training in November and continuing through the Russian winter. The team would train for 20 to 30 hours per week. They called it the workweek. Under a normal routine, the team would train for intensity lasting up to a full hour at the hardest effort, combined with lower intensity training; but Zachariah would always push for more effort, lasting at times two hours. As the race neared, most teams would taper back the training, but not Zachariah. His team would continue the high-intensity training until a few weeks before the race. There are three major races in the cycling world: the Giro d' Italia, Vuelta a Espana, and the most prestigious, the Tour de France. Zachariah and Alexi insisted that their athletes compete in all three events. The abnormal rigorous training combined with the three events would be nearly impossible for any athlete to endure, but Zachariah found a solution.

Since 2010 Zachariah had been a member of the FSB (Federal Security Service) which had replaced the KGB as the security force in Russia. They specialized in tracking and capturing spies, cracking down on dissidents, and protecting Russian oligarchs, always brutally and ruthlessly. It was here that he met Alexi who would later become his assistant coach and accomplice in several murders. In this mix, Zachariah thrived. He had an interest in mind-altering and performance-enhancing drugs. His position in the security force allowed him to use all of their resources to develop and refine these drugs. He studied chemistry entirely funded by the FSB. Eventually, his expertise in developing these drugs enabled him to curry favor with the upper echelon of the agency. They saw these drugs as an interrogation weapon, a modern truth serum, and a way to control enemies of the state. He was given diplomatic credentials that allowed him to travel at will. He perfected a blend of these different drugs to enhance endurance beyond what was possible before. All that was left to do was to make them undetectable. Unfortunately, he began to experiment on himself which started his downward spiral into paranoia, schizophrenia, and sociopathic behavior.

The war in Soviet Georgia, though short-lived, allowed Zachariah to use these drugs on subjects other than himself, mostly prisoners of war. The FSB recruited a well-known Georgian doctor, Dimitri Fedorov, who was forced to supervise these experiments. While Fedorov was working on a truth serum for the FSB using a combination of KGB and CIA formulas, Zachariah was experimenting on making the mind-altering and performance-enhancing drugs impossible to detect in the drug screens of the day. As a reward for his service and loyalty to the state, he was given the position of coaching the Russian cycling team by the oligarchs that owned the team. He recruited Alexi Petrenko to be his assistant coach. Not content with allowing the athletes to compete on their own merits, Zachariah began injecting them with his formulas. Soon he and Alexi had an unbeatable team, and the drugs went undetected until his fourth Tour de France. In 2012 Dimitri Semenov, the doctor who was forced to experiment on his fellow Georgians, was put in charge of the anti-doping controls. This choice did not sit well with Zachariah; but despite numerous protests, Dr. Semenov remained in charge. The good doctor was determined to carry out his duties to the maximum with a special animus toward the Russian team. He took the anti-doping testing to the next level and began testing for obscure and outlawed components that were thought to be impossible to find. In secret tests, he was able to find these components and went to the Cycling Anti-Doping Foundation to allow for broader testing. Permission was granted, and the tests began in secret with the Russian team in his crosshairs. Dr. Semenov reported his findings to the CADF, and they were disqualified from the competition. Despite Zachariah's continued testing and efforts to make the drugs impossible to find, the next four years saw more disqualifications for the Russian team. The drugs and the disqualifications began taking a toll on Zachariah's mind, and he became more sociopathic and paranoid. In 2017 he started the Cyclist Club in Russia. He convinced Alexi to join him in this endeavor with promises of glory and money. Alexi went along and helped him kidnap and train the athletes. He discovered that it was Dr. Semenov who reported his findings to the CADF for three consecutive years. He found him and murdered him and his wife using the same drugs but in stronger doses. In late 2018 with the authorities in pursuit, Zachariah used his diplomatic credentials to escape Russia, leaving behind a trail of victims. His name was removed from any connection to the Tour de France, and all records of his participating in the event in any form were destroyed. Alexi stayed in Russia and was able to escape capture by moving around Eastern Europe and Germany.

Marco returned to the office. "I went back ten years, and there's nothing on a Zachariah either as an entrant or a coach. Whatever team photos I was able to grab don't show anybody fitting his description."

Rodriguez leaned back in his chair. "What teams did you check?"

"I started with Russia, Ukraine, Serbia, and Georgia but got nothing. There was one thing that stood out, though. Team Russia was disqualified four years straight."

"Did it say why?"

"No."

"That's bullshit. They covered it up. I think I know why they were kicked out. They were doping; and Zachariah, or whatever his name is, was in charge. Marco, I need you to do something else for me. I know the Tour de France organization is headquartered in Brussels. See if you can get me a number. The guy in charge is Professor Jurgen Freidlich

"I'll get right on it, Sergeant."

"Make copies of everything you find. Thanks."

Marco returned with a folder full of printouts. "Here are the race records from the last ten years: winners, rankings, race times, all that shit. These are the disqualification records."

Rodriguez looked them over, "You're right, no names of coaches or trainers, and no team group pictures."

"I also found some newspaper clippings on the internet. These disqualifications were a big deal in Russia but not so much here. I guess we just figured it was business as usual. The only coach mentioned was an assistant coach named Alexi Petrenko. He's the third one from the left, bottom row. He was an assistant coach in 2012."

Rodriguez looked over the copies. "I'm convinced they scrubbed the records of Zachariah, which indicates doping wasn't his only problem. Were you able to get that number for me?"

"Not yet, I got Will working on it."

Rodriguez checked his watch and noted, "There's a six-hour time difference. It's 4:00 in Brussels."

Will entered and handed Rodriguez the number. "I hate dialing international numbers."

A woman's voice answered, "Hello, Professor Friedlich's office. May I help you?"

"Good afternoon. My name is Sergeant Rodriguez. May I speak to the Professor?"

"What is this regarding?"

"I'd rather discuss it with him if you don't mind. It's very important."

"You said 'Sergeant.' Is that a military Sergeant?"

"No, I'm a police sergeant from the United States. Can you put him on, please?"

"I'll see if he can come to the phone. Please hold."

"I'm on hold, and hold music is shitty all over the world."

Professor Friedlich picked up, "Good evening, Sergeant Rodriguez. What can I do for you?"

"Thank you for taking my call, Professor. I apologize if I interrupted something important."

"It's quite alright, Sergeant. Go ahead."

"I'm conducting a homicide investigation on Long Island, New York; and I need your help. I believe our chief suspect may have been either a coach or an entrant in the Tour de France beginning in 2012. The only name we have is Zachariah. We don't have a surname. We're working on a description now. Does the name sound familiar."

"Zachariah, no last name. That's not much information. You said you had a description."

"Yeah, he's tall, about 6'3", bald, with crooked teeth. Works out a lot. We're not sure if he was an entrant or a coach."

The Professor was silent.

"Professor, are you there?"

"Yes, Sergeant, I'm here. That description could fit several entrants."

"There's only one entrant I'm interested in, Professor."

"Sorry, Sergeant, I can't help you."

"What about coaches? Anybody fit that description?"

"No."

"Okay, let's try this. Does the name Alexi Petrenko sound familiar?"

"Petrenko? No, I'm not familiar with him."

"He was an assistant coach in 2012. You were in charge of races then and you still are. Correct?"

The Professor was silent once again.

"Sergeant, you're right. I was in charge, but these names don't come to mind."

"Are you sure? Because I'm holding a clipping from a French newspaper that has a team picture, and you're directly in the center of the group. Alexi Petrenko is to your right. You're separated by two officials. Do you remember him now?"

The Professor was quiet for a while. "Sergeant, can you please stay on the phone while I close my office door?"

"Sure, go ahead. I'll wait."

"Let me begin by saying that no one except a select group of officials in the Tour de France and the Russian government knows what I'm about to tell you. As you probably figured out, Zachariah is not his real name. It's Ivan Fedorov. Ironically, Fedorov means Gift of God. This is a gift the world can do without. Alexi Petrenko was his assistant coach."

"What can you tell me about Fedorov?"

"His father was in the KGB beginning in the '60s until his death in 2010. He was dispatched to Cuba where he was given the task of perfecting a mind-control drug. His subjects were political prisoners of the communist regime. Ivan was born in Cuba in 1980; and as soon as he was old enough, he went to work with his father. His mother was Cuban, and people who knew the family said she protested her son taking part. She went back, or shall I say, she was sent back to Russia and was never heard from again."

"Was his father a chemist?"

The professor laughed, "Chemist, pardon my laughter, but everyone in the KGB at that time considered themselves a chemist. They were butchers with no regard for human life. Ivan was born into this world of human experimentation. After a while, he became indifferent to it all. According to people who knew Ivan, his love was cycling, much to the disappointment of his father. His father wanted him to become a military man and follow in his footsteps.

Eventually, Ivan became intrigued by the effect of these drugs on the mind and human endurance. He wanted to develop an undetectable drug that he could take back to Russia to help athletes become the best in the world. He did this with his father's blessing, of course, with no thought to the physical and mental effects these would have on his victims. When they began to run out of political prisoners, Ivan began to test these drugs on himself. Not only did his father encourage it, he demanded it. When his father died, he returned to Russia and became an agent with the FSB, the new and improved KGB. He combined his love of cycling with his experimentation using these drugs, and he became the monster he is today."

"Was he ever tied to any specific murders in Russia?"

"He was a suspect in Russia, Georgia, and Ukraine; but there was not enough evidence, so they said. That's how things work in Russia, Sergeant. If you are connected with the oligarchs or the government, well, I believe you understand. Before he fled Russia, he killed the man in charge of testing the athletes for doping. His name was Dimitri Semenov. He killed the doctor and his wife. I suppose that was the last straw for the Russians. At that point, he and Alexi Petrenko became hunted men. No one has seen either one since."

"Mind if I ask you a personal question, Professor? What is your background?"

"My background is as follows, Sergeant. I have a Ph.D. in Psychology and a Masters in Psychiatry. I've been a consultant in various cases involving serial killings for the last ten years. I've had an interest in the workings of a serial killer's mind. There are nights where I don't sleep."

"How would you categorize Ivan's mental state?"

"That's a complicated question, I don't know where to begin. I'll say one thing before I hang up this phone. If you find him, please keep this in mind. You must kill the beast because prison will never contain him. Good night, Sergeant, and good luck."

Rodriguez hung up the phone and sat back in his chair. He paused. "Gentlemen, our Zachariah's real name is Ivan Fedorov. He left Russia a few years ago because he was being hunted for killing a doctor and his wife. Professor Friedlich told me that he was testing mind-control drugs on live subjects. David and the other cyclists were under his control."

The men were silent, then Will asked, "How do we catch a guy like this, Sergeant?"

CHAPTER 39

IT'S JUST BUSINESS

Eric escorted Mercedes to the library to begin her shift. As they were walking, Mercedes asked him, "So, Eric, did you think about what we talked about?"

"What's that, inmate?"

"Stop calling me 'inmate.' What the fuck is wrong with you, Eric? Are you pissed about something? What did we talk about? That conversation we had about getting me involved, you know, bringing me in. It's funny that only one of us remembers that conversation."

They arrived at the library and Mary was waiting for them. "Show Mary how we catalog these books and file them."

Mercedes turned her back on Mary, "What are you doing, Eric? If you want to teach me a lesson, I get it, but stop ignoring me."

Eric was quiet and then suddenly slammed the books down. "Both of you come back here now." They went to the area of the library that didn't have cameras. "Okay, let me straighten something out.

First of all, Mercedes, I already have a partner in my business. I can't afford another one. Second of all, Aunt Shauna."

"Aunt Shauna? What the hell are you talking about, Eric?"

"I know you and Aunt Shauna set up the hit on Rodriguez." Mercedes was silent. "And I know you're the one that killed her."

"I didn't kill her. I told you what happened." Eric looked at Mary, "Meet my partner, Mary. She saw and heard it all: the plan to kill Rodriguez and the murder of Shauna Wilson."

"Your partner? She's your partner? What the fuck does she bring to the table?"

"Do you remember me telling you that she works Mondays and Wednesdays. She was working both those days. Looks like you were unlucky twice, Mercedes."

"Fuck you, Eric. And you, you little bitch, were you watching me?" Mercedes lunged at Mary but was stopped by Eric. Mercedes continued fighting to get to Mary.

Eric ordered, "Stop, Mercedes. Nobody knows except us. We can work this out."

"Are you fucking her, too, Eric?"

"No, it's just business. Calm down and I'll let you go. If not, you'll be restrained and taken to the prison shrink." Eric had Mercedes pinned against the wall. "Calm down." After a while, he asked, "Are you calm? Can I let you go?"

"Okay, okay, Eric. Let me go." Eric relinquished his grip and stood between them.

"Stay where you are. You attack her again and I'm going to spray you, got it?"

Mercedes replied, "I got it, Eric. What do you mean, 'we can work it out?' What are you talking about?"

"$25,000 each, Mercedes. That's how we work it out."

"I can't get that kind of money, it's all frozen. That's why Rodriguez came to see me, to tell me that somehow he froze the accounts."

Eric responded, "So."

"So, were you listening? I don't have the money. I can't access the accounts, Eric."

"You said you still had contacts on the outside. Can't you get it from them?"

"I'm in prison, in case you haven't noticed. Why would anybody give me $50,000?"

"I'm thinking Friday should be enough time. What do you say, Mary?" Mary nodded in agreement. "Mary, show her how we conduct business." Mary selected a book from the cart and handed it to Eric. He, in turn, gave it to Mercedes. "Open it." Mercedes opened the book and discovered it was hollowed out. "We've got about twenty books just like this one. We deliver the book, and we pick it up with the money. When we get paid, Mary delivers the book to the animals in their cells with the merchandise inside. Every guard and every inmate has their own title, so we know where the money came from." Mercedes looked at Eric and then back at Mary. Eric continued, "Remember when I told you it was just some booze or smokes and maybe a little weed? Well, that was bullshit. It's drugs, pills, coke, whatever. When you killed Aunt Shauna, our source dried up. She had a contact on the outside, a crooked cop. It was a perfect operation. We were pulling down some nice bucks till you fucked it up by killing Shauna. That's going to cost you, Mercedes. Now, both of you get to work."

Mercedes and Mary worked quietly in their sections of the library. Eric stopped in from time to time to make sure they were working. The lunch bell rang, and Eric escorted the women to the cafeteria. Mercedes sat with her prison gang. She addressed the women at the table, "Shauna had a contact on the outside, a crooked cop. Does anybody know who he is?" The women looked around the table at each other.

One of the women said, "The only guy I can think of is a dirty cop she knew on the outside. I think his name is Mitchell. From what Shauna said, he was her connection. They were moving some illegal shit in here, you know drugs. Shauna and this dude figured out a way to bring them in."

Mercedes replied, "Did Shauna tell you how they were doing it?"

'No, she didn't tell anybody. She kept it a secret. I know she had a few guards on the inside helping her."

Mercedes asked, "I want to get in touch with this cop. Anybody know how?"

CHAPTER 40

GO WITH JAH

Darren Mitchell was on his way to Queens to meet with a drug dealer nicknamed Stilts. Since Aunt Shauna's death, he'd been thinking about revamping his drug business. No more shaking down rival drug dealers to steal their merchandise. He wanted to move his business out of Suffolk County and into Manhattan. With Rodriguez breathing down his neck for what he did to his father, he couldn't afford any mistakes, and nobody knew him in New York. He was meeting with Stilts, whose real name was Palmer Gordon, to set up a pipeline from Jamaica to Queens and eventually to New York City. Stilts was from Montego Bay, and he wanted to expand his business. He was willing to listen to Mitchell's proposal.

Mitchell arrived at an address in Queens surrounded by pawn shops and fast food joints. As he exited his car, the smell of weed permeated the air. When he got to the building, he was greeted by two men sitting on the steps. As Mitchell attempted to enter the building, one of the men blocked his way with his leg. Mitchell pulled back his jacket and showed him his gun. The man said, "If your name is Mitchell, you can go up."

Mitchell sighed and pulled out his badge to show the men, "I'm here to do business with your boss. Now move your fucking leg."

The man slowly moved his leg and said, "Respect, man, it's all about respect."

Mitchell replied, "Yeah, where do I go, which door?"

"Upstairs, first floor, number six. He's expecting you, my man."

Mitchell looked up at the abandoned building, "What a shithole. Does he do business out of this rathole?"

The men looked at each other and smiled, "Yes, it's low key. It keeps the Agents of Babylon away."

"Agents of Babylon? What the fuck are you talking about?"

The men smiled again, "The police, my man, the police."

As Mitchell climbed the stairs, the pungent smell of marijuana and urine became heavier. He noticed that the other apartments were empty and in disrepair. The first floor was dimly lit with green peeling paint. Mitchell removes his gun and holds it at his side. The door to number six was ajar and reggae music blared from the apartment. Mitchell pushed the door open slowly with his gun in hand. The door was pulled open the rest of the way from the inside; and a voice said, "Mitchell, my brother, enter." "I see you're armed, give it to brother Antoine or we don't do business." Antoine walked over with his hand out and Mitchell gave him the gun. He looked around the apartment and noticed men and women sitting on the floor and two bedrooms with people having sex on the beds. Most of the people were smoking weed and others were doing lines of cocaine. Stilts got up and extended his hand to Mitchell. Mitchell was surprised to see that Stilts was very short, and the surprise showed on his face. It didn't go unnoticed by Stilts. "Are you surprised by my short stature, Mitchell?"

"Now that you mentioned it, I was expecting someone taller." The people in the room laughed. Stilts tried to hand Mitchell a joint, but he turned it down.

"You don't like weed, Mitchell? Perhaps some cocaine or a nice Jamaican mommy."

"Do you want to talk business, Stilts, or do you want to talk shit?"

Stilts scowled at Mitchell. "Okay, okay, man. Let's talk business."

Mitchell began, "I heard at one time you guys controlled part of Suffolk County until the Colombians moved in and now you're selling nickel bags in Queens…"

Stilts cut Mitchell off, "You have an insulting way about you, Mitchell, you're disrespectful."

"Listen, Stilts, Shauna, and I had a good thing going on Long Island. Between the street sales and that pipeline into Suffolk Prison, we were pulling down thousands a week. Now she's dead and her source died with her."

"No, Mitchell, you're mistaken. The source stands before you very much alive."

"You were her supplier?"

"In the flesh. Let's just say that Auntie knew how to diversify. She had many sources."

"Shit, she never told me."

Stilts stared at Mitchell, "So, Mitchell, what deal do you want to strike with me?"

"It's simple. I supply the network and you supply the product."

"What's your poison, Mitchell? What do you want to sell?"

"I want to move to New York. Fuck Long Island. Things are getting hot for me out there. New York is a cocaine and heroin paradise. That's my poison; that's what I want to sell. Let me know how much you can handle."

"The Big Apple? I'm impressed, Mitchell, but what about the competition? How do you deal with them?"

"I'll get a network set up in the city. I've got police contacts there. They'll keep the competition to a minimum."

Stilts replied, "Crooked police bumbaclots everywhere I try to do business."

"Yeah, well, that's how it is if you want to move your product. I'm out of here. Call me and let me know how much weight you can give me." He handed Stilts a card.

Stilts asked, "So, Mitchell, who killed my Auntie Shauna?"

Mitchell was surprised by the question. "What?"

"My auntie. I want to know who killed her, Mitchell."

"Shauna was your aunt?"

"Yes, Mitchell, on my dear mommy's side. Find out who took her from this earth, Mitchell."

"I heard rumors, Stilts; but nobody knows, maybe it was one of her prison gang."

"If you want to partner with me, that's the one thing you need to do. Find out who killed my auntie and make them dead. Come back when it's done."

"I'll find out and I'll take care of it."

"Good, Mitchell, good. Now take your weapon from Antoine and go with Jah."

"Jah?"

"God, Mitchell, God."

Eric was approached by his contact while in the prison library. "I heard from Mitchell. He wants me to find out who killed Shauna. What do you know about it?"

Eric responded, "Me? I don't know shit. It was probably one of those dykes in her gang. Why are you talking to Mitchell about this? It's case closed."

"It seems Shauna's drug dealer nephew wants whoever did it dead. If we don't give him a body, it dries up. No more deliveries and no more money."

Eric interrupted, "Like I said, it's a closed case."

"Wasn't Delacruz's niece here when it happened?"

"Yeah, she was. If I didn't show up, they would have killed her, too."

"Was anybody else here?"

"No, just Delacruz."

"Well, Eric, you need to do something. We got to satisfy Shauna's nephew. It's just business. It's all you, Eric."

The guard handed Eric an envelope and warned, "Do the right thing or that's the last one."

Zachariah was in the basement with his athletes as they were training. "Very good, Sara. I think you'll be ready in time for the next meeting of the Cyclist Club. Keep up the training and soon you'll be competing."

Jennifer asked, "What happened to David?"

Zachariah sighed, "He died at the hands of a policeman who's been pursuing me, but soon we'll have our revenge."

"Does that mean we're all going to die?"

"Now, now, Jennifer, you know how much I hate negativity. You're not all going to die. In fact, it's a happy time for us. I have friends coming from Russia to assist me in the training. You see, I want to add more competitors and expand membership to the Cyclist Club. They'll be here on Wednesday. Do any of you have friends who might want to join us? Think about it. Come on, now, less talk and more training. Let's go, Kim, faster."

He went upstairs and prepared his usual half dozen eggs and vegetable smoothie and sat on his balcony overlooking the ocean. The water was calm today and the waves were softly breaking on the shore. He tilted his head back and let the warm sun hit his face. Next to him on a small table is a radio receiver. He turned up the volume and listened to the captives in the basement. He sipped his smoothie and smiled.

CHAPTER 41

A KILLER IS BORN

Mercedes was working in the library when Eric came in and pulled her by the arm into the maintenance closet. "What's your problem, Eric? You horny or something?"

"Shut up and listen. When you killed Shauna, you started a shit storm."

"I told you, Eric. I can't get to the money. It's all frozen, even my uncle's."

"Yeah, I know."

"So what do you want from me? Why did you pull me in here?"

"I'll tell you why if you'll shut up and listen. Because Shauna's nephew, a Jamaican drug dealer, wants the person who killed her dead." Mitchell was trying to strike a deal with this guy and no deal unless that happens."

Mercedes looked nervously at Eric, "Her nephew?"

"Yeah, her real nephew. Some crazy drug dealer from Queens. If we don't give him a body, it all goes away. No more side business and no more money. It all dries up. Matter of fact, he may find out it was you and get some fucking lifer in here to kill you. Either way, the business is gone. So give me a reason why I shouldn't tell this drug dealer asshole it was you."

"Me? You want to sacrifice me? Let me tell you something. My family kicked those dreadlocked assholes out of Suffolk County and into Queens. Even Shauna told me that we fucked up her business. That's right, Eric, the Delacruz family, my family. You think you're some big-time drug dealer moving a few ounces in this joint. My brother Diego and I moved tons of shit all over Long Island. If he wants a body, we'll give him a body."

"What are you talking about?"

"Think about it, Eric. Who can hurt us the most right now? Who knows all about us?"

Eric thought quickly and replied, "Mary. Are you talking about Mary?"

"Yeah, Mary."

"No way, Mercedes. I can't get anywhere near that after Shauna got killed on my watch."

"I'll take care of it, Eric. Just disappear. Go get yourself an alibi. After it's done, I'll run the business for you, and I'll triple your take. I know what I'm doing. My uncle taught me well."

Eric paced back and forth thinking, *Why the fuck did you have to kill her? Now it's all screwed up.*

"So, Eric, what's it going to be?"

"I got into this thing to make some extra cash and now I may have to kill somebody. This is so fucked."

"Like I said, leave it to me."

"You? What do you know about killing?"

"Do you really want to know, Eric? Okay, let me tell you. When we were young, our parents were killed by a rival cartel. A hit squad was sent to kill our whole family. They broke into the hacienda and killed our bodyguards and then our parents. My brother Diego and I hid because they would have killed us, also. My uncle found out who they were but kept it to himself. When I was 18 and my brother was 16, our uncle tracked them down. One by one we killed them slowly, tortured them. My uncle said we should be the ones to kill them, my brother and I. My brother wanted to kill their families, but my uncle felt this was enough bloodshed. They were sent by a rival drug dealer named El Moreno who had a hacienda across the Medellin River. From that day forward, there was an uneasy truce between him and my uncle, neither one daring to cross the river. And now my uncle is dead. So that's what I know about killing."

Eric was shocked. He stared silently at Mercedes and then uttered, "You were 18?"

"Yeah, and my brother was 16. So do you think some Jamaican assholes scare me?"

"So how can you triple my business?"

"Remember those contacts I told you about, we can make our own deals."

Eric replied, "I've got to be careful here. Mitchell can't find out. I've got to think about this. Let's go, Mercedes. You've got to get back."

CHAPTER 42

BEDROOM ROULETTE

Marco walked into Rodriguez's office. "Ivan Fedorov is off everybody's radar. If he's anywhere on Long Island, he's invisible."

"What about real estate companies? Anything there?"

"No, if he bought anything on Long Island, he didn't use his real name or somebody else was involved in the transaction. It seems like Zachariah is a ghost. He doesn't exist."

Rodriguez responded, "He's real and we're going to lock him up. I got word earlier today that the trooper who was shot at Mrs. Mayhew's house the night of her murder is doing better, and he's ready to give us some information. Take Will with you. Get to Hampton Hospital and talk to him."

"I'll be in touch."

Rodriguez was in his office when Detective Spinelli called, "Trooper Jensen is doing well, Sergeant."

"That's good news. Did he offer any new information?"

"Yes, he said something interesting about that night. Jensen told me that Mrs. Mayhew got a call earlier that day from an officer recommending that she sleep in a different room that night, one at the rear of the house—the guest room where she was killed. The officer that suggested it said that it was safer for her."

"Did she tell Jensen the officer's name?"

"Jensen seems to think she did, but he can't remember. Body Bag gave him a pretty bad concussion."

Rodriguez remarked, "Whoever told her to change rooms told her she'd be safer in the rear of the house because the trooper on duty was in closer proximity to the back bedrooms. She was set up, Marco. The officer that told her to change rooms is our connection to Zachariah. That's how the shooter was in and out so fast. Body Bag knew exactly where she was. All he had to do was overpower the trooper."

"How do you know it was Body Bag, Sergeant?"

"Connect the dots, Marco. Body Bag was found after we visited the hospital with half a cell phone shoved in his mouth. The nurse on duty said she dialed a number for him. I'll bet that call went to Zachariah and he wasn't happy about it. Body Bag was one of the cyclists that attacked me, and he fucked up. Zachariah made an example out of him. Find the officer that called Mrs. Mayhew and we'll find Zachariah."

CHAPTER 43
EVIL CLOAKED IN LAUGHTER

The flight from Russia was delayed for over an hour due to bad weather. Zachariah was wearing a suit and carrying a briefcase which gave him an air of importance. He walked to the Aeroflot Airline customer service desk and presented his diplomatic credentials. An official of the airport was summoned and he ushered Zachariah through the TSA checkpoint. While he waited, Zachariah browsed the high-end shops located on JFK's many levels. He noticed a black Balmain designer leather jacket modeled after a Harley Davidson motorcycle jacket. The price tag was $2,800. He entered the store and made the purchase. He disposed of the suit jacket he was wearing and donned the new Balmain to meet his friends. As he strolled through the airport, he heard the announcement that the flight had arrived. He was meeting his former assistant coach, Alexi Petrenko, and Mika Sokolov, an acquaintance who Alexi liked to have around because she was beautiful and good for his ego. The problem with Alexi was he loved himself too much to recognize her existence. Alexi was big in stature like Zachariah. He was 44 years old with brown hair, dark blue eyes, and a handsome face. A few scars, grim reminders from the war in Soviet Georgia, added to the air of mystery surrounding him. Mika was younger, a Russian beauty with dark hair and hazel eyes. In Russia, she was a model and a B actress. Zachariah used to call her the seductress.

As they walked through the airport, heads turned to look at them. They met Zachariah and he asked them about the flight. They made small talk as he led them to a waiting limousine which then headed east towards Montauk. Zachariah remarked, "Unfortunately, it could take us almost two hours to get to your hotel. First, though, we'll go to my house and drink vodka and talk about our time in Russia."

Mika admired his jacket and asked where he got it. "Do you like it? I picked it up while waiting for you to arrive. It's modeled after a Harley Davidson motorcycle jacket."

Mika replied, "They're very popular in Russia and very expensive. That one is a bit fancier than the typical ones."

Alexi chimed in, "Speaking of cycles, how is the club? The last time we spoke, you were doing quite well. You had many members and were recruiting more athletes. Is that still the case?"

"Yes, but I'm having difficulties with a certain policeman who is incessantly pursuing me."

"So buy him off like we did in Russia. Everyone has a price."

"Not this one, Alexi. He's a different type of policeman."

"Do you recall what we did in Russia, Zachariah? If we couldn't buy them, we killed them. We used to call it option two. Remember?"

"Oh, yes, I remember. But what if I was to tell you that there has been one attempt to assault him that ended badly for the two competitors I sent. A few weeks ago I had two very evil men working for me, and he and his fellow policemen killed them both.

There was another attempt to kill him, but he killed the two assailants instead."

Mika, uneasy, asked, "So much killing and for what?"

Alexi glared at her and questioned Zachariah, "Were they your cyclists?"

"No, not these two. Someone else hired them."

Alexi responded, "It seems that many people want this man dead."

"So it would seem. I was told he killed one while he was lying injured on the ground, and he showed no mercy. He chased my newest competitor to his death just the other night. You see, Alexi, this is not your normal American policeman." Mika and Alexi glanced at each other. "And you, Alexi? How are things in Russia? Did you bring some entries for us to screen at the next meeting?"

"Yes, I have four, all champions as you will see. It's good that I was able to come to America. I'm being hunted just like you. I had to disband the club and release the athletes. Luckily, I was able to purchase false documents and obtain a passport."

Mika asked, "So tell me, Zachariah, what does this policeman look like?"

Alexi remarked, "Why, Mika? Are you interested in jumping into the fray?"

"Why not? It seems that brute force isn't working. Perhaps a gentler approach might be more successful."

Zachariah replied, "Wait, I almost forgot. Mika, behind you in that cabinet I placed a few bottles of vodka. Let's have a drink and then we'll listen to your plan." They toasted, downed the vodka in one swallow, and slammed their glasses down.

"So you didn't answer my question. What does he look like?" Alexi looked at Zachariah and he filled the glasses one more time. They drank them down in one gulp. "I'm waiting."

The men chuckled and then Zachariah responded, "Well, he's tall and big like Alexi and me. He has dark eyes that pierce your soul and control your mind." The men laughed as Zachariah poured more vodka. "His name is Rodriguez and he's Spanish; and unlike us, he probably tans in the sun." They drank the vodka and began laughing again.

"Does he have hair or is he a bald ape like you?"

Zachariah and Alexi laughed hysterically, "She called you an ape, Zachariah, a bald ape."

"I know, isn't she beautiful?" The men quieted down and Zachariah replied, "Yes, he has hair. It's as black as your soul, Mika." And the men laughed again. "So what is your plan? Seduction, then you fall in love, get married, and have little Rodriguez's running around?" The men drank again and were howling. They finally calmed down when they noticed that Mika was getting angry. Zachariah placated her, "Go ahead, play the seductress; but I want to know everything you're doing. I have a plan, Mika. Why don't you seduce him and lure him to his death? How could he resist your charms?"

"What are you talking about?

"I have the perfect drug to give him, an agonizing death after you make passionate love to him, of course."

"Yebat' sebya."

"Alexi, did she just tell me to go fuck myself in Russian?"

"I think so."

They continued drinking for the rest of the trip. "We're a few minutes from my home. I think I've had enough vodka. I'm going to bed. In the morning you'll meet the athletes, and we can plan the demise of this nuisance with clearer heads." Zachariah instructed the driver to take them to the Lighthouse Inn. "I've reserved a suite with two private bedrooms. It has a view of the ocean and the lighthouse. It's reserved under the name Dimitri Semenov."

Zachariah handed Alexi forged papers to use as identification. "Semenov, the doctor that disqualified us all those years."

"Yes, Alexi, the same. Mika, stay away from Alexi. I think all that vodka has made him randy." The men began to laugh hysterically, and Mika replied, "Go home, Zachariah. You're a bit drunk."

"Okay, till tomorrow. Good night."

CHAPTER 44

FRIEND OR FOE?

The next morning Zachariah sent a limousine to pick them up. When they arrived at the house, Zachariah said, "I'm going to make you a traditional Russian breakfast."

Mika replied, "I'm tired of Russian food. Let's go out. I want an American breakfast."

"Good idea, Mika. I know just the place." Zachariah took them to the Route 25A Diner hoping to run into Detective McGraw. They walked into the diner and Zachariah scanned for McGraw. He spotted him sitting at his usual table chatting with the waitress. The waitress approached them. "You can sit anywhere."

"I see a friend of ours sitting there. May we join him?"

"Of course, I'll bring your menus."

McGraw sat upright with a look of disgust when he saw them approach. Zachariah greeted him, "Detective McGraw, what a coincidence. May we join you?" McGraw said nothing but gestured for them to sit down. Everyone sensed the tension in the air. "I'd like you to meet some friends from Russia."

After the introductions, Mika asked, "So what type of Detective are you?"

"Type? What do you mean by type?"

"You know, drugs, homicide, people who are missing."

"I'm a homicide detective. What brings you to America?"

"Us, we're just visiting our friend here."

"How long are you staying?"

Mika responded, "Depends on how long it takes for us to tire of Zachariah."

Alexi asked, "How do you know Zachariah?"

"Do you want to answer or should I, Detective?"

"Go ahead, you answer."

"The detective works for me. I pay him to look the other way, distribute misinformation to investigators, and destroy evidence. Isn't that right?"

McGraw appeared embarrassed by the answer and looked down at his coffee. "Yeah, something like that."

"We've had our differences, but we both hate Rodriguez. Don't we, Detective?"

"Yeah, that's right."

Alexi inquired, "Is that swollen lip one of the differences?" There was silence as the waitress approached the table to take their orders.

Mika asked, "Detective, what do you recommend? We're so tired of Russian food."

"Try the French toast or the pancakes. This place is famous for 'em."

Zachariah looked at the menu and replied, "Mika will have the Spanish omelet."

Zachariah and Alexi laughed, and Mika responded, "Idiot."

McGraw instructed the waitress to put the meal on his tab. He said goodbye and took his leave. Alexi questioned, "I assume he knows about the Cyclist Club?"

"Yes, he's been valuable to me in the past; but lately I'm not so sure about his loyalty. I may have to rethink our bargain with each other. Let's eat and then I'll introduce you to my latest team of competitors."

CHAPTER 45

TATTOO OF DEATH

Rodriguez was speaking with Dr. Aslam about the dead cyclist, Hatchet Man. Dr. Aslam updated Rodriguez about the toxicology findings. "This victim, like the others, had the greatest concentration of the drugs in his thighs. However, I want to make note that his dosage seemed to be greater than the others. I believe it was administered no more than a few hours before his death. He also had a tattoo of 'Hatchet Man' located across his upper back. It was fairly fresh."

"Did the tattoo have a signature?"

"Signature?"

"Yes, look closely for the letters 'MOS' in all caps somewhere on his body."

"He does have a hatchet tattooed on the left side of his chest. It's rather a nice job. It has blood dripping from the blade; and yes, I see the letters 'MOS' on the handle."

"Man of Steel, Doctor. That's who we're looking for. All of the cyclists had the letters 'MOS' on their tattoos. I'll need the toxicology report, Doctor."

"Sure, Sergeant, as soon as I conclude my testing."

"What about his victim?"

"You mean the night watchman? He had significant trauma to his head and neck. Multiple lacerations to his scalp and back. It seems the first blow rendered him unconscious."

Rodriguez remarked, "The guy never knew what hit him. I have one more question if you don't mind."

"Of course, what do you want to know?"

"Do these drugs have an antidote or a vaccine?"

"Since our last conversation, I've sent our lab results to some colleagues on the outside under strict confidence, of course. They're analyzing the compounds as we speak; but even if they can separate them, it would still take months to have enough information to put together a testing protocol and eventually an antidote."

"Unfortunately, the victims have weeks, not months, Doctor."

"We're moving as fast as we can. Is that all, Sergeant?"

'Yes, thank you."

CHAPTER 46
TWO COSSACKS

Zachariah arrived home with Mika and Alexi. He took their coats and returned with glasses containing a vegetable and protein concoction. "Here, Alexi, and this one's yours, Mika. Cheers. Let's drink to Russia and the success of the Cyclist Club."

"I remember this drink," remarked Alexi, "it's the one we used to make in Russia."

"It's green? Why is it green?" questioned Mika, eying the drink with distaste.

Alexi answered, "Because it's made from vegetables. Please taste it before you make faces at it."

Mika passed the drink to Alexi, "You can have it."

Zachariah asked, "Perhaps you'd prefer vodka?"

"No, thank you. It's too early for me. So where are your athletes, Zachariah?"

"My athletes, I almost forgot. Yes, come with me. I'll introduce you." He slid the bookcase back and they proceeded down the stairs. "Everybody up, I have someone I'd like you to meet." The captives stood as if on cue. "May I present my dear friends from Russia: Alexi and Mika. Remember, I told you that I coached athletes for the Tour de France. Well, Alexi was my assistant coach. Here we have Stacy, Andrew, Sara, Jennifer, and Kim. Sara will be the next athlete to compete. Kim is our newest athlete, and I'm expecting great things from her." Zachariah instructed his athletes, "Now, get on your bikes. You need to train for two hours and then I'll bring your breakfast."

They returned upstairs and Zachariah offered, "Why don't you two relax while I make breakfast for my athletes."

While Zachariah was cooking, Mika asked, "When do I meet this Rodriguez?"

"All in good time, Mika, all in good time" responded Zachariah.

Alexi looked at Mika and asked, "When it comes time to kill him, can you do it? Did you ever kill anybody before?"

'I'll do it the way Zachariah suggested, one injection and I'll leave him to die. I'm not going to watch."

Zachariah laughed, "You see, Alexi, she does have the instinct. I never doubted it. I've been watching this policeman's movements. I know where he buys his coffee in the morning, what time he goes to work, what time he leaves, all of it."

"So why don't we just shoot him and be done with it?"

"No, Alexi. Let Mika have some fun with him for a while and let's see where it leads. You know, a cat and mouse game. Tomorrow I'll show you the places where you can meet him and charm him. Charm him like the black widow you are, Mika. We met a cyclist on the boardwalk. His name was Will, but it turned out that he was a policeman working for Rodriguez. He would have made an excellent addition to our team."

"We?"

"Yes, David and I. He was my newest competitor. Unfortunately, his first competition was his last. Rodriguez chased him down in an automobile, and he was struck and killed. I saw his body mangled and twisted before they covered him. This policeman Will was there telling people to stand back. I saw his face clearly, but he didn't see me. Soon I'll have my revenge on all of them." Zachariah's eyes welled with tears, "I went home and wept that night. Breakfast is done. Please excuse me while I feed my athletes and then vodka."

They had been drinking vodka for hours and Zachariah and Alexi had passed out. Mika paced herself and was sober. She sat on the balcony overlooking the ocean.

A few hours later Alexi woke up, stretched, and said, "I'm so hungry I could eat a Russian bear." The sun was beginning to set, and the room was bathed in a warm glow. Alexi walked over and sat next to Mika.

"While you two were sleeping, I've been watching the sunset. It reminds me of the sunsets over Sochi." Mika paused and then asked, "How many people have you and Zachariah killed, Alexi? You do realize that you can never go back to Russia."

"Yes, we will, Mika. Zachariah is arranging for me to get diplomatic credentials."

"How many were policemen, Alexi?"

"Two, perhaps three. Now let it go, Mika."

"If you go back, they'll hunt you and kill you. They won't arrest you. You killed some of their own. They'll want revenge. Credentials or not, they won't stop till they find you."

Alexi was staring out at the ocean and repeated, "I told you to let it go, Mika. Besides, I'm counting on it. Death is better than a Russian prison." He continued to stare out at the ocean. "Mika, you do realize that if you fail to kill this policeman, Zachariah will hurt you; and I won't be able to stop him. Call it off, and I'll finish it. I'll kill the policeman." Neither one said another word; the only sound in the room was the sound of Zachariah snoring loudly.

"I'm famished. Let's wake him and have dinner, Alexi. I need to eat."

'Okay, I'll get him up, and then I'm going to take a shower. Care to join me, Mika? You could scrub my back," he said laughingly."

"I took one while you two Cossacks were sleeping. Ask your friend, perhaps he'll scrub your back. Please hurry, I'm starving."

———

The next morning as Sergeant Rodriguez was getting coffee from a Starbucks a block from the precinct, he called Detective Spinelli, "I'm on the way. I'll grab some coffee for you guys."

He didn't notice the car parked across the street with Mika and the men inside. "That's him, the tall one with the sunglasses."

Mika replied, "I love his suit. It fits him so well."

"His suit? What about him, for Christ's sake? Mika, do you think you can handle this?"

"He's very handsome. This is going to be more fun than I thought. I like him. He's dark and mysterious."

"Don't underestimate him, Mika," responded Zachariah. "This has to be the performance of your life. He arrives every morning at about the same time and leaves the precinct at approximately six."

"Do you know where he lives?" questioned Alexi. "Have you followed him home?"

"No, he would know he's being followed. I prefer to stay in the shadows. If he sees me, he would know it's me. Besides, I enjoy playing this game with him. So Mika, when do you want to play the black widow?"

"I'm thinking in a few days. I want to look glamorous when we meet."

"What about your accent? He'll know it's Russian, and he's heard me speak. That would be too obvious."

"I'm an actress. Accents are my specialty. Don't worry, perhaps I'll be British or French." Mika laughed, "I'm going to enjoy this."

Alexi scoffed, "She wants to look glamorous. It's ridiculous. I still think we save all this time, follow him home, and kill him."

"And deprive me of my fun, Alexi? How could you?"

"I'm planning a Cyclist Club meeting in a few weeks," said Zachariah. "I expect that his death will precede that meeting. If not, we do it Alexi's way. If this policeman was out of the way before the meeting, it would make my members and myself very happy. It would be wonderful if we could film his demise, wouldn't it?"

Rodriguez walked into the precinct and was greeted by Will who handed him a folder, "Detective Martino from Missing Persons asked me to give you this."

Rodriguez took the folder as they both entered the office. He explained, "My neighbor Vivian said a friend from college named Jennifer has been missing for about two weeks now."

"Vivian, your cat sitter?"

"Yeah, they share a few college classes; and Jennifer stopped coming to class a few weeks ago. Vivian's worried about her. I told her I would look into it and asked Detective Martino for some help." Rodriguez opened the folder, "So let's see what he found." Rodriguez was skimming through the papers and stopped on one paper in particular. He looked up at Will excitedly, "Will, ask Martino to come in here right away."

Detective Martino entered the office, "You wanted to see me?"

"Yeah, Detective, it's about Jennifer Morse. I see you were able to find out where she lives and also that her roommate, Gina Lee is, in the hospital. Do we know why?"

"Doctors aren't sure. It's some kind of drug overdose. Their landlord found her on the floor. He hadn't seen them for a few days; and last Friday when he went to collect the rent, nobody answered the door. He let himself in, and there she was on the kitchen floor."

"Is she able to communicate?"

"Not as of Monday. I spoke to the doctors, and they're evaluating the toxicology report. The lead doc said it's some sort of a drug cocktail he's never seen before."

Rodriguez jumped out of his chair and grabbed his jacket, "Let's go, Will. Which hospital is she in, Martino?"

"It's South Shore General. The doctor in charge is Dr. Chang."

"Will, I need you to drive. I have to make a few calls." Rodriguez dialed Dr. Aslam, "Good morning, Doctor. I apologize for the early hour, but this call is regarding the Mayhew case."

"Yes, go ahead, Sergeant."

"You said that the drugs found in the cyclists would eventually cause brain damage and death. Is that right?"

"Well, first these drugs would manifest in dizziness, severe headaches, and hallucinations before resulting in death. Depending on the dosage and the person's size, it could take six months to a year if used continuously. Why, do you have someone showing these symptoms?"

"I think so. We're going to the hospital now. I'll get back to you. What about that antidote you guys are working on? Any word when?"

"No, we still have a way to go before we have a sample we can even test."

"Thanks, Doctor. I'll get back to you."

Rodriguez called Detective Spinelli, "Marco, I need you to see Martino in Missing Persons regarding Jennifer Morse. Her disappearance may tie into the Mayhew case. Have Martino call the judge at the court and request a search warrant for Jennifer's apartment. Ask the judge if she can expedite it. If she has questions, she can call me. The address is in the file. We'll meet you there in about two hours. Find the landlord, he'll let you in. Detective Martino has all the information."

They arrived at the hospital and were greeted by Doctor Chang. The men introduced themselves and Dr. Chang led them to a private office. "So how can I be of assistance?

"Last Friday Gina Lee was brought in with symptoms of a drug overdose."

"Yes, I believe she was found unconscious on the floor of her apartment by her landlord. Right now, she's still in a coma. We're monitoring her heart and brain waves, but I'm afraid her brain waves... Rodriguez interrupted, "are getting weaker."

"How did you know, Sergeant?"

Rodriguez didn't answer. "Can you tell how long these drugs were in her system?"

"Some, others are still being analyzed."

"Tattoos, Dr. Chang? Does she have any tattoos?"

"Yes, she does. She has a full sleeve on her left arm and across her upper back is tattooed 'Red Widow.' Rodriguez glanced at Will. Dr. Chang continued, "We conducted the usual drug screens to find what drugs she used, but there are some that are foreign to us."

"I can help you there, Doctor. The person you need to speak with as soon as possible is Dr. Basheer Aslam."

"Dr. Aslam, the Medical Examiner?"

"Yes, call him as soon as you can. He'll have a lot to tell you about these drugs. Tell him that I suggested that you call. It's all related to a case we're working on."

"Okay, gentlemen. I'll call him immediately."

"Thanks, Doctor. Come on, Will. Let's go."

They arrived at the apartment to find Detective Spinelli waiting for them. "Hey, Marco. Did you find the landlord?

"Not yet, I just got here."

"Was Judge Williams able to get the warrant done?"

"Yep, I got it right here."

"Great, she came across again. Let's get the landlord to let us in. Don't forget to wear your gloves." As they a\were led into the apartment, the first thing they noticed was a beautiful foyer with the kitchen and dining room directly ahead of them. To the right were two bedrooms and a large living room was to the left.

Edgar, the landlord, asked, "Mind if I stay while you search?"

Marco answered, "Yeah, we do."

"I think that legally I can stay while you search my property. I know my rights," Edgar challenged, his voice raised.

Rodriguez looked at Detective Spinelli, "It's okay, Detective. Let him stay." The apartment was clean but sparsely decorated, with a few antique pieces, a comfortable-looking couch, and a couple of chairs. There were well cared for plants throughout the apartment. The kitchen was small, but the apartment had high ceilings, giving it a pre-war feeling. Edgar watched them like a hawk as they searched the living room.

Will asked, "What are we looking for, Sergeant?"

"Not sure, but I assume it would be in liquid form and injectable. The only way those drugs could have gotten into that girl Gina's system is by injection."

"Who would have injected her?"

Rodriguez responded, "She injected herself."

They continued searching the apartment under the watchful eye of the landlord Edgar. Eventually, Rodriguez opened a closet and discovered a box of syringes. He called Will over to show him what he found and whispered, "Somewhere in this apartment there are vials of drugs. The question is where."

Will responded, "My grandmother used to keep her diabetes medication in the fridge when I was growing up."

Rodriguez opened the door and noticed how well-stocked the refrigerator was. Some of the food was old and beginning to smell. On the top shelf in the back, they located a box with 48 vials of a clear liquid. "That's what I'm looking for, gentlemen. Let's go, Will. Take it to the car. Edgar, we're done. Thanks for your help."

"What was in that box you took out of here?"

Rodriguez responded, "Sorry, we can't say." He handed Edgar his card and added, "If Jennifer comes back, ask her to call me. It's important."

Edgar replied, "They owe me rent for this month."

"Sorry, Edgar. I can't help you there. Don't forget to tell her."

———

Zachariah was on his phone pacing the floor. Mika urged, "Why don't you take a break and try again later."

Alexi agreed, "Yeah, have a drink, and try again after dinner."

"You don't understand. I'm trying to reach one of my athletes, and she's always answered when I call. I want to make sure she's keeping up with her training and using the formula. She'll be competing soon, and I want to be sure she's ready."

"Who is the athlete, Zachariah?"

"It's Red Widow, another of my newest competitors. She debuted not too long ago, and she was wonderful."

Alexi replied, "Remember in Russia when we couldn't reach Yuri for a few days, and we found him on a farm near Moscow."

"Yes, I remember him. One of our better competitors. We discovered him in Soviet Georgia."

"I believe he was shagging the farmer's daughter."

Zachariah laughed, "Yes, I thought you were going to kill him, Alexi. I think he learned his lesson that day. He always answered his phone after that."

Mika asked, "What happened to him, Alexi?"

"It's not important what happened to him."

"I want to know, Alexi. What happened?"

"Do you really want to know, Mika? I'll tell you. He died. He's dead. That's what happened to him. He was a drug addict."

The room was silent. Zachariah dialed the number again. The phone continued to ring with no response. Zachariah turned the phone so they all could all hear the ringing. "No answer." After a few more rings he said, "After I feed my athletes, we'll go to dinner."

He delivered the food to all of his captives except Jennifer. He held her food back and asked, "Your roommate Gina is not responding to my calls. Why do you suppose that is? I'm trying to reach her and she's not answering. It's very unusual."

Jennifer responded," I don't know. I've been locked up in this fucking cage. She told me she was going to visit her family in China, and then one day she injected me with something and I woke up in here, you sick fuck."

"I suggest you watch your mouth, Jennifer. I can starve you if I choose. Since we're being honest with each other, I'll tell you where she really was those six weeks. She was here in your room under my coaching and training; and she competed beautifully, as you will when the time comes. Now here, eat your dinner."

CHAPTER 47
STALKING RODRIGUEZ

Rodriguez walked into the Starbucks downstairs from the precinct. He was buying coffee for his detectives, something he did most mornings. This morning he noticed a beautiful woman impeccably dressed browsing the menu. He got to the counter as she placed her order. The scent of her perfume attracted him, and he inched closer. When it came time to pay, she went through her purse and frantically searched for her money, "My God, I can't find my money. I can't pay for the coffee. I must have left it at my apartment. I'm so sorry."

The barista said, "Don't worry, you can give it to me next time."

Rodriguez intervened, "It's okay, I got it. No problem."

"This is so embarrassing. This has never happened before." Rodriguez placed his order and paid for their purchases. "I appreciate it so much, thank you Mr..."

"Rodriguez."

"Rodriguez, is that your first name?

The barista said, "It's just Rodriguez. He doesn't want to tell us his first name, so we just call him Rodriguez."

Rodriguez smiled, "Thank you, Sandra. See you tomorrow." As they were leaving, Rodriguez asked the woman "What's your name?"

"My name is Mika."

"Is that your first name?" They both laughed as they walked toward the precinct.

From across the street, they were being watched. Zachariah said, "See, Alexi, she has him caught in her web already. She's good and she's deadly."

Alexi replied, "A total waste of time."

"Come on, Alexi, don't worry. I'll let it go to a point; and if she fails, he's yours. I don't think he'll survive Mika. Now let's go eat."

Rodriguez and Mika stood in front of the precinct. Rodriguez said, "This is where I get off," and he pointed to the building.

"Are you a policeman?"

"Yes, I'm a sergeant."

"Oh, I guess I had better pay for my coffee or I'll be in trouble."

"You won't be in trouble if you have dinner with me tonight."

She looked at Rodriguez, "Well, I don't want to be in trouble."

"Great, how about 7:00? Where can I pick you up?"

"Do you mind if I meet you here at 7:00?"

"Sure, Mika. See you then."

Mika arrived back at Zachariah's house and flaunted her successful meeting with Rodriguez.

"You see, Alexi, I knew the brute couldn't resist such a beauty. Have your fun, Mika; but I want him dead by Friday. The thought of him dying at the hands of such a delicate creature makes me giddy."

"Did you say 'delicate?' Please, Zachariah, she's a woman. They deceive and connive. They can't be trusted."

Zachariah descended to the basement and prepared a special syringe for Mika. Alexi glared at Mika, "The end of the week, then I'll do it my way."

Returning from the basement, Zachariah instructed, "Here, take this, Mika. But be very careful, a small amount can kill very quickly. If there is any way you can capture his death on your phone, we can share it with our members."

"No, I can't watch anyone die. Excuse me, I'm going to take a shower."

Alexi looked at Zachariah, "You're making a big mistake. Let me follow her tonight, and I'll kill him."

"No, Alexi. I decide how and when he dies."

"Sure, just like home when you killed the doctor and his wife and brought the authorities down on our heads."

"Enough, Alexi. Perhaps you should do some time on the bike. It'll help you relax. Friday is the deadline. If she fails, they're both yours."

CHAPTER 48
RED OR WHITE

Rodriguez was in his office shaving when Detective Spinelli entered. "Are you shaving?"

"Yes."

"Did you change your clothes?"

"Yes."

"You gotta date?"

"None of your business," he said, laughing.

"Okay, Sarge, I'm out. Have fun."

"Good night, Marco." Rodriguez exited the building to find Mika waiting outside. "Hi, Mika, you look great. Are you hungry?"

"Yes, I'm starved."

"I know a great restaurant on the water not far from here. It's French. Is that okay? You can order for us."

"Can we go somewhere else? I'm so tired of French cuisine, perhaps Italian."

"Sure, I know a place also on the water. It's very nice."

As they were driving to the restaurant, Mika asked, "How long have you been a policeman?"

"Most of my life."

"Do you like it?"

"I love what I do. I wouldn't do anything else. What about you, Mika? Are you on vacation?"

"Yes, I'll be here for a few weeks. I'm visiting friends."

"Where are you staying?"

Mika wasn't prepared for that question, but she remembered Gold Street near the Route 25A Diner. "My friends have an apartment on Gold Street near the diner."

"The Route 25A is a good diner. Great breakfast. Well, here we are."

Theresa's is a high-end restaurant overlooking the ocean. They entered and the maitre'd recognized Rodriguez. "Good evening, Rodriguez. Welcome back. Who is this lovely lady?"

"Mika, I'd like you to meet Luciano, the best restaurateur on the Island."

Luciano smiled, "It's my pleasure, Mika. Now follow me. I have a table with a view of the beautiful sunset. Tonight there's no menu. I'll have Roberto, our chef, prepare a special dinner. I'll bring a bottle of wine from our wine cellar. Does the lady prefer red or white?"

"White for me. Thank you, Luciano."

Rodriguez replied, "White is fine for me, too. So Mika, how do you like the view?"

"This is a nice restaurant and the view is wonderful. I like Luciano, he's quite a gentleman. Do you eat here often?"

"Sometimes I have dinner with the mayor or the police commissioner. It's mostly about work, very boring."

Mika admired the view, "God, I love that sunset."

"So tell me, where are you from in France?"

"I was born in Paris, but now I live in D'Orsay. It's a suburb just outside of Paris."

"What kind of work do you do?"

"I was a model but now I'm a clothing designer. I did some acting in what you would call 'B' movies."

"Did you design the jacket you're wearing?"

Mika laughed, "No, I bought it at a discount shop on the Champs d' Elysée."

Rodriguez was looking at Mika and she seemed uncomfortable. She asked, "Is something wrong?"

"You look beautiful in the sunset." She blushed and looked away.

Halfway through dinner, she remarked, "You seem very serious about your police work. What do you do for fun?"

Rodriguez grinned, "I don't have any fun."

Mika laughed, "Come on. How do you relax?"

"I always make time for exercise no matter how busy I am."

She smiled, "It shows."

"Are you ready to go? I'll get the check."

Mika replied, "Can we walk? I ate so much."

"Sure, let's go to the boardwalk." They were walking for a while when Mika challenged him, "I'll race you to the water." She bolted toward the shore, removing her shoes as she ran. Rodriguez chased her and caught up as she reached the water.

"Now I have sand in my shoes. I hate sand in my shoes."

"You were supposed to take your shoes off."

"Well, Mika, you didn't give me a chance."

"I beat you, Rodriguez. Now you owe me."

"You owe me for the coffee, so we're even."

"It's chilly by the water." Mika looked at him and Rodriguez removed his jacket and wrapped it around her.

"Come on, let's go. Where are you staying on Gold Street?"

"I'm around the corner from that diner." They arrived at the location and Rodriguez walked her to the door, "Thank you, Rodriguez. I had a great time," and they kissed good night. She watched him leave, then walked around the corner, got into Zachariah's car and drove to her hotel. Alexi had been drinking vodka and was waiting for her. When she walked in, Alexi asked sarcastically, "Is there a dead policeman somewhere?"

"I'm going to bed, Alexi. I'm not in the mood."

"I have my answer, Mika, and it's no. The policeman lives, of course." "Go to sleep, Alexi, you're drunk." Mika slammed her bedroom door and locked it. She tossed and turned, unable to sleep. She was thinking of Rodriguez.

The following morning Marco walked into Rodriguez's office. "You got a message earlier from Dr. Chang from South Shore General. He's anxious to speak to you. It's important."

Rodriguez called, "Dr. Chang, you have some news for me?"

"Yes, but it's mixed. Gina Lee's condition has improved, and her condition has been upgraded to serious. The bad part is that she has severe memory loss."

"Is it permanent?"

"Time will tell, Sergeant. If anything changes, I'll be in touch."

"Marco, ask Will to come in here." Will entered and closed the door. "Dr. Chang called. Gina Lee is responsive but has severe memory loss. We'll have to wait and see."

Marco inquired, "So Sarge, how did your date go? I saw her as I was leaving. Wow, she's something else. Where did you meet her?"

"Downstairs at Starbucks."

"Starbucks?"

"Yeah, she was in front of me on the line. When she tried to pay, she didn't have any money so I picked up her tab. She's French. Her name is Mika."

Will teased, "Ooolala, she's French."

Rodriguez said, "French, gorgeous, and in Starbucks. What's wrong with this picture?"

"I see that look, Sergeant. What's on your mind?"

"Short answer, Marco. Zachariah and his cat and mouse games.

CHAPTER 49

WHO'S BOGIE?

Rodriguez had just finished a meeting with Detective Spinelli when Detective Martino shouted, "You got a call on line 4, Sarge."

"Hi Rodriguez, it's Mika. Am I interrupting something?"

"No, I just finished a meeting. Nice of you to call."

"I know you're at work. Do I call you Sergeant or Rodriguez?"

"Rodriguez, please."

"Okay, Rodriguez. I would like to take you to dinner tonight."

"Sounds great, but I've got a better idea. Let me make you dinner tonight at my place. I'm about ready to leave. I have to stop at the market and then I'll come by and pick you up, okay?"

"Is it okay if I come to your place instead? I'd like some time to get ready."

"Sure, I'll text you my address. Is 7:00 okay? You can meet Bogie."

"Bogie?"

"He's my roommate."

"You have a roommate?"

"Yes, he's my cat, the best cat in the world."

They laughed and Mika responded, "I'm looking forward to it, Rodriguez."

Rodriguez hung up the phone and grabbed his jacket. "Marco, I'm out. Keep an eye on things."

Mika arrived right on time and Rodriguez welcomed her. She looked even more beautiful than the night before. "Would you like a glass of wine before dinner?"

"Yes, thank you. What did you make for dinner? It smells amazing."

"I made lemon garlic chicken and roasted vegetables. It's a French recipe. I hope you like it."

"I'm sure I will. So where's Bogie?"

"He'll be around. He's a bit shy at first." Rodriguez poured the wine and they toasted to Bogie.

Mika asked, "So where did you learn this recipe?"

"I learned it in France. I used to spend summers there with some friends when I was in college. We would stay at a youth hostel in Toulouse. There's a beautiful beach not far from town. We would ride our bikes there early in the morning, swim all day, and be asleep by 9:00."

Mika agreed," "I heard that is a great place to swim and not far from Toulouse." She continued with a laugh, "But college students asleep by 9:00, I doubt it."

"Cooking is kind of a hobby of mine."

"I'm sure it'll be a wonderful dinner."

"I'll be right back. I think it's ready." When Rodriguez returned, Mika stood in front of him, put her arms around him, and kissed him passionately. He returned the kiss and picked her up as she wrapped her legs around his waist. He carried her into the bedroom. Rodriguez woke to the sounds of Bogie purring. He looked over at Mika, who was sleeping. His watch on the bedside table read 3:30 a.m.

He moved Bogie off the bed, waking Mika. "Was that Bogie? He finally got over his shyness, I see."

Rodriguez said, "We never did get to have our dinner." She beckoned for him to lie down and then climbed on top of him. Bogie was at the end of the bed, his purring louder. They both collapsed into each other's arms laughing.

CHAPTER 50

TUPAYA SUKA

It was early morning when Mika arrived at the hotel. The room was empty. She removed the syringe containing the clear liquid, replaced it with water, and returned it to her bag. She showered, changed her clothes, and drove to Zachariah's house. On the way, she called the precinct. Detective Martino answered the phone, "Is Sergeant Rodriguez there? I must speak to him."

"I'm sorry but he's out in the field. I'll take a message."

"My name is Mika. It's important that he calls me." She attempted to text and call him but received no reply.

When she arrived, she found Alexi sitting on the balcony looking out at the ocean. In his hand was a small knife that he was using to slice sections of an apple, a half bottle of vodka by his side. She joined him on the balcony and nervously sat next to him. The only sound was of Alexi slicing and chewing the apple and the soft sounds of waves breaking on the shore. The air was cool, and a salty mist was coming off the ocean. She asked, "Is Zachariah asleep?"

"No, he's out on his morning ride."

She looked at Alexi and observed, "You look like you haven't slept."

"Correct, Mika. I've been sitting here wondering if you finally did it. You didn't do it, did you? I knew you couldn't. Go back to Russia, Mika. This isn't for you."

"I'm not going anywhere, especially back to Russia."

"Tell Zachariah you're leaving, and let me take care of this policeman. Tell me where he lives, Mika."

"No Alexi." Alexi got up and grabbed his jacket. Mika noticed a gun tucked into the waistband of his pants. She shouted, "Where are you going, Alexi?"

"I'm going out."

"Why do you have a gun?"

"Stay here. I'm going to finish it before Zachariah gets back. Give me his address."

"No, Alexi. You're drunk, and you're tired. They'll kill you. It's not worth it; please stop."

Alexi pushed her out of his way. "I'll find him myself."

Mika grabbed the knife from the table and confronted Alexi with it. "Put the knife down and get out of my way. You'll never use it. Move, Mika."

"No, Alexi. I won't."

"You slept with him once and now you're in love. You're a tupaya suka, Mika."

"Fuck you, Alexi. Don't call me a stupid bitch."

Alexi screamed at her to get out of the way and then slapped her across the face. He grabbed her by the throat and squeezed. "How does it feel, Mika? Are you afraid? I knew we couldn't trust you."

Mika was scared and, in a panic, stabbed Alexi in the leg with the knife. He screamed in pain, "You bitch!" and slapped her again. He then lunged at her and grabbed her again by the throat. Mika was terrified that Alexi was going to kill her and she stabbed him in the neck. The knife found its mark and blood poured from the wound. Alexi's eyes were wide open in shock, and he tried to stem the flow of blood with his hand, to no avail. In a blind rage, he attempted to grab her by the throat yet again. He staggered a few steps and collapsed on the floor. Mika was sobbing loudly and calling Alexi's name. He crawled on the floor, reaching for her. Finally, he stopped moving, his eyes open and staring blankly at Mika. Blood was pooling on the floor and she tried to compose herself. She knew she couldn't call the police, and Zachariah would be back soon. She decided to call Rodriguez, but she was panicked and couldn't find her phone. She grabbed the car keys and was headed for the door when she heard Zachariah coming up the stairs. She had to think quickly, and she tore her clothes to make it appear that Alexi tried to rape her. She threw herself on the floor to soak up Alexi's blood. She heard the keys in the door. The door opened and Zachariah shouted, "What the fuck is this? Alexi, Alexi! What the fuck happened? All this blood. Mika, are you hurt?" He called Alexi's name over and over. He checked Alexi and declared, "He's dead. Fuck, why Alexi?" He ran to Mika and she appeared wide-eyed and frantic. She ran to him and he held her, "What happened here? Tell me, Mika. Who did this? You're covered in blood and you've got bruises on your face. Did Alexi do this to you?"

"Yes, he attacked me and tried to rape me. When I fought back, he beat me."

He poured her a glass of vodka. "Here drink this. It will help you relax." Her hands were shaking, and she could barely hold the glass. "Drink it slowly, Mika." He soaked a rag with cold water and instructed Mika, "Here, put this on the bruises. It will keep it from swelling." Zachariah left the room and returned with some clothes for her. "Take a shower and wash off the blood. Here, I have some fresh clothes for you." He walked her to the bathroom, "I'll be right outside if you need me. Go ahead. Don't be afraid." Zachariah covered Alexi's body with part of the rug. He went through Mika's bag and found that the syringe was still full. Enraged, he hurled it against the wall, shattering it. Then he grabbed Mika's cell phone and demolished it.

Mika came out of the bathroom to find Alexi's body covered by the rug. Zachariah was sitting on the balcony drinking vodka, a syringe hidden by his side. He coaxed, "Come here, Mika. Sit next to me; don't be afraid. Are you better?" Mika shook her head yes. "Good. Tell me what happened. Do you want to talk about it?"

"Yes, it's okay. When I got here, he asked me about the policeman, if I had killed him."

Zachariah said, "I assume the policeman is still alive."

"Yes. I started to tell him, and he attacked me. He began to tear at my clothes. He was upset that I didn't kill the policeman. He accused me of sleeping with him and called me a whore. He said he always wanted me, and he was going to show me how he treats whores. I grabbed the knife and...," her voice trailed off.

Zachariah sat staring at the ocean. Finally, he asked, "How long have you known Alexi?"

"What do you mean?"

"Tell me, Mika. How long have you known him?"

"Almost a year, I guess. Why?"

"And anytime during that year did he ever try to fuck you?"

"No. Why are you asking me this, Zachariah?"

"Because I would have, but not Alexi. Do you know why, Mika?"

"I don't."

"Because he was a homosexual, a faggot as they say. The thought of touching a woman was repulsive to him. Didn't you get the signals, Mika? It was obvious."

"No, it can't be..."

Zachariah cut her off. "Mika, it's true. He hated women." Zachariah stared sharply at Mika.

Mika got up and tried to run; but Zachariah grabbed her, knocked her to the floor, got on top of her, and held her down. "Where are you going, Mika, to your policeman friend? Perhaps I should rape you, but I have something else planned for you." He then injected her with the syringe and released her. She rose and got as far as the door before collapsing. He carried her downstairs and placed her into an open cell, slammed the door, and locked it. "Get on your bikes, all of you, and exercise. Do it now."

Stacy shouted, "Did you kill Robert? Where's Robert?"

"Shut up and get on your bike." He unlocked Andrews' cell and commanded, "Come with me upstairs." Andrew was shocked by all the blood and he froze. "Come on, Andrew. Help me. Let's roll him up in the rug."

As they moved the body, Andrew recognized Alexi. He jumped up and asked, "Isn't that your friend from Russia?"

"Yes, it is. It's my dear friend, Alexi. He was murdered by an evil witch. Come on, Andrew. Let's finish. When it gets dark, we'll go to the bridge; and I'll say goodbye to my friend."

The next morning Mika awakened as the effects of the drugs started to wear off. Zachariah was sitting in front of her cell eating an apple. He was using the same knife that killed Alexi to slice it. The handle was still bloodstained. She sat up on the bed and looked around, not knowing where she was. "Why am I in this cage and where is Alexi?"

Zachariah laughed, "Alexi is dead, Mika." He paused and stared at her. "You don't remember. You killed my friend yesterday with this very knife." She got to her feet. "How ironic. You were supposed to kill this fucking policeman and instead, you killed Alexi."

Mika was upset and pacing, "That's impossible, I couldn't."

"You did, and we disposed of him by throwing his body into the ocean not far from here." He cut another wedge of the apple and called for Andrew. "Andrew, would you tell Mika what we did with Alexi's body last night. Did we not throw it into the ocean?"

From one of the rooms came a voice, "Yes, we did. It was a little after midnight."

"You see, Mika, Andrew even remembers what time it was. Sara, you come with me. Everybody else, inject yourselves and get on your bikes."

They got into Zachariah's car and drove to the Lighthouse Inn. Sara was getting nervous and asked, "Why are we here?"

"We're going to room 325 to remove clothing and luggage. If anybody asks you your name, it's Mika; and I'm Alexi. Don't say anything else. I'll do the talking." They took all the baggage and clothes from the room. As they were walking toward the exit, a security guard stopped them.

"If you're leaving, you need to check out at the front desk."

"Of course, we seem to have lost our way. Can you lead us?" Zachariah looked around for the security cameras and spotted one at the end of the hall.

"Sure, just follow me. Did you just come out of room 325? Where's the couple that checked in?"

Zachariah looked at Sara, "Oh, they decided to stay with us. You know how tourists are. They can't make up their minds."

"Yep, so let's go to the front desk and they'll help you check out." The security guard turned his back and Zachariah waited until they were out of camera range and grabbed the guard by the neck and slammed his head into the wall. The security guard fell unconscious, and they ran for the emergency exit. The door opened, triggering an alarm. They sprinted for the car and tore out of the parking lot.

CHAPTER 51
THE LIGHTHOUSE INN

Rodriguez got the call. "Sergeant, this is Trooper Barrett. We've got an incident at The Lighthouse Inn. Somebody beat up the security guard. He's hurt pretty bad."

"Can't the local guys handle it?"

"Well, Sergeant, from the description you might want to get involved."

"I'm on the way." He called Will. "Meet me at the Lighthouse Inn."

Rodriguez was getting a description from the trooper as Will arrived. "The guard said they weren't the same couple that checked in, but they were leaving with their luggage. According to the front desk, they registered as Dr. Dimitri Semenov and his wife. They arrived last Tuesday."

"What about the couple that took the luggage out of the room?"

"He said the guy was big and bald, tall with a scary smile; and the woman was short with blondish hair and a light complexion. He remembered she had freckles."

"That's not Mika, and I doubt it was Alexi. It was Zachariah and one of his so-called athletes. Come on, Will, let's check the room." They entered the room and asked the maid, "Did they sleep in the same bedroom?"

"No, she was in this one." Rodriguez and Will searched the rooms. "When was the last time you saw them?"

"Two days ago. They always had a 'Do Not Disturb' sign on the door."

A trooper came into the bedroom with a few bottles in his hand, "We found these in the bathroom. They left them behind."

One of the bottles was a Russian perfume called Krasnaya Moskva. Rodriguez removed the top of the bottle. "She was wearing this perfume a few nights ago."

"Sergeant, he registered with a diplomatic passport from the Russian Consul. She had a standard Russian passport."

Rodriguez asked, "Which one paid for the room?"

"Neither one. It was paid for by Dimitri Semenov with an American Express card over the phone."

"Did anybody see the car they were driving?"

"No. They were in and out so fast, they must have come in through the front. It's the start of the season and it's busy, so nobody paid attention."

"Thanks, Trooper. What kind of shape is the guard in?"

"In and out of consciousness, Sergeant."

"Come on, Will. Let's go." As Rodriguez drove back to Oceanview, he called Marco. "Marco, I need you to check with as many real estate agents as you can on this part of the island and find out if anybody bought or rented property in the name of Dimitri Semenov."

"You got some new information, Sergeant?"

"No, old information. Dimitri Semenov is the name of the doctor who was murdered in Russia by Zachariah two years ago. He used the doctor's credit card to pay for the room at the Lighthouse Inn."

"Sergeant, there's a lot of real estate agents in Oceanview."

"I know. I suggest you get an early start in the morning. Let me know how you make out." Rodriguez called Dr. Chang to check on Gina Lee's condition. The doctor informed him that there had been a slight improvement, but she was still unable to speak.

Rodriguez arrived home. He was tired and laid on his bed. His phone rang. He looked at his watch and he answered, "Yeah."

"Congratulations, policeman. You charmed the black widow, Mika."

Rodriguez was up and pacing. "I have her now; but don't worry, she's well. I wouldn't hurt such a delicate flower...yet. I have something planned for her. You have two weeks to find her, policeman. Are you up for the challenge?" Zachariah hung up. Rodriguez returned to bed but couldn't sleep.

CHAPTER 52
AUNT SHAUNA SAYS HELLO

Mercedes entered the prison library, and Eric motioned for her to go to the maintenance closet. "I have to see the warden in about an hour."

"That's good, Eric. I'll do it, then. Don't forget our deal. You and your friends get me out or I'll take everybody down with me."

Eric stared at Mercedes, "Rodriguez is right. You are a black widow."

"Remember our deal, Eric. I'll get rid of Mary and set up the contacts. Just make sure you keep your side of the bargain."

Eric placed his hand on her breast and tried to kiss her neck. She moved away. "Not now, we've got things to do." Mercedes worked returning books to shelves and delivering books to inmates. An hour passed, and Eric was leaving to meet with the warden. "Where's Mary?" asked Mercedes. "She was supposed to be here."

"I don't know. I'll check with her CO. I have to go. She should be here soon. I'll stall the warden as long as I can, but I don't want to be late."

"Go keep the appointment and don't worry about me." Eric left and Mercedes was alone. She removed the knife from between the books and tucked it into her scrubs. She walked around the library waiting for Mary. She had to figure out a way to lure Mary over to the steps. She went through the exit door and looked around. She was concocting a plan when the exit door slammed behind her, startling her. Suddenly, the lights went out and the emergency lights flickered on. Her heart was racing, and she sensed someone standing behind her. She felt large hands on her shoulders as the figure leaned over to sniff her hair. Mercedes slowly turned and saw the guard that had been talking to Eric a few days earlier. She tried to run back inside but the man blocked her path. She kicked him, but he was unfazed. Panicked, she attempted to stab him with the knife, but the attempt was blocked. He twisted her wrist and disarmed her then grabbed her by the neck. "Aunt Shauna says hello."

Mercedes had her back to the stairs as he pushed her. She screamed and the sickening sound of her body hitting the marble steps filled the deserted hallway. She fell at the base of the stairs, and blood began to pool around her head. The guard went back inside, took a stack of books, and threw them down the stairs. He put the lights back on and left the library, avoiding the cameras.

Eric was in the warden's office when an alarm sounded. Suddenly, her assistant rushed into the office. The warden exclaimed, "now what the hell is going on?"

"Bad news, Warden. An officer found an inmate on the steps behind the library. It seems she was carrying a bunch of books and she fell. For some reason, the lights went out and triggered the alarm. She's dead, Warden."

"Shit, do we have an ID?"

"Yes, it's inmate Delacruz."

"Order a lockdown. What the fuck? It's always something." Eric heard the name and stared straight ahead. He didn't hear the warden calling him. Finally, her voice penetrated his fog. "Pullman, Pullman, let's go." She looked at him and asked, "Are you alright? Let's get to the library."

When they arrived, Mary was talking to the officer that found the body. The warden studied the scene. "Was anybody else here? Was she working alone?" Eric looked at Mary suspiciously. The warden turned to Mary, "How long have you been here, inmate?"

Eric interjected, "She was supposed to be here at 3:00, but she was late."

The warden glared at Eric, "Thanks, Pullman; but I asked her."

Mary responded, "I was late, and I started working when I got here."

"Did you see Delacruz?" Mary shook her head no. Eric glared at Mary and she hung her head. The warden looked at both of them, paused, and observed, "There's some shit going on here." She shouted, "Everybody out, and don't touch a fucking thing. Get the coroner's team in here and lock it down. Take her back to her cell." She eyed Eric suspiciously. As she left the scene, she shouted, "Lock it down now!"

The next morning Captain Ebersole called Rodriguez, "Sergeant, I have some news about Mercedes Delacruz."

"Talk to me."

"She's dead. She fell down a flight of stairs in the rear of the prison library. A CO found her yesterday on a routine check. They say she was carrying books and lost her balance. There were a bunch of books scattered all over the stairs."

There was a pause then Rodriguez said, "I know that library, Captain. The elevator is only a few feet away. Why would she carry books down the stairs? I'll bet there are no cameras there. Call the warden and have Officer Pullman, the CO that found the body, and whoever else was there brought to the library tomorrow morning."

"What's going on, Sergeant?"

"Tell her around 11:00 a.m. I'd like for you to be there, as well."

"Okay, Sergeant. I'll see you there."

Rodriguez arrived at the Women's Detention Center and was escorted to the library. In the room were Warden Russell, Captain Ebersole, Eric Pullman, Correction Officer Davis who found the body, and Mary. After introductions, Rodriguez turned to Warden Russell and inquired, "Mind if I ask a few questions?"

"Feel free, Sergeant." The warden turned to the assembled group. "If anybody feels they need legal counsel, speak up now."

The room fell silent. Rodriguez turned to Eric, "Where were you when it happened?"

"I was in the warden's office; we had a scheduled meeting."

"Who called for the meeting?"

The warden answered, "Officer Pullman."

Rodriguez turned to Mary, "Did you see Mercedes yesterday?"

Mary looked at Eric, "No, I was late."

"Why?"

The warden interrupted, "She had some feminine issues. She was in the infirmary until 3:30."

"What is it that you and Mercedes did, exactly?"

Eric spoke up, "They deliver books to inmates and pick them up when they're finished reading them. The books are logged in and out and returned to the shelves."

Sergeant Rodriguez continued, "I understand that she was carrying books and stumbled. Is that right?"

"We're still investigating, Sergeant," responded the warden.

"Do you normally carry books up and down the stairs or do you use the elevator?" Nobody answered. Rodriguez turned and pushed the button on the elevator. The doors opened. "The elevator works, so why would she take the stairs? Do you have the books that were found with the body?" The warden motioned to books stacked on a wagon. Rodriguez read the titles aloud and fanned the pages of the book. Eric watched nervously. "Do you keep a record of which inmates request books?"

Officer Davis replied, "I don't know."

Warden Russell stated, "You're supposed to keep records so we can account for these books, you know, taxpayer dollars and all that shit. Pullman, do you have the list?"

Eric admitted, "I have it" and took a clipboard from the wall above his desk. He showed Rodriguez a list of books and the inmates who were reading them.

Rodriguez studied the list and noted, "Most of these books have been signed out to the same inmates continuously for weeks at a time. One book stands out. It's a hardcover version of *To Kill a Mockingbird*. The book has been signed out to the same inmate every week for the last seven months. You must have the slowest readers in the world or nobody's reading these books at all." He turned to the warden, "Is this one of the books found on the stairs?" The warden nodded yes. "It feels a little light." He leafed through the book and fanned the pages, discovering that the center had been hollowed out. It was one of the decoy books that was used for smuggling drugs to the guards and inmates. CO Davis had thrown it down the stairs by mistake.

Rodriguez held up the open book, "This one would be tough to read, don't you think?"

"Damn," declared Captain Ebersole.

Warden Russell questioned, "What the fuck? Does anybody want a lawyer now?"

Mary shouted, "It was Eric! He set the whole thing up."

Eric screamed at Mary, "Yeah, and you delivered the books. You knew what was inside. Did you push her down the stairs?"

Mary angrily replied, "I wasn't going to wait till you and your girlfriend killed me. That's right, I told Stilts it was Delacruz that killed Shauna; and he hired Davis to kill your fucking girlfriend."

Davis roared, "Shut up, you little bitch!" Taking a knife from behind his back, he tried to run but was overpowered by Ebersole and Warden Russell and then handcuffed. Ebersole was holding the knife and Mary revealed, "That's the knife that killed Shauna."

Once they were taken away, Warden Russell declared, "What a shit show."

Rodriguez was about to leave when Russell inquired, "Sergeant, how long have you known about this?"

"I had a hunch about Pullman and Delacruz."

"I heard you visited inmate Delacruz a few weeks ago. Do you want to tell me what that was about?"

"With all due respect, Warden Russell, perhaps you should clean your own house before questioning me. Maybe keep an eye on some of your guards."

"What do you know about Pullman and Delacruz, Sergeant?"

"Ask Pullman. My visit with Delacruz was personal. If you need me to make a statement, Captain Ebersole knows where to find me." He pointed to the ceiling, "You might want to put more cameras in here. See you, Warden."

CHAPTER 53
THE INVITATION

As he was driving back to Oceanview, Marco called. "Hey, Marco. How's the real estate thing going? Any luck?"

"I stopped into a few places on Gold Street. A place called Ocean Realty remembers showing a property to a guy that fits his description. I spoke to the agent, Susan Sanders; and she said he was strange."

"How long ago was this?"

"She said it was about a year and a half ago.

"She remembered that far back? Do you think she could give us a description?"

"She said she doesn't remember details, just that when he smiled he was scary. She avoided eye contact. She said that he was big, bald, and had an accent. She showed him property at the end of the boardwalk near the marsh. She remembers him saying he liked it because it was quiet and out of the way. She showed him three houses, and none were good enough."

"Why?"

"Only one had a basement, and it was too small. He said he needed a large basement. She said she couldn't get rid of him fast enough. He was creeping her out."

"Keep at it. Check more places today." Rodriguez then called Will, "I need you to see if there are any properties owned by Dimitri Semenov in Oceanview. Go through tax records, deeds, liens, whatever you can get your hands on. We're against the clock. I'll explain later."

The Cyclist Club will hold a meeting on Friday, May 13th, at 7:00 p.m. Attire is black-tie for the gentlemen and evening gowns for the ladies. Upon arrival, the valet will provide a Venetian mask that must be worn for the entire evening. No identities will be revealed and your past will not be discussed. All other conversations are welcome. Address to follow.

Darren Mitchell was reading his text while having breakfast at the diner. He finished and headed for Queens to meet with Stilts. Antoine was there to greet him, and Mitchell gave him his weapon. They went into a private room. "What's on your mind, Mitchell?"

Mitchell looked at Antoine standing by the door. "Does he need to be here?"

"Yes, he's my brother from another…you know the rest, Mitchell. He stays. So, what's on your mind?"

"So are you happy that Delacruz is dead and that you fucked up a really good thing?"

"I don't like your manner of speaking, Mitchell. I've told you in the past you're disrespectful."

"Don't you think they're going to point the finger at me to save their asses? You fucked me good because you wanted revenge for your fucking Auntie. I told you I would take care of it. Now I gotta disappear for a while and my business will dry up."

"What business, Mitchell, shaking down dealers for their merchandise and hookers for twenty bucks? Isn't that why you came to me for professional guidance? It's too bad, Mitchell; but I don't think we can work together. You're too popular now, and your popularity is bad for business. Go hide, Mitchell; and don't come back here. Our business is finished. This is what happens when you can't control your people. Antoine, give him his gun back and see him out."

"Fuck you, Stilts. You'll hear from me again."

"Leave, Mitchell, while you can; and take your disrespect with you."

Once Mitchell left the building, Stilts instructed Antoine, "Keep an eye on the bumbaclot. If he puts us in jeopardy, you know what to do." Antoine followed Mitchell for a while as he drove along Queens Boulevard but eventually pulled into an abandoned service station and went around the back. He dialed a number in New York. "Mr. Washington, how's your day going?"

"Fucked as usual. It seems Stilts got a second visit today from Darren Mitchell and things got heated."

"Heated. Yeah, all that bullshit about working together apparently got all fucked up. Stilts had Delacruz's niece killed in prison. It was all about revenge for his Auntie. Mitchell was moving drugs into that prison, and it fucked up his game. What about you guys? You got anything on him."

"Not much. He's ex-DEA from Florida. If he's dirty, he's under the radar. The locals in Oceanview are investigating Delacruz's murder. They got people in custody, but Mitchell's name hasn't turned up yet. Listen, when the shit hits the fan we're going after Stilts. For right now, we're looking at Jimmie Velez, one of Mitchell's buddies. See if we can work him."

"Be careful Agent Washington."

"Yeah, later."

CHAPTER 54

THE DEAL

Rodriguez called his men into his office. "Close the door and have a seat." He took his phone and played back the call from Zachariah.

Spinelli leaned back in his chair, "Motherfucker."

"Yeah, that's not much time. Will, how did you make out with the real estate records."

"Nothing with that name, Sarge. No tax records, liens, or deeds, I went as far back as last year." Somebody is making these transactions for him."

Detective Martino yelled, "Sergeant, call on line 2."

Rodriguez picked up. "Hi, Sergeant, it's Ebersole. Eric Pullman wants to have a chat with you. They're holding him in Suffolk Prison. He doesn't want to talk to anybody else, just you. I'll set it up for tomorrow morning at 10:00. See you there."

Rodriguez arrived at the prison to find Ebersole waiting for him. "Follow me." They were directed to a conference room where Eric was being guarded by an officer. Ebersole flashed his badge, "We'll take it from here."

Eric remarked, "I only wanted you here, Sergeant."

"Sorry," replied Rodriguez, "he's got to stay." They sat down and Rodriguez pulled his chair in close. "So what's on your mind, Eric?"

"I guess I fucked up bad, didn't I?"

"Yeah, you did; but I warned you. I told you to watch yourself around her. Let me ask you a question: were you and Delacruz planning to kill Mary? I want the truth or I'm out." Eric nodded yes. Rodriguez and Ebersole exchanged glances. 'Was she the one who was supposed to go down the stairs?"

"Yeah, she was supposed to die."

"Did you tell anybody else about your plan?"

"No, it was between me and Mercedes."

"What did she promise you, Eric?"

"She said she could triple our business with the contacts she had on the outside."

"What was she getting in return?"

Eric looked back and forth between both men. "She wanted us to break her out of there."

There was a pause and then Ebersole inquired, "How were you going to get her out?"

"I don't know, we didn't have a plan yet."

"Why did you want to talk to only me?"

"I heard a guy named Mitchell hired some people to kill you."

"What else did you hear?"

"I heard he was trying to make a deal with Shauna Wilson's nephew, a guy named Stilts from Queens."

Rodriguez looked at Ebersole and he shook his head no. "So Mitchell's responsible for the drugs coming into prison."

"Yeah."

"Do you have an address?" Eric shook his head no. "The problem is without an address for Mitchell, there's not much we can do." Rodriguez began to get up, "Without an address, we don't have much, so I guess that's it."

Ebersole was surprised but also began to rise. Eric shouted, "Wait, wait, please. Davis knows where he lives. Davis knows."

Ebersole stated, "I got it."

A short time later Davis was brought in and provided the men with the address and was then led away. Rodriguez requested, "Captain, can you excuse us? I need a few minutes with Eric."

"I'll give you a couple of minutes. I'll be outside."

There was a pause then Rodriguez stated, "Here's what I'm going to do, Eric. So the plan was the warden was going to be your alibi while Mercedes killed Mary."

"Yeah, Mercedes said she was going to do it."

"So nobody knew about this plan except you and Mercedes. You got sucked in by her, but you're not the first. I'm going to forget this conversation ever happened. You're going to prison, but you'll avoid a conspiracy to commit murder rap. That's the best I can do. I think I can convince Ebersole to look the other way. I'm giving you a big break. Don't fuck it up."

As Ebersole and Rodriguez walked to their cars, Rodriguez remarked, "I want to give the kid a break, Captain."

"How do you want to handle it, Sergeant. It's your call."

"No conspiracy to commit murder rap, Captain. You good with that?"

"Like I said, your call."

"I'll get the necessary warrants for Mitchell. I'll let you know when to move on him." Rodriguez called Detective Spinelli, "Marco, grab Will and meet me at 513 Seaview Drive. Park down the block and don't get out of your car. We're gonna keep an eye on the house."

"We got Zachariah?"

"No. Meet me there." Rodriguez was the last to arrive. He parked and walked past the house, noticing activity inside the garage. When he reached Detective Spinelli's car, he told them, "Looks like he's going on a trip. He's loading his car."

"Who's in there, Sergeant?"

"A suspect, that's all I can say right now. Hold tight. If the doors go up, I'm moving in."

"What about the warrant?"

"Ebersole's working on it."

"Aren't we screwed without a warrant, Sarge?"

"Maybe."

"What's the story with this guy?"

"Smuggling drugs into Suffolk Prison."

The garage doors opened and Rodriguez directed Marco to cover the house. Rodriguez walked to the garage entrance and stood directly in the path of the car. He yelled, "Close the doors, Mitchell. I just want to talk." Will ran to the garage. As he got close, Rodriguez shouted, "It's okay, stay outside." His weapon was aimed at the car. The doors closed. "Darren Mitchell, you're under arrest." He walked toward the car.

With the car in park, Mitchell gunned the engine. He lowered the window and yelled, "Get out of the way. I swear I'll run you down." Rodriguez walked further into the garage with his gun still trained on Mitchell. Will parked his car across the street and got out with his gun at his side. The sounds of sirens in the background were getting closer. "Did you call Suffolk PD on me?"

"No, it wasn't me or my men, probably one of your neighbors."

Mitchell took his gun from the seat and pressed it against his head. Rodriguez shouted, "Wait, let's talk." He continued to inch closer. Mitchell was staring straight ahead, the gun still at his head. Rodriguez approached the car and asked, "Do you know who I am?"

"Yeah, you look just like your old man, 'the Saint.' I heard you were looking for me. So now what? Is this about revenge, Rodriguez? All this to avenge your old man."

"No, Mitchell. It's about breaking the law. Are you gonna go out like Persaud?"

"Listen, Rodriguez. I didn't think your old man was gonna kill himself." Rodriguez was silent. "I'm sorry about that, but it was out of my control. So now what do I do? Give myself up? You know that ain't happening."

"Come on, Mitchell. Put the gun down and let's talk."

"We're not talking, Rodriguez. There's a message on my phone I want you to see. It's in my jacket pocket. Can I get it?"

"Go ahead."

He handed Rodriguez the phone with the gun still against his head. "You're looking for a piece of shit named Zachariah. Well, I can deliver him to you." Rodriguez paused and looked at Mitchell. "Yeah, he invited me to join some fucking club. Scroll down to the heading Cyclist Club. There's a message from the man himself. Friday, he's all yours."

Rodriguez stared at the message in disbelief. "Shit."

"Yeah, Rodriguez. That's the devil himself."

"Thanks, Mitchell. Now put the gun down. Don't go out this way. What you gave me is big. Maybe we can work something out. Put it down."

"A deal? Don't make me laugh. I know how those turn out. Giving you Zachariah is my way of balancing the books."

"Listen, Mitchell. If you die, Zachariah finds out and I'm back to square one. You said you wanted to balance the books, then do as I say. Put the gun down and listen."

Detective Spinelli contacted Rodriguez. "What's going on? Are you okay, Sarge?"

"Yeah, Marco, we're okay. Keep everybody outside. I don't want anybody moving on the house."

"What's the plan?"

"I'm winging it, Marco. I'll let you know."

"Okay, Rodriguez, go ahead and talk. I'm listening."

"You need to stay alive, and the press can't know about this. If Zachariah finds out, I'll never get close to him and he goes away. First, I'm gonna pull everybody out so it's just me, you, and two of my men. I'll keep Suffolk PD outside the perimeter. Then I'm gonna call Captain Ebersole and see if we can use a safe house in Brooklyn. You need to be under wraps till I get Zachariah. Give me your gun, Mitchell, handle first."

Mitchell hesitated then handed Rodriguez the gun. "Marco, have Captain Franklin pull his troopers back past the perimeter and let me know when they're done. Tell him the request is coming from me. I'm gonna open the garage doors halfway. Tell Will to come inside."

A short time later Marco called, "They moved out and Will is coming in."

Rodriguez called Captain Ebersole, "What's going on, Sergeant? I'm hearing there's action in your neck of the woods. What's it about?"

"Mitchell was trying to run, but we got there first."

"Why did you move in? We don't have warrants yet."

"We had probable cause and a witness. That should be good enough. I need your help one more time, Captain."

"Go ahead."

"I need to put Mitchell on ice in your safe house."

"For how long?"

"Till Friday the 13th."

"Lucky me, but why?"

"I'll explain when I see you."

"Alright, Sergeant. I'll meet you there"

"Open the door halfway, Mitchell; and let my man in."

Will entered and asked, "Okay, Sergeant, what's the plan?"

"We're going to Brooklyn. Captain Ebersole has a safe house there. When we get there, I'll explain it to everybody. Is Marco outside?"

"Yeah, waiting for the word."

"Alright, tell him we're coming out. You drive. I'll sit in the back with Mitchell. Sorry, Mitchell, I gotta cuff you."

"No professional courtesy?"

"Sorry, turn around."

The cars slowly drove away as the bystanders began to disperse. Some of the more curious tried to get a glimpse inside the cars. The flashing lights of the Suffolk County P.D. were visible well outside the perimeter. "Turn left here, Will. Let's take 25A." The interior of the car was silent, then Rodriguez asked, "How did you get involved with Zachariah?"

Mitchell answered. "I gave him to you wrapped up, so why don't we leave it at that."

They arrived at the safe house and Captain Ebersole greeted them. Ebersole addressed two of his men, "Check him out, take him upstairs, and keep an eye on him. Don't let him get close to a phone. So, Sergeant, what's this about?"

"Mitchell's story starts with my father, but let me give you the short story. Somehow, Mitchell got involved with a guy named Zachariah who's responsible for homicides in Oceanview."

"Yeah, we heard about 'em in Brooklyn. Is he connected to the Mayhew killings?"

"Yes, he is, there's no doubt." Rodriguez showed Ebersole the text on Mitchell's phone.

"Cyclist Club? What the fuck is that?"

"In Zachariah's mind, it's his Tour de France, his competition where people are killed by cyclists. They film it and show them at these meetings. I get the feeling that I'm in Friday's show."

"Did these guys try to kill you?"

"I think they were sending a message, but they got hurt; and Zachariah killed one of them."

"So Friday you're going to this meeting posing as Mitchell?"

"Yep."

"Do you know what you're getting yourself into?"

"I'll find out Friday. He's got a hostage, and he's going to kill her if I don't find him."

"Why don't we just put a team together and hit the house on Friday?"

"No, It's gotta be me alone in the beginning, I have to find the hostage. When I find her, Suffolk PD can bust down the doors."

"If there's any help you need, Rodriguez, you can count on me."

"Thanks, Captain."

One of Ebersole's men shouted for them to come upstairs. "It's. Mitchell, he wants to talk to you guys."

They sat across from Mitchell and Ebersole said, "Okay, Mitchell, go ahead."

Mitchell looked at both men and requested, "Just us, okay?"

Ebersole instructed his men, "Go downstairs, fellas. Give us a minute. Shut the door when you leave. Okay, Mitchell, they're gone."

Mitchell began, "There are two bodies in the marsh down by Dock Street. They're about 100 yards from the road."

The men looked at each other and Rodriguez asked, "Who killed them?"

"I was there, but it wasn't me."

"Then who?"

"A guy by the name of Jimmie Velez."

Rodriguez said, "Are you talking about Icepick Jimmie? I heard he went south a few years ago and was hiding out in Florida."

"No, he came back last year. I hired him to watch my back. He did the killings, I swear."

"What was it about?"

"Territory, Rodriguez, drug territory. They were working my turf. We set up a meeting to talk, just talk. I sat in the car and Jimmie went ahead to see what was up. You know, talk shit out. Next thing I know, Jimmie ice picks the guy in the throat. I jumped out of my car screaming at the dumb fuck. The other guy shot at me but missed, and Jimmie put a couple of slugs in the guy. We dragged them into the marsh and got out of there. It's across from the abandoned mill."

Ebersole said, "I'll get Suffolk PD on it."

"Thanks, Captain; but keep Mitchell's name out of it."

"Sure, Sergeant."

CHAPTER 55
CHANGE OF PLANS

Justine Godfrey was lounging on the terrace of her Greenwich, Connecticut mansion. The groundskeepers were working to make sure the landscaping was perfect. It had to be because Justine had a way of berating people around her if things weren't done her way. One of her maids brought her the newspaper. Justine was bored and she quickly skimmed the paper. One news story caught her eye and she came to a full stop.

The headline read:

> *Augustus Becker, an official with the Las Vegas Gaming Commission, has been arrested on human trafficking charges in Reno, Nevada. Authorities are eyeing a link to a ring in the Northeast.*

She dialed a number on her phone. "We have to talk now."

"What's going on, Justine?"

"That fucking Augustus may have just fucked everything up."

"Okay, go ahead talk tell me what Augustus has done to prompt such a reaction from you."

Justine paused, "He got arrested in Reno on trafficking charges."

The man reacted, "Oh, my. That is a problem."

"The paper said that authorities are looking at a link in the Northeast. That's us. We're that link."

The man paused, "Justine, do you remember what I said to you when you wanted to bring him into our organization."

"Yes. I do."

"I told you he was a degenerate gambler and was not to be trusted. He lost his family and his home because of his addiction. I doubt he even has enough money for bail, if there is any. You see, the authorities are tough on human trafficking these days. I suggest you get a legal team together and get to Reno. Bail him out before he opens his big mouth and we have to shut it understand?"

"I can't go to Vegas. I have a meeting of my private club coming up, and immediately after that I'm flying to Saudi Arabia."

"Saudi Arabia? Why?"

"It seems my dear departed mommy has oil interests there."

"More money, dear, more money. "Justine the next time you have the urge to get laid, pick a married salesman from Kansas instead of some fucking unstable degenerate like Becker."

Justine wasn't listening, "Imagine me with my looks and killer body around those repressed men in Saudi Arabia."

The man chuckled, "My dear Justine, it's not the men who are repressed in that part of the world, it's the women. This is your mess. Get it straightened out before Becker tells all. I believe you should rethink your trip to Saudi Arabia." The man warned, "Fix this; and use your funds, not the organization's. I'll be in touch."

CHAPTER 56

#82

It was three days to the meeting of The Cyclist Club. The embossed invitations had reached the members days ago. All were attending. Rodriguez was in the precinct reading Mitchell's invitation. "Marco, grab Will and come in. I need you guys." The men were seated in the office and Rodriguez slid the invitation across the desk. "Mitchell gave me his invitation. Friday night I'll be attending Zachariah's party as Mitchell. Zachariah has never seen him, doesn't know what he looks like. I'm going in blind, and I'm not sure what to expect. He's got a hostage, so we can't go kicking doors down. When I find her, I'll give you the signal. The house, #82 Maple Court is just outside of town. Marco, when we're done, find out who owns the house."

On the desk was an open map. Rodriguez pointed to the map. "This is a real estate map of the area. The area is hilly, and the ocean is directly in front. There are only two ways we can approach and that's from the hilly areas around the property. There's an access road here behind these trees. Put your cars up here. You can't see them from the house. Marco, from this vantage point here, you'll see the entire house. Put your cars behind this row of trees here and here. There's a road on this side that leads straight to the front. On my signal, bring your team down that road and seal off the area. Will, there's a road around the back here on Cherry Street. Stay off the road and wait here with your team. When you see Marco move, come down here and cover the back. Nobody in, nobody out. Captain Franklin with Suffolk PD will be providing backup. I'll be wired, and I'll be communicating with Marco, but it has to be one way. I can't receive, only send. I'll tell you when to get your men moving. I'll be unarmed in case they frisk me or wand me."

Marco asked, "Will you be able to get a gun in there?"

"I don't know, Marco. I'm not sure what I'm up against. When I get there, they're going to give me a mask to wear."

"Mask?"

"Yeah, one of those Venetian masks. According to Mitchell's text, I'm supposed to be anonymous. That works in my favor. The rest I'm not sure about."

Zachariah was sitting in front of Mika's cell. He'd been keeping her sedated ever since she killed Alexi. She slowly awakened, saw Zachariah, and her body tensed. "Good morning, Mika my dear. I hope you slept well. Would you excuse me?" Zachariah shouted to his other captives, "On your bikes! Let's exercise. Two hours now. You see, Mika, how they're under my control? They would do anything for me."

"Is that what you're going to do to me? Place me under your control?"

"I considered making you one of my competitors as a tribute to Alexi's memory, but I've changed my mind."

"Are you going to kill me?"

"No. I made you a wonderful breakfast." He unlocked the door, "Come upstairs. We can watch the ocean and have breakfast together." Mika slowly walked through the door. "I trust you will be a good guest and not attempt anything." Mika nodded and Zachariah took her arm. She almost pulled away but stopped herself. They sat in silence and ate their breakfast. The ocean was unusually turbulent, and the wind was blowing from the northeast, the clouds moving fast across the sky.

"Zachariah, can we go inside? I'm cold."

"Yes, of course. I want you to be comfortable, my dear. Breakfast is done, and it's been a while since you've had a shower, hasn't it? Come with me." He took the cup of coffee out of her hand.

"I can take it down..."

Zachariah cut her off, "I insist, Mika. Besides, the bathroom up here is so much nicer. You can lock the door. I won't disturb you." He put his hands on her shoulders and squeezed.

Her voice quaked, "Okay, thank you."

"Excellent, I'll give you some clean clothes."

Mika went into the bathroom, locked the door, then tried the doorknob to be sure. She ran the water and debated what to do. From outside, she could hear "Flight of the Valkyries" playing loudly. She suddenly noticed that the doorknob was slowly turning; and as the door began opening, the music got louder. Mika trembled as she watched the door slowly open. Zachariah entered the bathroom naked and stopped at the door. In his hand was a pair of scissors. "Why are you not in the shower, Mika? You promised. All that water is being wasted." She noticed multiple scars on his body. "Do my scars frighten you? Let's just say my father believed in discipline and I thank him for it. Get out of those old clothes and get into the shower now, Mika."

"Please, I'd rather shower in my room."

"No, Mika, I insist." Mika was still trembling as she began to undress, looking at the scissors as she disrobed. Zachariah spoke softly, "You'll feel better after a nice hot shower." She got into the shower and Zachariah joined her. He placed the scissors on the edge of the bathtub. She turned her back, covering her breasts, looking over her shoulder. "Mika, do you wash your hair first or last?"

She paused and then in a trembling voice said, "Last."

"Then allow me to wash your back. Is the temperature of the water comfortable?"

"Yes, it's okay" He washed her back making circles with the washcloth. "Did the policeman wash you as gently as this?" "Flight of the Valkyries" continued to play in the background. "See, Mika, I'm not a brute. I was in love once. She was from Ukraine. Her name was Natasha. She was beautiful like you."

Mika quietly asked, "What happened?"

"My father despised her because of where she was from." Zachariah was massaging her shoulders, "Does that feel good." Mika nodded yes. "You can turn around and rinse now." Mika turned to face him. He looked her up and down, "My, you are exquisite." Zachariah picked up the scissors. Mika tensed, her breathing became heavier. "I've always felt that you would look better with shorter hair." He raised the scissors and she recoiled. "Don't be afraid." Zachariah began to cut her hair, "I won't cut it too short." Her hair filled the shower floor and began to clog the drain. "Your hair is so thick." He cut her hair as "Flight of the Valkyries" continued to play. "Do you like the music?" Mika nodded yes just to placate him. Zachariah ran his fingers through her hair and remarked, "There, just as I thought. It makes a big difference." He put the scissors down. "I did your back, would you mind doing mine?" Mika picked up the washcloth and began to wash his back. "My mother used to always say you must use soap. Come on, Mika. I think you should use more soap." Zachariah rinsed, then said to Mika, "You can wash your hair now. I'm leaving. Use the black towel. It's big and soft. I'll make smoothies for us and meet you on the terrace."

He left the bathroom without drying himself off. Mika leaned against the shower wall and cried, her heart raced with fear. She found Zachariah dressed and sitting on the terrace, his feet up on the railing, as she joined him. "Come, Mika, sit. Look, the clouds have parted and the sun is shining." Mika's hair was not quite dry, and it hung to her shoulders wetting the top of her blouse.

Zachariah offered her a smoothie. It was green and smelled like apples. "What is this?"

"It's a combination of apples, bananas, and green vegetables. I give it to my athletes; they love it. It's good for them as they train."

"I thought I wasn't going to be one of your athletes."

"You're not, Mika. You're special. After all, you're the one who killed Alexi." Mika looked at Zachariah. He continued, "Friday night I want you to be my guest at The Cyclist Club meeting."

"I don't want to go. I don't like all that killing."

"Oh, but I insist, Mika. You must be there, you're the star attraction." Zachariah took a syringe from alongside his chair. She tried to run, but Zachariah grabbed her by the hair and pinned her against the chair. She fought him, trying to bite and punch him. She kicked him in the groin, and he let out a maniacal laugh. He injected her easily and she succumbed to the sedative as he talked to her. He sounded as if he were in an echo chamber, "Did you think you would get away with killing Alexi, my closest friend? Friday night you'll meet the Cyclist Club members. Sorry, Mika, but you'll be sedated till then. It's beginning to take effect. Sleep now, Mika

CHAPTER 57

THE STAKEOUT

Marco strode quickly into Rodriguez's office, "Sergeant, guess who signed the deed for 82 Maple Court?"

"Josh Solomon."

"Shit, Sergeant, how did you know?"

"I took a ride out there this morning. I spoke to the caretaker and asked a few questions. I told him I was a real estate investor looking for properties in the area. He said the owner was having a party on Friday night; and since Josh Solomon is dead, I'm assuming the new owner is Zachariah. He showed me around the property and left me alone long enough for me to unlock a window at the back of the house. It's open just enough to get your fingers underneath and open it all the way. I know how we can hide a gun until I need it."

"How?"

"*To Kill a Mockingbird.*"

"What, Sergeant?"

"Let me make a call. I'll explain later."

Rodriguez called Warden Russell, "This is Warden Russell."

"Good morning, Warden. This is Sergeant Rodriguez."

Coldly she says, "Yeah, what can I do for you?"

"I need that book *To Kill a Mockingbird*. The one with the hollowed-out interior."

"Why, Rodriguez?"

"Because I want to hide a gun in it."

"A what?"

"Don't ask. It's a case I'm working on."

"You do realize this is evidence."

"Come on, Warden. There's probably 20 more just like that one."

"Well, not quite twenty. But okay, Sergeant, it's yours."

"I'll send one of my men, Will Jankowski, to pick it up."

"Come to the third floor, I'll clear him through."

"Thanks, Warden."

"By the way, Rodriguez. I put more cameras in the library."

"Great, he's on his way."

A short time later Will returned with the book. Rodriguez opened it and Will reacted, "What the fuck?"

Rodriguez explained, "Great way to transport drugs in a prison, don't you think?"

Marco took the gun from his ankle holster and inserted it in the hollowed-out section. "Wow, just right."

Rodriguez nodded his head and unlocked his bottom drawer. He removed a Springfield Armory XDs 45 handgun and an extra clip. "This baby has amazing stopping power. Let's see if it fits." The gun fits perfectly, "Bingo."

"Shit, Sarge, is that gun regulation?"

"Probably not. The caretaker told me that on Friday morning there'll be food and tables and chairs being delivered. On the second floor, there's a meeting room with two bathrooms. Right next to the bathroom across from the door there's a large antique bookcase. Put the book on the second shelf from the top all the way to the right."

Marco's phone rang. He spoke for a while and then hung up. "You're not going to believe this, Sergeant, but Josh Solomon owns another house on Shore Crest Drive, number 26." The agent told me that Solomon insisted that it have a large basement."

"Nice work, Marco. On Friday night we hit both locations. Detective Martino will be the lead on that operation. Ask him to come in."

Will asked, "So Sarge, who gets to go in on Friday?"

"It can't be you, Will. He's already seen you."

Marco offered, "I'll do it. I'll get in there and make sure the gun gets inside. I'll wait till Friday morning when there's activity."

Rodriguez advised, "I checked out the grounds, and there's a small growth of trees not far from the house. They'll give you partial cover. Get in and out as fast as you can."

Detective Martino entered the office and was briefed by Rodriguez. "You're probably going to find kidnap victims in the basement. Beyond that, I don't have a clue. Just stay alert. You know what to do, Martino. See how many men Captain Franklin can give you."

"Okay, Sergeant."

Rodriguez received a call from Ebersole, "Sergeant, our guest is singing like a canary with a hard-on. He rolled over on a guy named Palmer Gordon, aka Stilts, a dealer from Queens. He's Shauna Wilson's nephew, and he was Shauna's supplier on the outside. It seems he and Mitchell were about to make a deal to increase distribution when Stilts wanted to know who killed his Aunt. I called the New York DEA, and they've had a guy in there for several months. Their man on the inside said that there's a warehouse in Queens where the stuff is kept. Mostly weed and heroin and according to their man, it's a lot of weight. Stilts is stiff-lipped when it comes to the location, but their man is working on it. When Stilts found out that Delacruz killed his aunt, he paid Davis to kill her. That put a crimp in Pullman's and Delacruz's plans. Mary was the target, not Delacruz. Pullman was in charge of logging and keeping track of donated books. Davis hollowed some out to move drugs around the prison."

"Thanks, Captain. I'll keep you posted about Friday." Rodriguez hung up and headed for the door. "Spinelli, you're in charge for a few hours. I'll be back."

Will asked, "Where're you going?"

"To rent a tuxedo for Friday."

"You need backup, Sarge?" and the men laughed. Rodriguez ignored them and left.

CHAPTER 58

BOOKMARK

It was the day before the Cyclist Club meeting and Zachariah was on site making sure everything was being handled according to his instructions. He was barking orders as he walked around the grounds. He always used the same event planners for these meetings; and as far as they were concerned, it was a private masquerade event. Although creepy, it was nothing out of the ordinary for them. They knew the rules. No one was allowed in the screening room except for the members and there was no talking to the members. The food must be cooked to specifications put forward by Zachariah. After serving brandy and cigars, they were to leave the premises except for the valets and private security, all armed, of course. "Tomorrow I want everybody here at 4:00 p.m. Any lateness will not be tolerated."

Zachariah returned to his house and went to the basement. He unlocked Sara's cell, "Come upstairs with me, Sara. I have something for you to do. The woman in the room next to yours is going to be my guest tomorrow at a meeting of the Cyclist Club.

Tomorrow at 6:00 p.m. I want you to dress her in a beautiful gown that I've bought for her. Then you will help me put her in my car. You'll return to your room and I'll lock you in. I won't be gone for long; and when I return, I'll have a surprise for all of you: ice cream."

"Where are you taking her, Zachariah?"

Zachariah gave her a cold stare and said, "To her death." Sara showed no emotion and Zachariah continued to stare. Sara stared back, and Zachariah let out one of his maniacal laughs. "Wonderful. The thought of death and murder doesn't shock you. You're perfectly ready for competition. You see, she killed my good friend Alexi; and she must pay."

Sara replied, "I understand. I'll kill her if you want me to."

"I know you would, and tonight you'll sleep in my bed. Does that shock you?" Sara shook her head no. Zachariah moved closer and whispered, "Excellent."

Friday morning arrived and the leaders of the assault teams met in Rodriguez's office. Marco was at the house to plant the gun. He called Rodriguez. "Sarge, there are cameras hidden in the trees in the back of the house. I see two of them, and one on the side hidden behind some fucking gargoyle must be modeled after Zachariah."

"Shit, Marco. I must have missed them. Can you work around them?"

"Negative, Sarge. They're aimed directly at the back windows. I can't go in that way."

"How the fuck could I have missed them? Come back. We'll figure something else out."

"No, Sarge. There's no time. I'm going through the front."

"Marco, don't go through the front. It's too dangerous."

"I'm going to walk this fucking gun inside right under their noses."

"Marco, don't goddammit. Martino, take a couple of men and drive past the house in case shit gets out of hand."

"You got it, Sarge."

Marco worked his way down to the front of the house where they were unloading. He made his way to a truck, grabbed two chairs, and followed the caterers into the house. In his backpack is the book. They went upstairs, and he deliberately dropped one of the chairs. One of the workers exclaimed, "Hey, what the fuck are you doing? If Joey catches you dropping shit, he'll can your ass."

"Sorry, it's my first week."

"It'll be your last if you keep dropping chairs. Set up the tables. We'll get the rest."

"Okay, sorry about that." The men went downstairs to continue unloading and one of them remarked, "Fucking rookie."

When they were out of sight, Marco reached into his backpack and pulled out the book. He was about to put the book on the shelf when he heard a voice, "What are you doing? Put that book back." It was one of the security guards coming up the stairs.

"I'm sorry, it's my favorite book. *To Kill a Mockingbird*, have you ever read it?"

"No, and I don't give a fuck. Put it back where you found it and get back to work."

"Okay, I'll put it back. It was on the second shelf from the top, all the way to the right. I wasn't trying to steal it."

"What was that crash I heard?"

"Oh, that was me. I dropped one of the chairs."

"Be careful and get back to work or I'll tell your boss."

Marco continued to unload and slowly made his way back to his car parked nearby. The trucks were leaving, having unloaded everything. The driver looked for Marco and asked, "Did anybody see the rookie? He disappeared." The men laughed, "He couldn't handle two chairs. Fuck him, let's go." The men laughed as the trucks drove away from the house.

Marco called Rodriguez, "Mission accomplished, Sarge."

"Fuckin-ay, Marco. Nice job. Gentlemen, the gun is inside. When Marco gets back, we'll brief him." Marco returned to the precinct and the final plans were set in motion. "Captain Franklin has 14 men for us. Marco and Will take four men each. Martino, the rest will be with you. Get to Shore Crest at 7:00 and observe but do not engage. The meeting is at 8:00 and it's half an hour from Shore Crest to the house on Maple Court. Move in a few minutes before 8:00. I want to make sure he's close to the Maple Street house before you go. Marco, when I find Mika, I'll send you a hit from my watch. Will, when you see Marco move, secure the front. Team leaders, get your teams together at 6:00 in the parking lot downstairs."

"What about you, Sarge?"

"I'm going to pick up Mitchell's car in case they're checking plates. The invitation is my ticket in. I'm going in light, no badge and no gun. Okay, gentlemen, are there any questions?"

The men were silent, and Martino said, "I think we're good, Sergeant."

"Good, now get some rest. Let's get this guy tonight and wrap this shit up."

CHAPTER 59

DRESSED FOR THE KILL

Zachariah was pushing his captives harder than usual. He was yelling at them, "Pedal faster, more energy, come on, move." He continued to nervously look at his watch. At precisely 5:00 he screamed at them to stop and the captives breathed a sigh of relief. "Cool down, my champions. I'll bring your dinner soon." At 6:00 Zachariah appeared with their dinner. He was dressed entirely in black. He opened Sara's door and said, "It's time. Go upstairs and wait for me there." He opened Mika's door. The drugs were beginning to wear off. He picked her up and carried her upstairs.

Jennifer screamed, "Where are you taking her?"

Zachariah turned with Mika in his arms and said, "Andrew, if she speaks again, I will open your door and ask you to kill her." Zachariah carried Mika upstairs and laid her on his bed. He called her, "Mika, Mika, look at this beautiful dress I bought you. You're going to wear it tonight. Sara, please help her put it on. I think red is her color, the color of blood." Zachariah closed the door and put on "Isle of the Dead" by Rachmaninoff. He sat on the terrace, put his head back, and listened to the music. The door to the room opened and Mika walked out being helped by Sara. Zachariah motioned to Sara to bring her closer. He gently lifted her head and looked at Sara, "I believe with a little makeup she will be even more beautiful. "Apply her makeup something appropriate and then, Sara, go back to your room and I'll lock you in." He spoke to the other captives, "Everybody, listen to me. I'll be gone for a while. I would expect you to abide by the rules. The cameras will assure that you do," and he pointed to the cameras above them.

Zachariah helped Mika to the car. She was becoming more lucid and she asked Zachariah, "Where are we going?"

"To a party, my dear."

"I'm tired. I don't want to go to a party, I want to go to bed."

"No, my dear, tonight you are the life of the party," and he flashed a sinister smile, his crooked teeth even more horrifying in the streetlights. They arrived at the house and Zachariah drove into the garage. He helped Mika to a room on the second floor. This room was outfitted with exercise equipment, a high-tech training bike, and a camera focused on a large chair. "See, I gave you a nice comfortable chair so you can go to sleep." He injected her with just enough serum for one hour. "When you wake up, you will have a big surprise. Go to sleep now." He exited the room and called over one of his security guards, "Make sure nobody goes into that room."

It was 7:45 and the guests were beginning to arrive. As they left their cars, they were checked for weapons and given their masks. The security guards then ushered them into the main atrium. Champagne and hors d'oeuvres were served as the guests mingled. Rodriguez arrived and went through the same formalities. He noticed that at least one of the valets was armed. He walked through the front door where two of Zachariah's guards stood watch. The bulges in their jackets signaled a weapon. Once inside, he avoided mingling with the other members. He excused himself and went upstairs under the pretense of going to the restroom. He used his watch to text Marco: *3 valets armed 2 at the door armed.*

He went to the bookcase and made believe he was looking at the books when he heard people coming up the stairs. A couple approached him, and the woman said, "Hi, is this your first meeting?"

"Yes, it is."

"That's quite a collection of books, isn't it."

"Yes, it certainly is."

"Well, enjoy."

They split up and went to different bathrooms. He removed the book and put the gun in the waistband of his pants under his tuxedo jacket. As he descended the stairs, he ran into Justine Godfrey. She stopped and looked him up and down, "Hello, you're not familiar to me. Is this your first time?" and she paused, "at the meetings, I mean," and let out a laugh.

"Yes, it's my first."

"Well, I can't see your face; but you look like quite a specimen. I love those broad shoulders. Have fun tonight, you're in for a treat."

"Thanks."

A voice boomed over the speakers. "Members, it's time to proceed to the screening room. It promises to be a most entertaining meeting. Fill your glasses and bring your drinks into the screening room and enjoy." They filed in and Justine made sure she sat next to Rodriguez. The members settled in and a figure all in black walked onto the stage. The spotlight went on and illuminated the man with a bright white light. The light was a stark contrast against the black background. He, too, was wearing a mask; but unlike the others, it was more like a death mask. It was the face of someone who had died a painful death. The members were startled at the sight; and some stirred nervously in their seats, glancing sideways at each other. Rodriguez sat stoically, staring at his quarry.

The figure in black spoke, "Good evening, members. Before we begin, I would like to introduce a new member. Please stand so we can look at you." Rodriguez stood in the dim light and looked around the room. "Members, please welcome him. Tonight we have several exciting offerings, and some are international. My dear friend Alexi has brought us some dramatic competitions from Russia and Ukraine. Before we view them tonight, we are going to do something different. In the past, we've been voyeurs watching people suffer and die from afar. It's like an automobile accident. It repulses you, but you can't look away. Death will eventually come for us all; but when we watch it in its most primitive form, it shocks us and draws us in. You want more and more of it, and that's why you keep coming back. I provide you with a glimpse of death, and you squirm in your seats. You look away at times but leave with a clear conscience knowing you didn't kill them; and you console yourself with that thought, untrue as it may be. Most of you in this room have already killed, some of it was premeditated, some were in the heat of passion, and a few cases were the result of bad drugs. You know who you are. Tonight one of you will volunteer to kill a fellow human being who has done absolutely nothing to you. In fact, she is helpless and bound to a chair, a young and beautiful woman. If no one volunteers when asked, I will pick someone." The members were whispering to each other and squirming in their seats. Zachariah shouted, "Quiet!"

Rodriguez sat quietly, still staring straight ahead. Zachariah motioned to a person somewhere above and a screen dropped from the ceiling. The screen came alive and the club members gasped at what they saw. A single spotlight was focused on a figure tied to a large antique chair. The chair was throne-like in its appearance.

Mika was restrained with silver fabric that appeared to be silk knotted into ornate bows. As the effect of the drug wore off, she began to stir and then realized she was tied and unable to move her arms and legs. She strained against the fabric to no avail. Zachariah spoke to the members "Don't look away, don't you dare look away. There's a table next to the chair and on that table are instruments used by our competitors. We have a bat used by Red Widow, a hatchet similar to the one used by Hatchet Man who died at the hands of a policeman, and there are knives used by competitors in the past. So now you're asking yourselves, *Why is this happening?* Because that innocent-looking beautiful creature killed someone very close to me and lied about it. So the time has come for one of you to show the rest of us what you're made of."

Rodriguez was flanked by Justine Godfrey and Ali Bakar. Ali began to slowly and apprehensively raise his hand. Rodriguez leaned closer to him and said, "If you raise your hand, I'll break your fucking arm." Ali lowered his hand and folded his arms on his lap. Rodriguez raised his hand, and the eyes of the other members focused on him.

Zachariah began a slow clapping rhythm and the others reluctantly followed. "I had a feeling it would be our newest member. The rest of you can learn something from him." Justine looked up at Rodriguez with an admiring gaze. Zachariah pointed, "The door on the right leads to that room." He went to a console and "Flight of the Valkyries" began to play loudly, echoing through the screening room. Rodriguez entered the room and observed the camera over the chair recording the encounter. He saw the instruments Zachariah was talking about neatly laid out on a table in front of the chair. Rodriguez thought to himself, *Professor Friedlich was right. I have to kill the monster.*

Mika slowly regained her senses and fought against her restraints. Rodriguez turned his back to the camera and moved close to Mika.

He partially lifted his mask, "Mika, it's me. I'll get you out of here." Her breathing slowed down and was more measured knowing it was Rodriguez. He pulled his mask back down and went to the table with the instruments, picked up a large knife and showed it to the camera. He waved the knife around for dramatic effect. Zachariah was ecstatic. The members gasped. Facing the camera he moved the knife from hand to hand. Upon seeing this, Zachariah let out one of his maniacal laughs. Rodriguez moved to the chair, his back to the camera. He signaled Marco to move in. He cut the bonds holding Mika, removed his mask, and turned to the camera long enough for Zachariah to see it was him. In an instant, he pulled the gun and fired a single shot through the camera lens. Zachariah was standing eyes wide open, mouth agape, and let out a scream. He took a phone from the wall and screamed, "On the second floor, kill them both."

Rodriguez instructed Mika to hide upstairs. He heard footsteps coming from below. He opened the door and saw two of Zachariah's men coming up, guns in hand. They spotted him and he slammed the door and stood to the side. Immediately, five shots rang out, piercing the door. He knocked over a table with a lamp on it. It made a loud crash as it landed on the floor. From the stairs, he heard "I got him." The door opened and Rodriguez was waiting. He smashed the man in the face with the gun. The man desperately tried to grab the railing but missed and began to fall backward, his arms flailing. He was helped on his journey down the stairs with a kick to the chest by Rodriguez. His partner at the base of the steps fired two shots that wound up in the door frame. Rodriguez fired back, killing him. From outside, the sounds of gunfire shattered the night as Marco and his men engaged in a firefight with Zachariah's security.

Zachariah burst through another door screaming, "You fucking policeman!" Rodriguez turned and was slammed into the door with Zachariah's hands around his neck. Rodriguez head-butted

Zachariah, hitting him on the bridge of his nose. Zachariah backed off and Rodriguez went on the offensive. He hit Zachariah with a series of punches, but Zachariah seemed to shake them off. His crooked, misshapen teeth were bloody, giving him a vampirical look. He attacked and Rodriguez sidestepped him and smashed his head into the door leaving a blood-red stain. He smiled devilishly, "You fight good, policeman." He attacked again and knocked Rodriguez to the floor, attempting to stomp on his head; but Rodriguez was able to move out of the way and kicked Zachariah on the side of the knee. He fell to one knee and Rodriguez kicked him in the face. He grabbed Rodriguez's ankle and was able to take him down. Zachariah was on top punching at Rodriguez's face. Some of the punches were blocked and some connected. The power behind the punches was too much for Rodriguez and he was getting lightheaded. He pushed his fingers into Zachariah's eyes and Rodriguez was able to raise his leg and kick Zachariah in the face. Both men were now on their feet, and Zachariah grabbed a barbell and was swinging it wildly. Rodriguez moved around the room, avoiding Zachariah. He noticed the gun on the floor and dove for it. One of Zachariah's guards came through the door, gun in hand, and Zachariah shouted, "Kill him!" Rodriguez was able to grab the gun and he fired, hitting the guard who dropped his weapon and staggered down the stairs. Rodriguez was still on the floor as Zachariah attempted to bring the barbell down on his head. Rodriguez was unable to get on his feet and he rolled on the floor avoiding Zachariah. He warned him, "Drop it or I'll shoot." Zachariah continued his pursuit with the barbell. Rodriguez fired and hit Zachariah below his ribcage. Zachariah was unfazed and continued to swing the barbell. Rodriguez warned him again to no avail. He fired again and Zachariah dropped the barbell and walked toward the training bike. Rodriguez said, "You're under arrest. Get on your knees." Zachariah ignored the command and climbed on the bike. From outside, sirens blared as medical personnel arrived on the scene. Zachariah locked his feet into the toe clips and began to pedal. Rodriguez got on his feet, and with his gun trained on him, repeated, "You're under arrest." Zachariah flashed a sardonic smile, his eyes red and bloodshot, his face bloodied. He said, "I was beating you, policeman. So now you arrest me, and I go to a prison hospital where I'll be nursed back to health." Rodriguez said, "Get off the bike or you'll bleed to death. And you're not dying here, you're dying in prison."

"Prison won't hold me, policeman. I'll get out; and when I do, I'll get my revenge. I know all about Will, the young man I met on the boardwalk. Detective Marco has two daughters. The school they go to must be expensive. How old are they, 8 and 10? My vengeance is blind, policeman." The whir of the bike provided a fitting background for Zachariah's ramblings. He continued to pedal at a high rate of speed. Rodriguez issued one more warning, "Get off the bike."

"Did you know that Will has a beautiful girlfriend, but she's not as beautiful as Mika. Before I'm through, Mika will beg me to kill her."

"Get off the fucking bike."

"What happens if I refuse, policeman?"

Rodriguez paused then replied, "What happens? This happens." Four shots rang out and echoed in the room as all four hit their mark, the middle of Zachariah's chest. The smoke and the sulfur smell of gunpowder lingered in the air. Zachariah was still on the bike, his feet secured to the toe clips. The whir of the bike began to slow down. He was bent backward at the waist, looking like some demonic sculpture from someone's nightmare as the pedals moved his legs. A twisted grimace marred his face, not a latex face covering but a real death mask. Rodriguez stared at the macabre scene and lowered his weapon. He ran up the stairs and found Mika, "Come on, let's go." As he helped her down the stairs, he ran into Marco.

"Where's Zachariah?"

Rodriguez responded, "He's on the bike. Get the coroner up there." When they walked outside, it was clear that the troopers had the situation under control. Mika was taken away to the hospital.

Will hurried over to Rodriguez, "Zachariah?"

"He's dead, Will. How did we do out here?"

"We have two wounded, and three of his security are dead. You were right. Martino found five captives in the basement in the other house. They're on their way to the hospital. Martino found a box with a bunch of go-pros in it."

"Nice work, Will."

Blue and red lights illuminated the night, and the sounds of sirens pierced the quiet. When he got to the front gate, The Cyclist Club members were lined up with their hands behind their heads. A trooper with a clipboard was checking their names. Rodriguez approached the trooper, "I'll take over here. Get to the second floor and see Detective Spinelli. He'll tell you what to do."

Rodriguez walked up and down the line. "When I call your name, say 'Here' or 'It's me' or raise your hand. I don't give a fuck. I just want to know who you are. After you identify yourself, Trooper Evans will cuff you and walk you to the wagon. Once inside, we'll read you your rights." Here we go, 'Ali Bakar?'" Ali reluctantly raised his hand and began to sob. He was cuffed and led to the wagon.

Next was Carlyle Bolton III. Carlyle was not happy and said indignantly, "Do you know who my father is?"

"Well, if you're Carlyle Bolton III, your father must be Carlyle Bolton II. Trooper, cuff him."

The roll call continued until Justine Godfrey was called. She looked at Rodriguez and remarked, "Well, Mr. Broad Shoulders, now that I've seen you without the mask, you're an even finer specimen."

"It's not 'specimen,' it's Sergeant Rodriguez."

He just looked at her but she continued, "I have a strong feeling that we will meet again soon, Sergeant."

Rodriguez paused and replied, "If we do, it's going to end the same way. Cuff her and get her into the wagon." Justine looked him up and down and smiled as she was led away.

CHAPTER 60

REVEALED

One week had passed since the raid at The Cyclist Club meeting house. The headlines were slowly moving on to other news. Some of Zachariah's captives had been released from the hospital and were resuming their lives. Mika had decided to visit friends in Germany. Rodriguez was driving her to the airport. They were both silent. Finally, Mika asked, "When did you know?"

"Know what, Mika?"

"That I wasn't who I said I was."

Rodriguez smiled, "You mean French and here on vacation?"

"Yes."

"I knew it Immediately."

"I know you're a good detective, but are you really that good?"

Rodriguez smiled, "Well, what are the odds that I would meet a beautiful woman in Starbucks and wind up paying for her coffee?"

"It could happen; you're very handsome."

"Sure, it happens to me every day." They both laughed and Rodriguez continued, "You still owe me for the coffee."

"No, I don't. I won the race at the beach, so we're even."

"Remember when I told you about Toulouse and the beach? Well, the closest beach is a hundred miles away."

Mika replied, "I guess I should have done my research."

"I guess. The night we slept together I found the syringe. I emptied it and replaced the liquid with water." Mika laughed and he asked, "What's so funny?"

"I also emptied it and replaced it with water."

"So you replaced water with water?"

"Yes."

They both laughed and Rodriguez asked, "Would you have injected me?"

"No, I could never hurt anybody. I was stalling to keep Alexi and Zachariah from coming after you. They were talking about all of their victims in Russia, so much bloodshed. The morning Alexi died, he was coming for you. He was drunk, and he attacked me when I tried to stop him. His body was thrown into the ocean by Zachariah and one of his captives."

"I know it was Andrew, but he was under the influence of Zachariah. Do you think you'll ever go back to Russia?"

"I'll never go back. It's so dark and depressing with many bad memories. I need to take some time. I think perhaps I'll go to France after Germany. I've never been there."

"Obviously," they both laughed.

They arrived at the airport and Mika's flight was called. They stood facing each other, and Mika put her arms around his broad shoulders and whispered, "You saved my life. I'll never forget you." She walked quickly toward the gate, stopped, turned around, and walked back. She passionately kissed him and whispered in his ear. "I love you."

Rodriguez didn't have a chance to answer as she turned and hurried to the gate.

A few days later Rodriguez was sitting in his office when Detective Spinelli and Will came in and stood in front of his desk. Not looking up from his computer, he asked, "Can I help you, gentlemen?"

Will answered, "Marco wants to ask you something."

"No, I don't. I thought you were going to ask him."

Will replied, "You said you were going to ask him."

Rodriguez continued to work on his computer and said, "It's Humphrey."

"What's Humphrey?"

"My first name is Humphrey. Is that what you were going to ask me?"

"Your name is Humphrey Rodriguez?"

"Yeah, say another word and you're fired. My father was a big Humphrey Bogart fan, so he named me Humphrey."

Marco said, "You know you can legally change your name."

Rodriguez looked up with a scowl, "Why would I change it? I like it. Is that what you wanted to know?"

"No, Sarge. We wanted to know where you're going on vacation."

"Really? That's what you wanted to know? Nowhere. It's a few weeks off. Kind of a staycation, just me and Bogie. Now both of you get out of my office. Wait Will, get back here and sign these papers."

"What papers, Sarge?"

"I want you to be in my command. I've already discussed it with Captain Franklin, and he said he'd be happy to get rid of you."

"He said that?"

"Just sign the papers, Will, and welcome aboard." Will did so enthusiastically. "Thanks, Will." Rodriguez got up and shook his hand. "Before you go, sign these also."

"What are these, Sarge?"

"Congratulations, Detective Jankowski. You've been promoted."

"No shit, Sarge."

"You deserve it." Marco came in with a big congratulatory cake and the other officers in the precinct celebrated with them. In the middle of the festivities, Rodriguez received a call from McMahon. He took the call outside of his office. "McMahon, I wish you were here. You could have a piece of cake with us."

"Yeah, so do I. It would be a lot better than what the fuck I'm dealing with out here."

"Out where?"

"I'm back in Vegas; and by the way, congratulations on that Zachariah thing. Well done, Sergeant."

"Thanks. Why are you back in Vegas?"

"I got a call from Captain Steiner, Vegas PD. Remember him?"

"Sure."

"Well, it seems they've got what could be a serial killer on their hands. They found two bodies in Red Rock with the same MO. He asked me for my help, and I'm asking for yours. I want you to be on my team for this one. I spoke to your Commissioner. He said you're between cases and he can spare you; besides, you've got time coming. What do you say?"

Rodriguez paused, "Sure, McMahon. I'll get out there as soon as I can."

"Great. I'll book you a flight for tomorrow. I'll call back with the details. Thanks, Rodriguez."

"Anytime." Rodriguez walked back into his office and motioned to Will and Marco. "I'm going to Vegas, fellas."

"Nice. Have fun, go crazy."

"Well, it's not exactly a vacation. I just got a call from McMahon. She used to be my boss when I was with the Vegas DEA. She needs me to help her with a case. Spinelli, you'll be in charge while I'm gone. Hey Will, you like cats?"

"Sure, we'll take care of Bogie till you get back."

"Thanks, Will."

"Marco, I've got something for you. Wait here." Rodriguez came out of his office with an envelope and handed it to Detective Spinelli. "While I'm gone, you and Will get a team together and serve this arrest warrant. Captain Franklin has all the details."

Marco opened the envelope, "Shit, this is for Detective James McGraw."

EPILOGUE

Sergeant Rodriguez confronted the evil Zachariah and faced the biggest challenge of his career in this second installment and he prevailed. In the third installment Sergeant Rodriguez travels to Las Vegas. His objective is to unravel an intricate web of deceit and murder to catch a serial killer and break up an international human trafficking ring.

Red Rock Bleeds coming soon from George Marzocchi and Red Penguin Books.

ABOUT THE AUTHOR

George Marzocchi has authored the crime novel Stained Glass and Cyclist Club as well as a sci-fi short story titled Abduction at Loon Lake. Cyclist Club is the second installment in the Detective Rodriguez series.

He began writing with an eye toward crime and fictional detective genres.

George is an avid fan of cinematography and classic/nouveau film noir. He has a visual eye and he has spent many years as a professional photographer and is currently working in the large graphics display field.

George has a love of travel and recently enjoyed trips to Sardinia, Rome, Italy, Bruges Ghent, Antwerp, Paris and Cologne, Germany (taking photos throughout).

He studied photography and visual design at the New School in New York City. He resides in both Manhattan, New York, and Milford, Connecticut with his wife Terry and their two cats, Caribou Cody and Balkie.

He is the proud father of Damien and Julian.

George loves gardening, photography, cooking and tennis.

ALSO BY GEORGE MARZOCCHI

Available now

Stained Glass

Coming soon

Red Rock Bleeds

www.ingramcontent.com/pod-product-compliance
Lightning Source LLC
LaVergne TN
LVHW011927070526
838202LV00054B/4522